BARRY JONSBERG

PANDORA JONES
ADMISSION

BOOK 1

ALLEN&UNWIN

SYDNEY • MELBOURNE • AUCKLAND • LONDON

First published in 2014

Allen & Unwin
83 Alexander Street
Crows Nest NSW 2065
Australia
Phone: (61 2) 8425 0100
Email: info@allenandunwin.com
Web: www.allenandunwin.com

A Cataloguing-in-Publication entry is available from
the National Library of Australia
www.trove.nla.gov.au

ISBN 978 1 74331 811 9

Cover & text design by Astred Hicks, Design Cherry
Typeset by Midland Typesetters Australia

This book was printed in March 2014
at McPherson's Printing Group,
76 Nelson St, Maryborough, Victoria 3465, Australia
www.mcphersonsprinting.com

10 9 8 7 6 5 4 3 2 1

MIX
Paper from
responsible sources
FSC® C001695

The paper in this book is FSC® certified.
FSC® promotes environmentally responsible,
socially beneficial and economically viable
management of the world's forests.

For Jodie Webster

It took slightly under eight hours for Melbourne to die.

When Pandora Jones thought back to that day - something she did often - there were large holes in her memory. She definitely remembered sitting at the kitchen table eating breakfast and listening to the news on the radio, her mother bustling about and packing lunch for her brother Danny.

~~~

The reporter's voice droned in the background, but she wasn't paying attention. Danny was complaining that he wasn't feeling well and didn't want to go to school. His voice was rising in indignation as his mother insisted he would. They had been through this many times before. Danny often didn't want to go to school, and he had a limited imagination when it came to thinking up reasons.

'I've got a sore throat,' he pleaded. 'And a bad cough.'

He coughed to lend weight to his claim. Pan thought it was a pathetic attempt and didn't sound in the least convincing.

The reporter was talking about the election of a new Pope and relaying reactions to the appointment from prominent Melbourne clerics. Pan zoned out and pushed her cornflakes around the bowl.

'Not a chance, bucko,' said Pan's mum. 'The last time I swallowed that excuse, you spent the whole day playing games on the computer.'

'Not the *whole* day.'

'Yes, the whole day,' said Mum. 'You forget, Daniel, that I can check *exactly* how much time you were online. Fool me once, shame on you. Fool me twice, shame on me. Now go and get ready for school.'

'I'm sick!' But he went, stomping up the stairs, demonstrating an energy at odds with his supposed illness.

Pan's mum raised an eyebrow at her daughter and Pan smiled. Her attention was caught by the words 'breaking news' on the radio, but even then she didn't listen closely. Not at first. She took her bowl to the sink and washed it, placed it on the drainer. Then she opened her school bag, retrieved her diary and checked the timetable for the day. Pan knew she had double maths, but couldn't remember whether it was first up. The words from the radio drifted into her consciousness.

. . . from the eastern seaboard of the United States. Maine and Pennsylvania have confirmed cases and there are reports that parts of New Jersey are also particularly affected. More on this story from our North America correspondent, Mark McAllister. Mark.

Thanks, Jeanette. I'm in New York City where hospitals have reported significant increases in admissions. This flu virus – and I must stress that no formal identification of the virus has yet been made – seems to be spreading at a rate that has authorities alarmed. The Mayor has appealed for calm.

Are there any reports of fatalities, Mark?

Nothing official as yet, Jeanette, though it is strongly rumoured that a number of people have died in Maine over the last few hours and it's clear that authorities are taking the situation very seriously.

What is known about this virus?

Very little. It appears to have raised its head in a few areas of New England and spread rapidly. Fewer than twenty-four hours have elapsed since the first patient was admitted, so tests at the moment are necessarily inconclusive. We're in a developing situation and I'll bring all the news as it breaks.

Thanks, Mark. And look after yourself.

Mark coughed. Just once.

~ ~ ~

Pan couldn't remember anything else about that broadcast. She didn't recall her mum's reaction to the news, whether Danny actually went to school or not. She couldn't even remember leaving home. The more she tried, the harder it became. It was like a void, a stubbornly featureless blank.

The next thing she remembered about that day was walking to school from the station, though she could recall nothing of the train journey. She remembered a man following her through a pedestrian precinct a kilometre from her school. She remembered that it had started with a curious itch between her shoulder blades, a sense that someone was watching her. The feeling was so intense that she had stopped and turned, but at first could see nothing. Then she spotted him. A nondescript figure, moving no faster or slower than anyone else. A man in his early thirties, short-haired, wearing a suit, white cords snaking from his jacket pocket to his ears. Nothing in the least unusual in his manner. His eyes were cast to the ground and his head nodded slightly to a rhythm only he could hear. He didn't even glance at Pan, but she knew something about him was wrong. The difficulty was pinning down exactly what.

The precinct was crowded at that time in the morning. Retail workers were opening their stores and businessmen and women hurried past, takeaway coffee cups in hand. No harm could come to her with so many people about. She wasn't overly anxious, but she stopped and sat on a bench and opened her school bag. She rummaged into its depths, but kept one eye on the man as he walked past. He didn't break stride. He simply strolled past. Not too fast, not too slow. Didn't glance at her. She gazed at his back as he threaded his way through the throng, but he didn't turn. Within moments the crowd had swallowed him.

Her imagination was working overtime - not for the first time. This was something her mother and her teachers knew only too well. 'Pandora is gifted with a fertile and formidable imagination,' her last English report had read. 'But she would be well advised to exercise fuller control over it.' There was truth in that. She had to admit it. But she also knew an overactive imagination didn't explain everything.

She had experienced things like this before. Feelings. Intuition. Hunches. Pan had no name for it that quite expressed the way it *felt* inside. Maybe it was a heightened ability to read faces, body language, situations, the environment. But she couldn't pretend her ability didn't exist. There was too much evidence. Like the time she knew her best friend, Joanne, had split with her boyfriend. Pan knew before Joanne told her. Or when she could picture where her mum's misplaced keys were. And her maths teacher last year. He appeared the picture of health – always running to school. He'd even competed in the London marathon and finished in the top hundred. Yet Pan had sensed, as he stood at the whiteboard one day, that there was something ... broken inside. She had gone to his funeral, just one pupil among many. But she was probably the only one present who had not been surprised by his sudden and catastrophic heart attack.

It didn't always work. Sometimes these hunches, these intuitions, proved groundless. Yet she wasn't altogether convinced that just because no evidence came to light, she was wrong.

Pan sighed. There was no point going over all this. She had to trust her own feelings. The guy *had* been watching her. The fact that his eyes never appeared to fix on her didn't change that. Perhaps he was simply a freak, someone who got off on watching sixteen-year-old schoolgirls. That happened.

Pan picked up her school bag. Through the crowd a face appeared, smiled. Joanne waved and Pan waved back. She got to her feet and joined her friend.

~~~

Another break. Another void. Pan was sitting in class, but she had no idea which one. There was a relief teacher, a large woman with a prominent mole on her right cheek. Pan hadn't seen her before and she thought she knew all the relief teachers her school employed. The woman was talking at the front of the class. Pan gazed around the classroom. So many students were away. Her classes normally included twenty-five students, but today there were no more than six or seven present. Later, when she tried to recall their identities, she drew another blank.

'Turn to page one hundred and forty in your textbooks and read the chapter. Then answer the questions that I will write on the board. Write in your ...' The woman coughed. She brought her hand to her mouth and coughed again. She bent over slightly as she did so and placed her other hand against her chest. The class was silent. The woman drew a deep breath and straightened.

'I'm sorry. As I was saying ...'

The next coughing fit was more violent. This time she put both hands to her face, which had turned a pale shade of blue. Her eyes bulged. The coughing was tearing her apart. She stumbled forward and sat down heavily on a chair in the deserted front row. Pan stood, unsure whether the teacher needed help or whether the paroxysm would pass of its own accord. It didn't. Each cough racked her body and the woman was clearly having difficulty finding breath. Her complexion darkened and her body doubled over so far her face nearly touched the ground. Pan rushed to the front of the class. She was dimly aware that no one else had moved. What were you supposed to do in these circumstances? Pat her on the back and hope it would pass or go for help from the front office? She wasn't sure. The woman toppled from the chair and lay on her side, still coughing violently. Pan knelt at her side. The teacher's eyes were wide with fear. She took one hand from her mouth and reached out for Pan as if for aid or comfort. Pan grasped it. It took a few moments before she realised the hand was wet and sticky. Instinctively, she tried to withdraw it, but the woman's grip was too strong.

It didn't seem possible, but the coughing increased in violence and frequency. The side of the woman's face was badged in blood. Her other hand fell away from her mouth and it too was covered in a thick film of red. Pan felt sick, but she couldn't move. The woman was holding on so tightly it was like she was trying to draw Pan into a kind of perverse embrace.

The final cough wasn't as violent as the others, but it sent a spray of fine red droplets into Pan's face and hair. She recoiled and this time the woman's grip broke. Pan held her own hands up before her face, saw the blood. When she looked down, the teacher's eyes were wide open, as if astonished, glazed and staring through her.

~ ~ ~

Another gap. Pan walked down a city street. There were shops and cafes, seating areas along the pavement, bright with canopies and umbrellas. Birds hopped onto tables and pecked at plates. Most of the tables were deserted, only a few people sitting alone and curiously still. Pan put a hand to her forehead. She was feeling hot and her hand came away damp with sweat. There was something wrong with her vision as well. The world had a curious cast, as if she was somehow distanced from what was going on around her. It was difficult to focus on anything and her peripheral vision swam with lozenge-shaped forms, like bacteria swimming under a microscope. Was she sick? She seemed to remember that someone else had been very sick recently, but she couldn't pin the memory down. Her legs felt heavy and she had to physically force her body to take one step after another.

There was something wrong about the situation but Pan couldn't identify it at first. Something to do with sound. The birds were shrill, chattering to each other. Unnaturally loud in the surrounding silence. She forced herself to concentrate. That was it. The surrounding silence. At this time of day - she glanced at her watch to check, but there was nothing on her wrist other than a pale band of skin where sunlight hadn't touched - there should be traffic, the constant noise of conversation, the hubbub of a city in operation. Pan stopped and looked around. Cars were parked at illegal angles. A tram had stopped in the middle of the street, its doors open, and Pan could see the shape of the driver, a dark silhouette against the sun. He wasn't moving. Her attention was caught by a sudden movement further down the street. A person stumbled from a shop. It was a woman. She had a bundle of dresses draped over her arm. A jumble of coat hangers formed a kaleidoscope of metal that trailed behind her. The woman stopped and put a hand out to a lamppost, steadying herself for a moment. She hugged the dresses to her side.

A sound and a movement off to Pan's right. She turned her head but it was like forcing something that had seized up. She could feel the bones in her neck creak and click. A car swayed and swerved, though it was going no faster than twenty or thirty kilometres an hour. Sunlight blazed from its windscreen and Pan flinched as a dagger of reflected light stabbed her eyes. She couldn't see who was driving. The car scraped along a parked car and the screech of metal against metal was another source of pain. The car didn't stop. It bounced off the other car and sideswiped the tram. Even then it didn't stop. It kept going down the street at the same slow pace. Pan knew what was going to happen, but she didn't understand why she knew. The woman – a shoplifter? She wasn't carrying any bags – stepped out onto the road. Her eyes were fixed on the other side of the street as if salvation lay that way. She didn't glance to left or right. The car didn't deviate either. It caught her a glancing blow and the woman flipped into the air, performed half a turn. It was almost beautiful in execution. Until Pan heard the woman's head hit the bitumen. Even at a distance the crunch was sickeningly final. Immediately a pool of blood spread from the ruined skull and drew lazy patterns against the ground.

Pan couldn't move. She watched as the woman's arm twitched and reached for the pile of clothes. Her hand clutched the dresses and then stilled. The car continued down the street for another thirty or forty metres and then veered onto the footpath. It hit a parking meter, twisting it into a grotesque angle, before ploughing into a shop window. The window crazed and then fell in great lumps of powdered glass. It all seemed to happen in slow motion. The car's door opened, but no one got out. Pan watched for a few minutes, but nothing happened. Silence returned, broken only by squabbling of birdcall.

Pan was tired. Suddenly it was impossible to get her body to move. There were thoughts at the back of her mind, but they were slippery and elusive. She should help. She should go over to the woman, see if there was anything she could do for her. Go and check on the driver of the car. Isn't that what people did in these situations? But it was all too hard. She needed to sit down, gather her thoughts, find strength from somewhere. Even that was difficult.

She realised she was standing by a street-side cafe. There were metal chairs arranged under umbrellas advertising Italian coffee. She needed to sit. Just for a moment. Then she would go and see if she could be of any assistance. Pan was already forgetting why assistance might be needed. Sit down. Just for a moment. She forced her legs to move, but it was difficult to exert control. She almost fell, had to reach out a hand to steady herself. Finally, she slumped into a chair. The coldness of the metal against her legs was delicious. Pan put her hands down on the table and tried to resist the temptation to put her forehead against the cold surface. A nagging thought at the back of her mind warned her that if she rested now she might never get up again. But she closed her eyes anyway. The light was painful and there were thoughts she needed to sort out. A destination. A place she must get to. Home. That was it. She had to get home, but she had no idea where home was.

The hand that clasped her wrist did not even cause her to flinch. She opened her eyes and watched the hand incuriously. It was knotted with tendons and held onto her with a fierce and desperate strength. She could see her own hand blanching as blood flow was cut off. Pan followed the hand until she saw the wrist and then the arm. There was something familiar about the material of the sleeve that hovered in her vision but, once again, the memory eluded her. She turned her face upwards.

A police officer. Of course. A small part of her was relieved. Police sorted things out. They made things better, established order. Pan wasn't sure how she knew, but this was a situation that required the establishment of order. He was probably in his thirties and had a thin moustache. The skin on his face was pockmarked with old acne scars. But his eyes were what held her. They were wild with some emotion that was difficult to identify. Fear? Horror? His mouth opened and Pan noticed that a small trail of blood oozed from one side.

'All dead,' said the man.

Pan tried to remember how to talk and it was surprisingly difficult. At first she just managed a croak.

'Dead?' she said finally.

The police officer nodded vigorously and Pan was pleased she had understood. For some reason she felt it was important to impress this man with her grasp of the situation.

'Who?' Pan added.

The man let go of her wrist and motioned towards the street.

'Everyone,' he said.

Pan turned from those eyes with difficulty and forced her vision to focus on the street. This time she saw what had passed her by before. How had she missed that? How had she missed the car with a man hanging out of the driver's seat, his face like a bruise, eyes wide and unseeing? And the bodies in the middle of the road, surrounded by blood? The woman sitting in a chair almost opposite her, leaning back as if examining the sky, arms dangling by her side, her chest stained red? A bird was perched on her shoulder. As Pan watched, it darted a beak into a staring eye socket. Something burst and Pan looked away.

The police officer shuddered and sat in the chair next to Pan. He coughed a couple of times, covering his mouth with a sleeve. When he stopped, there was a broad and sticky band of blood on his arm.

'My wife and baby. Both dead,' he said. He started to cry, but made no noise. Pan watched as the tears rolled down his cheek. 'Drove home,' he continued. 'I can't tell you what I saw on that drive. Too many horrors. Too many. Found them in bed. Dead. My wife. Laura. She had the baby in her arms. So small. She had barely started living and now she's dead. I was too late, you see? You understand? I was too late to die with them.'

'I'm sorry,' said Pan.

'Me too,' said the policeman. He fumbled with something at his side, but Pan was still fixated on his haunted eyes and didn't see what he was doing. 'I came here,' the man continued. 'I have no idea why. Maybe to see if anyone survived. Who knows?' He looked into Pan's eyes. 'There will be no one to bury us, you know? You know that, don't you? We'll rot here.'

'I'm alive,' said Pan.

'Not for long,' said the policeman. 'We're all dead, but some of us don't know it yet.' He raised his arm and put something into his mouth. It was long and dark, but Pan took a few moments to realise what it was. Even if she'd had the energy to try she wouldn't have been able to stop him. The gunshot was loud and immediately the air filled with the bitter smell of burned flesh and gunpowder. The back of his head exploded in a mist of blood and bone fragments. For a split second he sat there, his eyes still fixed on Pan. Then he fell off the chair.

'I'm sorry, but I have to get home now,' said Pan. 'My mother and my brother are expecting me.' She couldn't remember her brother's name, but was confident it would come back to her in time.

~~~

Gaps. Whole featureless areas of memory. A plane crashing? Had she seen that? Something about a screaming noise that caused her to raise her eyes to the sky. A wing clipping a skyscraper, fragments of metal twisting and fluttering in the clear air. An explosion and a billowing column of dark smoke. Was that a memory?

The bodies littering an area of parkland. Someone with a gun staggering down a street, shooting into empty shops, laughing at the sound of windows smashing. A car speeding into a stanchion of a bridge, the vehicle disintegrating on impact, something flying through the windscreen. A girl in a white dress sitting in the road, playing with a doll and coughing. Holding onto the hand of a woman lying motionless next to her. A body dangling from a first floor window, knotted sheets around its neck. Pan didn't know what was real and what was the coinage of her fevered mind.

She had no recollection of how she got there, but suddenly there was a familiar street and a familiar house. The front door was open and part of her registered that as strange. Pan staggered from one room to another but no one was there. The television was on, but there was no picture. Only a hissing storm of white static. She went to the local park. Her mother sometimes went to the park and there was nowhere else Pan could think of to go.

It was as if, having decided to go there, she immediately found herself among trees and winding footpaths. The sun bathed everything in dappled light. Something attracted her attention - a distant noise, familiar yet elusive. It resolved itself into the creak of chains. She headed towards the sound, crossed in front of the lake and pushed through a barrier of low-hanging branches.

A playground. The creaking of chains was the passage of a child's swing. A boy swung himself back and forth, his legs flexing as he shifted weight, gaining greater and greater height. A woman sat on a bench close by. She had her hand to her mouth. Pan thought the woman was her mother, the boy her brother. But she couldn't be entirely sure. She took a few more steps towards them.

The woman was obscured regularly by the passing form of the swing, but she glanced up and smiled. It was a smile soaked in weariness.

'I knew you'd come,' she said.

Then she coughed. A couple of barks, her hand covering her mouth. The woman recovered, looked up at Pan apologetically. The swing passed across her face, regular as a metronome.

The second coughing fit was more intense. She doubled over, her head almost touching her knees. The cough this time was racking, painful. And it didn't stop. She tried to get her breath, but the next wave came too quickly. Pan watched her face turn red, swollen with blood, her hands cupped over her mouth, body convulsing with the strain of bursting lungs.

Pan moved past the boy on the swing. She sat next to the woman on the bench, took her in her arms and thumped her hand on the small of her back. Nothing changed, except the coughing redoubled in intensity. It was as if the woman was being shaken apart. A drop of blood oozed between the woman's fingers, dropped to the ground, a crimson coin between her feet. It was followed by another and another and yet another. The splatters were separate bright circles. Then their edges merged, puddled. Before Pan's eyes, the area of red spread, the drops no longer falling from the woman's hands individually, but in long strings. She glanced up at the boy on the swing.

He was describing a slower, lazier arc through the air now. He coughed, but she couldn't hear him. The woman was making too much noise. The boy took one hand from the chain of the swing and rubbed at his mouth. He was coughing all the time now. When he took his hand away, it was smeared with red. Pan stood, torn between the two - the woman on the bench and the boy arcing through the summer sun.

~ ~ ~

Perhaps Pan lay down in the park, caught between two deaths. Perhaps she stretched out onto the grass and let the sun play on her face. After a while, she was aware only of silence. Possibly she fell asleep. Or passed out. Nothing made any sense. She couldn't remember when anything had ever made sense. The silence wrapped her like a blanket and she surrendered to it.

Time had no meaning. But some time must have passed because she became aware, by degrees, of a change in the quality of the silence. Something buzzing. Another familiar sound, but she was far too tired to identify it. Pan just wanted it to go away, an annoying insect disturbing her dreams. It didn't go away. It became louder, the buzzing resolving itself into a drone. A small part of her conscious mind was aware of a wind against her face. It wasn't a sweet breeze. It smelled of oil and dust and made her cough. Then one final memory. Being lifted. Someone talking in her ear, though she couldn't make out any individual words. A sense of movement, the drone of rotating blades and the certainty that she was lifting further and further into the sky, the park shrinking beneath her, taking her away from the world.

Her mind was full of horrors and wanted nothing more than to shut down. But one image nagged away at her, like a dull toothache. Not her mother tearing her lungs apart on a park bench, nor her brother's blood-soaked hand. Not the spray of brains as a bullet tore through the back of a policeman's head. None of those curiously fragmented pictures of death.

She thought about the man in the pedestrian precinct, the one she believed had been following her. It was the most unremarkable of memories, but she felt it was important. More than important. Crucial.

But Pan gave herself up to the dark.

Chapter 1

A garden. Of sorts.

Flowers were growing from multicoloured pots. The ground was rough and solid rock. Here and there, small patches of lichen had found a foothold in a crack and struggled for life, but otherwise the terrain was barren. The garden lay on a fairly flat area on the summit of a mountain. It was as if someone had roughly chopped off the very tip of a pyramid, to leave an irregular patch a couple of hundred metres square. Standing in the centre of the garden, it was only possible to see that patch of stone, dotted with flower pots from which a variety of plants bloomed. They were mainly pink heathers in the pots, hardy plants to withstand cold and freezing winds, but there were also other flowers she couldn't identify, reds and greens and yellows. It was a grey canvas splashed with dots of brilliant colour at irregular intervals. The garden was an abstract painting.

Pandora Jones stood at the centre. The cold seeped into her bones and a thin wind slipped like a scalpel through her light ankle-length smock. It pressed the fabric against her body. Bare feet burned against the ground. She had no idea how she had got here. There was nothing in her head, no memory that connected the coldness of the present to anything before. She came to life slowly, senses clicking one by one into place. The knife of the wind, the solidity of the rock beneath her feet, the colours pressed against her eyes.

She moved without conscious thought. Her right foot lifted, took a step. And her left foot flexed at the ankle, lifted as the right settled on the rock. Her body obeyed commands she was not aware of issuing. She moved towards a grey horizon where stone met mud-coloured sky. As she did so, the scene was gradually exposed, each step revealing further details. Five paces from the edge of a cliff, she stopped and looked around. Her mind was beginning to process, but in a mechanical way. Her eyes took in details but she could relate them to nothing. At the centre of her consciousness was a series of horrendous images, but they seemed distant somehow. Like a nightmare dimly recalled, from which her mind shied away.

The mountain she stood on was dizzying in its height, but now she realised its true scale. Behind was a range of other mountains which made the one she stood on seem tiny in comparison, a child of the vast mass at her back, nestled up as if for protection. Their pinnacles were lost in cloud and there was no way of knowing their height. They punctured the grey sky and disappeared. Nothing moved against their sheer faces, except occasional swirls, tiny dots of birds against patches of snow or ice. The range defied understanding, so she turned her eyes towards something more easily understood. Something smaller. Pan gazed down at the world spread beneath her.

The mountain ranges hugged the scene as far as she could see from left to right, impossibly steep sides to a bowl that led to a distant sea. She fixed her eyes on that. Even from this distance she could see the faint ripple of waves against a rocky shore. Small flecks of white, the tips of swells, changed constantly so that the grey expanse of water seemed somehow alive. Then she noticed a place where the coast curved into a bay, a thin sweep of land that protected the waters within its embrace. Dotted in the bay was a fleet of boats, maybe a dozen in all. They looked like children's toys. And close up against the shoreline was a cluster of shapes, maybe huts and other larger buildings. A village of some kind, built around the port. The scene was familiar, yet at the same time utterly alien.

She moved her line of sight further up from the sea. The sense of cold was becoming more sharply defined with every passing moment. The next feature of note was puzzling. It was not something she immediately recognised. Her mind had to work on it. A strange structure had been built about one kilometre, maybe two, inland of the village. Her first thought was that it was a wall, but if so, then it was truly huge. It stretched from the mountain range on her left all the way across to the range on the right. It blocked off the sea and the village nestled up against it. There was no way to reach the water without crossing this structure. At regular intervals, slim towers sprouted from the building and pointed towards the sky. There was something strangely unsettling, disturbing even, about it. Was it designed to keep things out? Or keep things in? She didn't have the energy to explore the thought in more detail. But she filed the questions away for closer examination later.

On her side of the wall were a bewildering variety of buildings clinging to every patch of exposed rock. Strange buildings, some vast and sprawling. It was almost impossible to put things into perspective. The plateau she stood on towered above the buildings beneath and the height played tricks with her vision. Her eyes flickered over them, tried to find points of reference. The layout appeared chaotic. Some places were clustered together as if part of a specific community. Other buildings sprawled apart from the others. Thin tracks wove between the structures, forming maze-like paths that must serve as roads. Off to her left was a river, houses packed along its banks. A few patches of green here and there relieved the monotony of buildings. A forest, small and lush, crouched in the foothill of the mountain where the river seemed to have its source.

Pan was almost unaware of the coat being draped around her shoulders. Her mind was so occupied with trying to make sense of her surroundings that she scarcely noticed. But the sudden warmth made her start. She turned.

The man smiled at her. 'Hello,' he said. 'You must be cold.'

She pulled the coat around her and nodded. The wind still numbed her face, but she could already feel her body warming inside the new covering. She was dazed, as if waking from a long and deep sleep. There were questions she needed to ask, but it was too difficult to pin them down. So she simply nodded again and turned her eyes back to the view.

'Quite a sight, isn't it?' said the man. Pan said nothing.

'It's why I'm so pleased this is the Infirmary,' the man continued. 'The best view you'll get anywhere around here, in my humble opinion. I come out here as much as possible, provided the weather is good, which, to be honest, it hasn't been so far. And the flowers provide some colour. Living things. Beauty in the bleak terrain. The Garden on Top of the World. Cheers me up.'

The words buzzed in Pan's head. They were annoying and she wanted to wave them away. Instead, without thinking about it, the word spilt from her lips. It left a strange, metallic taste in her mouth.

'Infirmary?'

'Yes. A hospital. It's behind you. Where you were sleeping. At least where I *thought* you were sleeping. Until I came in to do my rounds and found your bed empty. I'm glad you've woken up. But I think it's time you got back to bed. You'll catch your death out here. In my professional opinion.'

Pan watched a speck in the sky swirl and ride the wind. It was too far off to see what type of bird it was.

'What is this place?' she asked.

'All of this? What you can see below you? This is The School.'

She absorbed his words, but they made no sense. She nodded and hugged the coat closer. The man moved in front of her and looked into her eyes.

'Do you remember your name?' he asked.

'Pandora. Pandora Jones.'

'Excellent,' he said and smiled. 'Sometimes our patients experience residual amnesia. I'm glad you remember.'

Pan said nothing.

'Pandora,' the man continued. 'A classical name. The bringer of mischief into the world.' He chuckled. 'I only hope you don't bring much mischief into *this* world. Can I call you Pan, for short?'

'Fine,' she said. The speck in the sky had disappeared. Pan tried to spot others but failed. The cold was invading the coat. She hugged it even closer.

'What happened to me?' she asked.

The man took her hand and Pan focused on his face. It was crisscrossed with wrinkles, around his eyes and across his brow. *A face made for laughing*, Pan thought. He was small and overweight, a pair of half-moon glasses perched on his nose, cheeks ruddy and bulging, hair parted in an unsuccessful attempt to hide a wide bald patch. When he parted his lips she caught a glimpse of discoloured teeth. He shifted his fingers onto her wrist, felt for her pulse. Pan glanced down at the white bandage on her forearm. Her hip ached.

'Do you remember what happened out there?' he asked.

Pan considered the question. Sudden images flooded in and she closed her eyes against them. She took a quick intake of breath and tried to close her mind to the memories.

'I see you do,' said the man. 'You have been through a lot, Pandora Jones. Like everyone here. But there will be time to come to terms with it. If that's possible. In the meantime, you need warmth and rest, my dear. Come on. Come with me.'

Pan allowed herself to be turned and led away from

the cliff's edge. A low, brightly lit building nestled against the mountain face behind. In front of the building was a paved area, with plastic tables and chairs dotted around, but it was deserted. Directly behind the area was a set of French doors, one side open and rocking slightly in the wind. The man led her past the cluster of outdoor furniture and through the open door.

A hospital ward. She let her eyes roam the room. Eight beds were ranged against the far wall, facing the French doors and their flanking windows. All were empty. The man led Pan to what was apparently her bed. The sheets were rumpled, presumably thrown back when she got up. She allowed herself to be helped back in. She *was* tired. A sudden weariness swept over her as he tucked the sheets in and fluffed the pillows.

'I think you might need a little something to help you sleep,' said the man. He opened a leather bag at the side of the bed, and took out a small case. Pan glanced at the window. From here she could see the white-shrouded mountain peaks against the muddy sky. The image blurred as she looked. Her eyes were too tired to correct it.

'No!' She sat straight up, back pressed against the hard bedhead. 'Get it away from me.'

The man paused. He had been tapping the syringe to remove an air bubble. The girl's eyes were wide and staring, her arms trembling as they braced against the bed, pushing herself back. He glanced at the syringe, hid it behind his back.

'Pan,' he said. 'It's okay. You don't have to have an injection if you don't want. It's fine. No one will force you to do anything. Here. I'm putting it away.'

But Pan only stopped trembling when the bag was firmly shut. She sank down into the bed, pulled the covers up to her eyes. The man leaned over her.

'Get some rest,' he whispered. 'And no more wandering, okay?'

'Hope,' said Pan.

'Hope?'

The man's face started to blur. She couldn't keep her eyes open. Her own words seemed to come from a long way away.

'Pandora brought mischief, evil into the world, but she also brought hope.'

'So she did,' said the man. 'So she did.'

But Pan was already asleep.

Chapter 2

Summer rain.

Holding her face up to the sky, the water washing her clean. She could taste the drops on her tongue, feel the pricks of impact on her skin. She closed her eyes.

A voice called to her. It called her name, but the sound was blurred around the edges. She opened her eyes and searched for the source of the sound. Far off to her right, a tree stood in the corner of a park. It was huge, its branches a massive canopy that freckled the sky. At the base a woman was sitting on a large chequered cloth. A boy sat next to her. He had blonde hair and he was toying with something in his hand. The woman was making movements with her hands. Join us. Come in from the rain.

The park stretched all around. The grass beneath her feet was coarse and yellow. Rain made the leaves jump. The girl had her arms spread wide, palms up. Her wet clothing clung to her body. She loved the feel of it. She laughed at the sullen sky. Then she ran to the tree, shaking her wet hair from side to side, drying it as a dog might. She collapsed on the cloth. The woman looked up and there was annoyance in her eyes, but its roots weren't deep.

'Don't you dare make me wet as well. Keep off.'

The boy glanced up at her. He was sulking, but there was also a small smile there. His face held a curious mixture of annoyance and mischief.

'Not fair,' he whined. 'I wanted to go in the rain, but she wouldn't let me.'

'Who's she?' said the woman. 'The cat's mother?'

This made the boy smile more, though he fought it.

'I'm starving,' she said.

'You're always starving,' said the woman.

And then, in the strange, unsurprising way dreams have, she looked at herself from the outside. She saw a girl, thin as a whippet, her face quite plain. She saw her hair, brown but streaked with natural bands of blonde, lying in wet strands on thin, bony shoulders.

Everything was entirely familiar, yet totally unfamiliar at the same time. She moved further from the small group picnicking in the summer rain. They shrank to small dots on the landscape, faded entirely, became nothing.

She felt close to knowledge. Names teased her. But the more she focused, the more elusive they became. Recognition was infuriatingly close. She could taste it, like a water drop on the tip of her tongue. She raised her head to the weeping sky, closed her eyes and put out her tongue. The sun's warmth dried it. She was running down a street in broad sunlight. Her shadow paced her, a slab of darkness tilted on her left. When she raised her eyes, a police officer was there. He had a moustache. When he smiled, a gold tooth glinted.

'I've always wanted to say that,' said the officer. He laughed and clapped a hand on her shoulder.

The jolt to wakefulness was painful, the sound of her hammering heart echoing in her ears.

Pan glanced around the room, chest heaving. The beds arranged along the wall, the French doors, the garden furniture, the snow-capped peaks. Her name was Pandora Jones. She remembered standing on a cliff. The School. A man with laughter in his face. There were other memories, too, from further back. An explosion of blood, an aeroplane's wing catching a building, a teacher slumped on a classroom floor. They were like images from a movie, but spliced together with no regard for narrative. There was a story there, but it was fragmented, chaotic.

She dragged aside her bed covers and stood. For a moment, she thought she might faint. Her legs were weak. But then she straightened. A towelling robe lay at the foot of her bed. She put it on, cinched the belt. Apart from the French doors that led to the courtyard, there appeared to be only one exit door, off to her left. Pan walked towards it and the weakness in her legs diminished. By the time she passed through the door, the sense of faintness in her head had faded.

There was a short corridor, with clean floor tiles and walls painted a light pink. Her brain processed a scent, recognised it. Disinfectant, with its artificial tinge of pine, and below that, the smell of sickness, of air breathed into ailing lungs a thousand times and exhaled, recycled. That curious smell of hospitals, decay and sterility mixed. There were no signs indicating which way to turn, but Pan glanced to her left and noticed, no more than five or six metres away, a nurses' station. Behind a desk, a woman in a light blue uniform sat, writing in a ledger. She glanced up as Pan took a step forward.

'Well, well,' she said. 'Our sleeping beauty awakens. How are you feeling, dear?'

'I need answers,' said Pan.

'You need *rest*, my lovely. That's what you need. Before The School takes you and, trust me, you won't be resting then. How about I take you back to bed, get you settled? There'll be time for questions and answers later.'

'No,' said Pan. 'Now. I need answers now.'

The nurse's smile froze for a moment, but she recovered quickly.

'I'll phone Dr Morgan,' she said. 'You sit, Pandora, before you fall down. You have been very ill, you know, and the body takes time to recover. You mustn't push yourself too hard, too early.'

Pan leaned against the desk, but said nothing else. She ignored the row of chairs to her left. The nurse frowned, picked up a phone and punched in a couple of numbers. The fingers of her right hand drummed a beat on the surface of the desk.

'Dr Morgan? Clare here. Our patient Pandora is in reception . . . Yes, she seems fine, possibly a little agitated . . . She wants to talk to someone as a matter of urgency . . . Uh, huh . . . Fine. I'll tell her. Okay. Thanks, doctor.'

She replaced the receiver.

'Dr Morgan will be here shortly, Pan. Now, please sit down.'

The nurse stood and walked around the side of the desk, took her by the arm. Pan allowed herself to be led to a chair. The dizziness had returned and so had the sense of weakness.

'Would you like a drink?'

It was only when the idea was suggested that Pan realised how thirsty she was. The back of her mouth felt thick and coated. When she swallowed, her throat felt raw.

'Water, please,' she said.

The nurse smiled. 'I'll get you some. Back in a moment.'

Alone in the reception area, Pan felt an almost overwhelming desire to go behind the nurse's desk, check what was written in the ledger, look at the charts and files bundled in a pile. But there was a pain, a pressure behind her eyes and she was just too tired. A minute passed and the nurse came back with a glass of water and a carafe.

'Here you are, Pan,' she said, handing her the glass. 'You are probably dehydrated. We've tried to keep you as hydrated as possible intravenously, but you've been unconscious for a long time. Drink as much as you can, my dear. Don't bolt it down. Sip. Small amounts, but regularly. We've no ice, I'm afraid.'

Pan paused with the glass halfway to her mouth. 'How long have I been unconscious?'

The nurse looked flustered. She put the carafe on the table next to the chairs and returned to her position behind the desk. 'You have been very sick,' she said. 'Anyway, Doctor will be here in a moment and I'm sure he will answer all your questions. Now, if you will excuse me, I must return to my work.'

Pan swallowed the urge to push for answers. Instead, she took a long draught of the water. It tasted wonderful. Slightly warm, but clean and pure.

A door opened behind the nurses' station and the man she remembered from the previous day - was it the previous day? - stepped into the reception area. Following him was a woman with bright red hair scraped back from her face and tied in a ponytail. Both of them wore doctors' white coats. Both were smiling.

'Pan!' said the man. 'You look remarkably well. I am Dr Morgan - your doctor. This is my colleague, Dr Macredie, who is our psychologist and student counsellor here at The School.'

The woman smiled and put out her hand. Pan shook it automatically.

'Nurse Watson tells me you have some questions.' Dr Morgan beamed at Pan. 'And who can blame you? Who can blame you? But before the interrogation - the understandable interrogation - I would like to check you over briefly. Not long, I promise. Pulse, shine a light into your eyes, smack your kneecaps with a hammer. I am joking, my dear.' He crouched down before Pan, slipped his fingers onto her wrist. 'Routine, that's all.' He took a pencil-thin torch from his top pocket and shone it into first one eye and then the other. 'Right,' he said, snapping off the torch and replacing it in his pocket. 'I have established beyond any reasonable doubt that you have indeed the correct number of eyes and that they are positioned as they should be - either side of your nose. Another triumph for medical science.' He smiled at his own joke.

'I need answers,' said Pan.

The doctor pushed his half-moon glasses further up his nose.

'Of course you do. Of course you do. But this reception area is perhaps not the best place to talk. Come with me. There's a conference room we can use. It will be much more comfortable. And private.'

He held out his hand and Pan used it to help raise herself to her feet. She followed the doctors through the door behind the nurses' station, along a short corridor and into a large, windowless room dominated by a long wooden table. A dozen chairs were arranged around its perimeter. A whiteboard stood to one side, a row of markers lined up on its metal ledge. She was ushered to a chair at the head of the table, the doctors sitting either side of her. The woman - the psychologist/counsellor - had brought in the carafe of water. She refilled Pan's glass and poured water into two glasses already arranged along the table. There was silence for a moment. The man sipped slowly.

'Pandora,' he said finally. 'Before we start, can I ask what you remember before you woke up in our hospital bed? As many details as you can. Start with your full name.'

'My name is Pandora Jones,' she said. 'I am sixteen years old and I live in Melbourne. I have a mother, and a brother called Danny. Where are they and what am I doing here?'

Dr Morgan held up a hand. 'Please,' he replied. 'We will answer all your questions fully and honestly. That is my promise to you.' He put a hand over his heart. 'But first, we need to understand how much you already know. It differs, you see. Some survivors remember everything that happened. Others ... well, there are gaps in their memories. I suspect that is the case with you, my dear.'

'Survivors? I don't understand.'

'Describe the last full day you remember. Indulge me, Pan.'

She frowned. 'I don't know. It's kind of hazy. I went to school . . .'

'Before you went to school?'

'Something on the news, I think. Something important, but I can't remember what it was . . . I was having breakfast. My brother Danny said he was feeling ill.'

'Okay. Excellent. You said you went to school?'

'Except I can't remember anything about it. I remember coming home.' Images flashed into Pan's mind. A police officer. A car hitting a bridge. A woman coming out of a shop. She shook her head. They were nightmares. They weren't real. 'I couldn't find my mother,' she finished. 'Like I said, it's all hazy. What happened? What is it? Why can't I remember?'

Dr Morgan glanced at Dr Macredie and ran a hand through his hair, smoothing it over his bald patch. Then he leaned forward and locked his hands together, rested his chin on upturned index fingers. He fixed Pan with his eyes.

'You *do* remember other things, Pandora,' he said. 'Unpleasant things, am I right? I can see it in your eyes. But you think they were nightmares. They couldn't possibly be real.' He paused and this time there was no laughter in his eyes. 'They weren't nightmares, Pan. They actually happened.'

'This isn't making sense.'

Dr Macredie spoke for the first time. Her voice was soft and Pan instinctively leaned forward to better catch her words.

'On 24 March, the last day you remember, there was an outbreak of a new flu virus. It seems to have originated in the north-eastern states of America, though no one can be sure. At any rate, that is where it was first reported.'

Pan's memory was jolted. The radio broadcast over breakfast. A man reporting from New York City. Something about deaths. She forced herself to pay attention to Dr Macredie's words.

'We have no idea what the virus is, though we have been conducting research. We can talk about that later, if you like. When you've had time to come to terms with what we have to tell you.'

She took a sip of water. Pan noticed that the doctor's hands were shaking. 'The bottom line is that the virus spread at a rate that was ... unprecedented. The symptoms initially were unremarkable. Coughing, sore throat, a mild fever. But within hours, people's lungs were effectively destroyed, eaten away. Most people died drowning in their own blood ...'

(The relief teacher, her face purple, struggling to get air, eyes wide with panic.)

'... and by the time the seriousness of the situation was realised it was far too late. Maybe the virus stayed inert for a time. We just don't know. The United States grounded all national and international flights later that day. But it did no good. The virus appeared in Europe, the Far East, Africa, Australia. Every country in the world.'

'My mother and brother are dead, aren't they?' said Pan. Her voice was wooden and it was as if her feelings had been anaesthetised.

Dr Morgan reached over to take her hand, but Pan snatched it away.

'Tell me,' she said.

'Yes,' said Dr Morgan. 'I wish I didn't have to say this, but when you were rescued, from a small public park in Melbourne, you were found close to the bodies of a woman and a boy. I assume they were members of your family. Pan, I am so sorry.'

(A drop of blood oozed between the woman's fingers, dropped to the ground, a crimson coin between her feet. It was followed by another and another and yet another. The splatters were separate, bright circles. Then their edges merged, puddled. Before Pan's eyes, the area of red spread, the drops no longer falling from the woman's hands individually, but in long strings. On the swing, the boy coughed once.)

The man's voice was muffled. It came as if from a great distance. When Pan looked up she couldn't see clearly either. It was like watching something underwater and her eyes burned. Everything was blurred and fragmented. There was a solid lump in her chest, constricting her lungs. Her mind seemed as inert as the lump. Pan registered dimly that Dr Macredie was speaking again.

'. . . just blind luck that we found you. A needle in a haystack really. Even with the heat sensor, the helicopter's equipment can't isolate people. Other animals don't seem affected, so the sensors constantly identified life. You are a miracle, Pandora Jones, and although you probably don't understand that now, you will give thanks in time. Trust me.' She spread her arms out. 'Some people, it seems, were resistant to the virus. Not immune, but they survived. People like you, Pan. Others weren't affected at all. Dr Morgan and myself, for example. We didn't even display any symptoms. As yet, we have no idea why. Maybe we will never know. Whatever the reason, we have come together. The School is a place for those who survived.'

'How many?' Pan didn't recognise her own voice in her ears. It was thin and croaky.

Dr Morgan glanced at his colleague. Neither spoke for a moment.

'I told you we wouldn't lie to you, my dear,' said Dr Morgan. 'We don't know how many survived. It's possible - probable even - that thousands are out there, in comas like the one you have been in for the past two months . . .'

(Two months?)

'. . . but we don't know where they are. We have people searching, but the more time passes, the less chance we have of finding more. You, yourself, were among the last of those we discovered. In the past two weeks, no one at all.'

'How many survivors?' Pan didn't know why she was so insistent. Under the circumstances, was it really important?

'Worldwide?' said Dr Morgan. 'Maybe ten thousand. Maybe more.'

Those figures were absurd. A part of Pan's mind understood that.

Dr Macredie put her hand on Pan's and this time Pan didn't have the energy to remove it.

'The virus has killed billions, Pan,' she said. 'There's no one out there. The world as we know it has been destroyed. Humanity stands on the edge of extinction. And that is why we have come to The School. To learn how to pull back from that brink.'

Chapter 3

Pan studied her reflection in the bathroom mirror.

The face that gazed back was familiar in a strange, dislocated fashion. She looked into her pale, green-tinged eyes, the long face with a nose slightly too large to be in proportion, the brown hair flecked with blonde. A plain girl. *I used to know you, but that was in a different time and a different world.* Her arms and legs were thin, wasted. Examining her eyes more closely, she noticed they too were pinched - eyes, she thought, that had seen far too much. It wasn't how she remembered herself - not really. There had been a time when she laughed, when her body was taut and muscular, rather than shrivelled, emaciated. But that had been a different girl entirely.

Because that girl is dead.

Pan shuddered and stepped into the shower cubicle, turned on both taps. The water wasn't hot and the pressure was weak, but the flow was restful against her skin. It helped drown out the clamouring in her mind.

Pan scrubbed her hair with coarse soap. She had asked the nurse for shampoo, but the woman had only smiled in a wry fashion and told her that supplies of luxury items were limited. It didn't matter. Nothing much mattered anymore. After her discussion with the two doctors, Pan had gone back to the ward and slept, though sleep was perhaps too benign a word for what was effectively a shutdown of body and mind. She'd slept for eighteen hours, though she was unaware of the time that elapsed. Nor did she care. It was not a sleep that relaxed and restored. It was torn by vivid dreams. She saw the same images over and over again, like scenes from a horror film on a loop, but among the replaying of a woman turning almost delicately in the air and a pool of blood tracing patterns in the street were other pictures. Pan running through an alleyway, her heart thundering in her chest. Someone was behind her and closing. She turned her head from time to time, but saw nothing. Her eyes fixed on the opening of the alley, legs cramping with acid, sure that someone would, at any moment, step in front of her, block her escape.

When she woke - sitting bolt upright in bed, her face covered in sweat and a cry dying in her throat - she didn't understand where she was. Then she saw the French doors, the rows of beds, and remembered. *When I was a child*, she thought, *and I was having nightmares, awakening was a blessing, a restoration of normality, a sense, finally, of being safe.* Now it was waking from one nightmare into another. She forced herself to get out of bed. The temptation to lie down again was strong, but the fear of what sleep would bring was more powerful. She found her way to the bathroom.

The soap stung her eyes and she reached blindly for the towel draped over the rail.

It was placed into her hands.

For one moment, Pan didn't understand. Then the knowledge that she wasn't alone hit her. Her heart quickened and she pulled the towel up against her body, scrubbed furiously at her face, working the soap from her eyes.

'Sorry to alarm you,' said a voice. It was a girl's voice. 'I forget sometimes that newbies are sensitive about such things.'

As soon as her eyes cleared, Pan wrapped the towel tightly around her body and blinked at her visitor. The girl was short and lean, jet black hair to her jaw line, cut, rather inexpertly, into a fringe that framed a face with small delicate features. Her eyes were almost as black as her hair.

'Where I come from,' said Pan. 'It's polite to knock.' She didn't attempt to keep the irritation out of her voice.

'But you're not there,' the girl pointed out matter-of-factly. 'You're in The School now.' She ran her eyes up and down Pan's body. 'We don't go for social etiquette much around here. If you don't mind me saying, you look like crap.'

'Thanks,' said Pan. 'Now, if *you* don't mind, I would like to get dressed.'

The girl didn't move.

'In private?' Pan added.

'I brought you some clothes,' said the girl. She pointed to a pile of army fatigues, neatly folded on a bench. The clothes seemed very similar to the ones the girl herself wore. 'Whatever you were wearing when you came in was burned. Standard procedure. And it's cold out there right now, so a hospital gown just isn't going to cut it.'

Pan hugged the towel tighter. 'I'm not going anywhere,'

she said. 'As you so tactfully pointed out, I look and feel like crap. Once I dry off I'm going back to bed.'

The girl shook her head. 'No,' she said. 'You're not. You are coming with me for orientation.' She smiled then and it brightened her whole face. Pan almost found herself smiling back. It was infectious. But she fought the impulse and won.

The girl held out her hand. 'My name is Wei-Lin,' she said. 'And you are Pandora Jones. I'm pleased to meet you, Pandora.'

Pan was tempted not to take the offered hand, but she couldn't bring herself to be deliberately rude. She shook and the girl's face brightened.

'I'll wait for you outside,' she said. 'Please be quick. The others are waiting and we have a lot to get through.'

'And if I refuse?' said Pan. She had decided that she would accompany the girl, but felt it was important to establish that she had a will of her own. The hospital bed had lost what few charms it ever possessed and she was curious about what lay beyond the Infirmary's walls. But she bristled against the assumption that she would simply follow orders without question.

Wei-Lin smiled. 'You'll come anyway.'

'You mean you'd physically force me?'

'Absolutely.' She appeared immensely cheerful at the prospect. 'But I don't think that would get us off on the right foot, do you? So I would much appreciate it if you got dressed and came with me, Pandora Jones. Please.' She moved towards the door, but immediately turned back. 'Haven't you done enough sleeping to last a lifetime?' She left without waiting for a reply.

Pan was grateful she didn't have to answer the question. She *had* done enough sleeping and, anyway, it had brought nothing but pain. She put the clothes on quickly. They were baggy in the body, but the length of the trousers was about right and the camouflage jacket's sleeves were only slightly too long. The dark combat boots pinched somewhat and Pan hoped they would break in quickly. She towel-dried her hair and pulled it back from her face. When she looked into the mirror she almost laughed. Her reflection was faintly absurd, an emaciated girl trying to look tough and failing spectacularly. Pan didn't laugh, though. She wasn't sure she would ever laugh again.

Wei-Lin was waiting outside the door. She glanced at Pan, but said nothing. Then she walked down the corridor, past the nurses' station and out the front door. Pan followed, struggling to keep up. Her leg muscles tightened and burned almost immediately. *I'm in really bad shape*, she thought.

'Don't we need to tell the doctors that I'm going?' she panted at Wei-Lin's back.

Wei-Lin threw her answer over her shoulder. 'They know. They weren't happy, but they know,' she said. 'Anyway, they're not doctors. Morgan and Macredie. They call themselves doctors in The School but out there...' she gestured vaguely towards the sea '...they were something else entirely. I think Macredie might have been a school nurse and Morgan was in hospital administration. The closest he came to medicine was a first-aid certificate that he had to have for his job.'

'Wait,' said Pan. She stood for a moment and resisted the temptation to bend forward and put her hands on her aching thighs. Wei-Lin turned. 'How can they be doctors here?' Pan added.

Wei-Lin shrugged.

'We've lost ninety-nine point something percent of the world's population. They have an interest in medicine and they have books. It would have been convenient if a few GPs had survived, maybe some surgeons. Perhaps they did, but they are not here. This is a new world, Pandora. We make do with the talent we have. And we learn.'

Pan took deep breaths and gazed out at the surrounding landscape. The view was as dramatic as it had been from the courtyard outside the Infirmary. The sky was overcast with low clouds that threatened rain and she could not see the sea. But the rest of The School was spread before her. And the wall.

'What's beyond that wall?' she asked.

Wei-Lin took a couple of steps back and stood next to Pan. She too looked out over the landscape.

'I'll answer your questions at orientation,' she said. 'But I don't want to repeat myself unnecessarily. Time is precious, so let's go.'

'How do we get down?' The question hadn't occurred to Pan before and she wondered why. The plateau that the Infirmary was on was bounded at the back by the mountain face. On the other three sides there was a sheer and precipitous drop.

'There are stairs.' Wei-Lin pointed to the left-hand side of the outcrop, but it was impossible to see anything from where they stood. 'Cut into the rock. Steep, and there are no handrails. I hope you're not afraid of heights.'

'Actually, I am.'

'Ah,' said Wei-Lin. 'That's something you will have to master then. Or maybe the simplest solution is not to get sick or injured. That way you might never have to visit the Infirmary again.'

The descent was terrifying. Pan kept to the right side of the steps, as close to the rock face as she could, but although the steps were broad, she could still see the edge and the dizzying drop. Her eyes were drawn to it. She focused on fixing her vision on each step and tried to regulate her breathing. One step after another, bringing both feet together before reaching for the next. It seemed to take forever. Wei-Lin appeared to have no concerns. On the few occasions that Pan looked up, her companion was almost skipping down, stopping every few minutes to allow Pan to catch up. If she was impatient with Pan's progress she hid it well. Finally, they reached the bottom and Pan let out a long sigh. Her legs were cramping, and she was grateful for the cold, clean air.

'Just a couple of hundred metres to go,' said Wei-Lin. She pointed towards a low-set structure down a dirt path strewn with stones. 'That's where we're going.'

The building reminded Pan of the drab portables at her school.

'It's time to meet the rest of our group,' said Wei-Lin. She set off down the path and Pan forced her aching muscles to follow.

~~~

The room was spare and cold. The few windows were uncurtained and festooned with cobwebs. A dilapidated desk was at one end, in front of an old-fashioned black-board and an assortment of plastic chairs arranged in a haphazard circle. Sitting on the chairs were three boys and three girls. They looked up as Wei-Lin and Pan entered. They appeared as dispirited as the room they occupied.

Wei-Lin walked briskly to an unoccupied chair, but she didn't sit. Pan took a place next to a tall, good-looking boy of about seventeen. She met his eyes and he nodded briefly before returning his gaze to the floor.

'Good morning,' said Wei-Lin. 'Welcome to our group and I'm sorry I have kept you all waiting. With the exception of me, you are all new to The School. Think of this as your very first day of school.'

The boy next to Pan snorted, but he didn't raise his head. If Wei-Lin heard him she didn't acknowledge it.

'My name is Wei-Lin and I am your mentor. This does not mean that I am in any position of seniority over you. The School doesn't operate like that. All it means is that I have been here longer. Five weeks to be precise. I know my way around The School and understand how it functions. The purpose of this orientation is for me to pass on what knowledge I have, give out important information and answer your questions to the best of my ability. Is that clear?'

No one said anything.

'Okay,' she continued. 'Some basic stuff to start. You've all been issued with one set of clothing. On the bench over there you will find another set and a backpack. When we're done here, please put your change of clothes into the backpack. This is all you'll be issued, so look after them. Sunday is the designated wash day so that means you'll have only one change of clothes per week.

Trust me, you get used to it. On top of the clothes, you will find a watch. Like the rest of the stuff here, this is army issue. The watch is tough and accurate. Wear it at all times. You'll also find a map of The School, to help you make your way around at the beginning. You probably won't need it after a few days.

'Right. Here's the idea. There are eight of us in this particular group. We live together, eat together, learn, study and work-out together. We'll be self-sufficient and we'll look out for each other. This is the smallest group in The School - most are around fifteen in number, but fewer and fewer people are coming in, so this is probably how we'll stay. Should there be a further influx then it is possible that one of you will be selected to leave this group and mentor another. But that probably won't happen, if only because we can't afford to lose anyone.'

Wei-Lin paused, but whether that was to allow anyone to speak was unclear. The group remained silent. Pan glanced around. Most still had their heads bowed, though one girl sat stiffly upright in her chair, her eyes fixed on Wei-Lin. Her gaze was flat and hard. *She is tough*, thought Pan. *Possibly troubled. Maybe even trouble*. The girl stared directly at Pan, who lowered her eyes instinctively. The silence stretched a moment or two longer.

'It is hoped,' continued Wei-Lin, 'that we'll become a tightly-bound group. A family.'

The boy next to Pan laughed outright at that. It was a bitter laugh, but it wasn't entirely without humour.

'They say you can't choose your family,' he said, 'so that's consistent. And I'm sorry to piss on your parade, *sister*, but I had a family and they were trouble enough. I'm not sure I want another.'

'Yes,' said Wei-Lin, calmly. 'But your real family is dead. We're not. That's an important difference.'

The boy shrugged, but he didn't say anything.

'Okay,' said Wei-Lin. 'We may become a dysfunctional family. Most are. But we need to get acquainted, if only so we know who it is we resent.' The boy laughed again. 'I will start and then we will go around the circle. It's basic information. Name, where we came from and what, if anything, we are good at. The School is keen on identifying skills and developing them. It could be anything. Green fingers, ability at maths, skiing, whatever. A word of advice, before we start. Try not to revisit your memories of the virus. Most of us, I suspect, have jumbled memories anyway – a side-effect of infection, it would appear.'

'Why?' interrupted Pan. 'I mean, why don't you want us to talk about it?'

'It's not that I don't want you to,' replied Wei-Lin. 'It's just that it's not productive. If you are anything like me, you visit some terrible places every time you fall asleep. Nothing useful comes of sharing it. We have all been through hell. We are still going through it. I can't cope with my own nightmares and I certainly don't want the burden of yours.'

'Okay,' said Pan.

'My name is Wei-Lin. I am fourteen and I lived in Hong Kong. I once came third in my age group for archery in a competition in China. Archery is a skill I've been learning since I was eight years old. I guess this means I am top in my age group now. I was rescued AV by a helicopter on reconnaissance for survivors and brought to The School just over five weeks ago. I remember little of my rescue and even less of the days before that.'

'AV?' asked the boy next to Pan.

'After Virus,' replied Wei-Lin.

The boy nodded. 'I feel so much better knowing we have an acronym for it,' he said. 'Makes me feel nostalgic for the old world.'

Wei-Lin smiled. 'You,' she said, pointing to the boy on her right.

He had spectacularly bad acne. Pan felt relieved that she would be the last to speak.

'My name's Karl,' he said. 'Fifteen. Wellington, New Zealand. Not particularly good at anything, unless you count computer games. I was hot shit at that.'

'Could be useful,' said Wei-Lin.

'You have computers here?' said Karl. Hope lit up his face.

'No,' said Wei-Lin. 'Not yet. But you will have developed some useful skills from playing. We'll talk later. Next.'

'Samantha, but everyone calls me Sam. Sixteen years old. Originally from the UK, but I was on holiday in Bali with my . . .' She stopped and swallowed. 'Can't remember how I got here. I was in the Scouts for a long time. I've done some orienteering.'

'Excellent. Next.'

For a moment it seemed the girl wouldn't say anything. She was pale, her face pudgy and coarse featured. She twirled a lock of hair around her index finger and was reluctant to meet anyone's eyes. It seemed she was on the verge of bursting into tears. *She is severely depressed*, thought Pan. *Though, then again, aren't we all?* Finally the girl opened her mouth, but everyone had to strain to catch her words.

'Cara,' she whispered. 'New Zealand. I can cook. A little.'

'Fantastic,' said Wei-Lin. 'The food here is disgusting, as you will find out. Anyone who can cook will be worth their weight in gold.'

If Cara was pleased at this, she gave no sign. She simply continued to twirl the same strand of hair round and round.

The next boy was almost as reticent. He identified himself as Sanjit from the Top End of Australia and that he was good with most things technological. Wei-Lin assured him that his skills would similarly be valued. The next was the girl with the hard stare. She was as loud as the previous two had been quiet.

'Jen, seventeen, from Sydney, Australia. I have a black belt in judo and a number of different martial arts.' *That would be right*, thought Pan. *She looks like someone who would be keen on inflicting pain, rather than someone who studied martial arts for self-defence or spiritual enlightenment. The aggressive, possibly bullying member of this new family.*

The good-looking boy to her immediate left was next.

'My name's Nate and I'm eighteen,' he said. 'I was in Singapore for an athletics meet, but I'm American. Sorry about that, though there's nothing I can do about it. Unlike everyone else, I remember everything – AV . . .' he made speech marks in the air with his fingers, 'perfectly, though most of the time I wish I didn't. I am a runner. It's all I'm good at. Give me a stretch of land and I'll run across it. If running is part of this brave new world, then I'm your man.'

Pan liked his accent. She liked the way he looked even more. Tall, dark, with a mass of black curls, and even though he was wearing the same fatigues as everyone else, they didn't hide his lean and muscular frame. He also appeared to have a sense of humour. *I bet he turns out to be a dick,* thought Pan. *The attractive ones always turn out to be dicks.*

She was unexpectedly nervous when it was her turn to speak. She kept it brief and then surprised herself when it came time to outline her skills.

'I find things,' she said.

'Sorry?' said Wei-Lin. 'You find things?'

Pan regretted her words immediately. In fact, she had no idea she was going to say anything at all about her hunches, her intuition, until the words spilled from her mouth. Maybe it was nerves. Now she felt the eyes of the rest of the group on her and felt obliged to continue.

'It's just that . . . well, I seem to know things other people don't. So when someone loses something I can often tell them where it is. No big deal, or anything. Lost keys, that sort of thing.' Pan could feel her face flush. *Why did I bring up this crap?* she thought.

'You mean you're psychic?' asked Nate.

'N . . . No,' Pan stammered. 'I get hunches, that's all. Feelings. And sometimes those feelings turn out to be . . . It's hard to describe. Look, forget it. I don't have any skills. Not really.'

Silence. Then Nate laughed. He lifted his hands and made wavy motions with his fingers. 'Doo, doo, doo, doo,

doo, doo, doo, doo,' he chuckled. 'Welcome to the *Twilight Zone*.'

But it wasn't said nastily. Pan found herself smiling, though when she glanced up she noticed a sneer on Jen's face. There was nothing friendly about *her* expression.

Wei-Lin clapped her hands together.

'Okay, everyone,' she said. 'I think we are in need of a break. Please collect your backpacks and change of clothes and follow me. I'll show you where we'll all be sleeping and then take you to the canteen for what passes for lunch. I know you have loads of questions and I'll answer as many as I can while we eat. After lunch, we'll go to our first and last lesson of the day. Actually, it's not really a lesson as such. I've arranged for us to observe a weapons-training class with Mr Gwynne to give you some idea of the curriculum. Lessons proper will start tomorrow. After that, we'll come back here and I'll finish this orientation by answering your remaining questions as best I can. All clear? Then let's go.'

They all packed the clothes, strapped on their watches and hefted the packs onto their backs. Wei-Lin led the way out of the building. A pale sun had emerged from between the clouds and caused Pan to narrow her eyes. She followed the Chinese girl down a rough track leading towards the distant wall. After a couple of minutes, Pan noticed that Nate was walking at her side. He was smiling broadly.

'You find things, huh?' he said.

'Sometimes,' replied Pan.

'Excellent. I think I've lost my mind. Any idea where I could find it?'

'This is where we girls will be sleeping,' said Wei-Lin. 'Dormitory D. The boys are next door in E. We're sharing our sleeping quarters with other groups, so you'll find most of the beds are already taken. I suggest you find yourself a bunk and put your backpack on it. Stake your claim.'

The dormitories were grouped together, about twenty of them. A fence separated the boys' from the girls' areas, though it wasn't a high fence and seemed to be more a symbolic barrier than anything else. Each building had a large capital letter printed on the roof. The dormitories were constructed of corrugated iron, each one painted a bilious primary colour.

'Cheerful,' said Nate. 'Hey, once we've checked in, how about meeting up at the poolside bar and ordering a few pina coladas?'

'Be sure to let me know if you find the pool,' said Wei-Lin. 'I haven't stumbled across it yet.'

'What's with the segregation?' Nate asked. 'I thought we were a team. Live together, work together, sleep together.'

'In your dreams,' said Sam.

'I mean,' Nate continued, 'with only a few thousand of us left, I would have thought we should all be getting on with the grim task of re-populating the planet. It's a dirty job, but I want it placed on record that I'm prepared to do my bit for the sake of humanity's future. I'm happy to take one for the team.'

'Are you going to be making jokes all the time?' said Jen. That hardness was back in her eyes. She put her hands on her hips. 'Because frankly, *pal*, I don't find any of this a bit funny.'

'So what do you want me to do?' Nate replied. 'Weep, wail, tear my hair out? You need to lighten up, sister.'

'What I *need* . . .'

'Okay, guys.' Wei-Lin clapped her hands together. 'It's great that we're already bonding, but I suggest we leave this discussion for another time. Check out the sleeping quarters and meet me here in ten minutes. Then I'll show you the shower blocks and we'll get something to eat.'

Pan was the first to open the door to dormitory D. The interior was dark and smelled of sweat and boiled cabbage. Even though it was fairly bright outside, the narrow, uncurtained windows did not admit much light. Pan ran her hand along the wall, looking for a light switch, but found nothing. It took her a few minutes to realise that there wasn't one. She made her way down the centre of the room, the other girls trailing behind her, looking at the rows of beds on each side. Nearly all were made immaculately. Even in the dim light she could see that none of them had so much as a wrinkle on the flat sheets.

Two-thirds of the way down the dormitory, she came across a number of beds that were clearly unoccupied, the blankets and sheets folded on the bare mattresses. Presumably, the pick of the beds were those closest to the door, closest to the toilets, she guessed. New students had to make do with what was left. She deliberately picked the bunk at the furthest end of the dormitory – maybe she would be given a small amount of privacy. She sat down on the bed. The mattress was firm, bordering on hard and the grey blanket was coarse and musty. Next to each bunk there was a basic locker. She opened it. Inside were a small torch, a pair of earplugs and a rough towel. She picked up the earplugs and examined them.

'It can get noisy at night.' Wei-Lin stood at the end of Pan's bunk. She nodded towards the earplugs.

'Noisy?'

'Most of us suffer from nightmares. Without those, your chances of getting any sleep aren't good.'

Pan nodded and placed the earplugs back. She turned on the torch. It had a narrow powerful beam. *For finding your way out in the middle of the night*, she thought. Without electricity the room would get very dark.

'Oh, yeah,' said Wei-Lin. 'You need to ration the use of the torch. Once the battery's gone, that's pretty much it, I'm afraid. We rarely get any supplies from the outside and torch batteries are not high on The School's list of priorities.' Pan switched hers off. 'There are flame torches,' Wei-Lin continued, 'for seeing your way around the grounds at night.'

'Flame torches?' asked Pan.

Wei-Lin smiled. 'You'll see,' she said. 'Old technology, but kinda atmospheric.'

The other three girls selected their bunks. Pan wondered if she wore the same expression as they did. As if they were in a nightmare and losing hope that they would ever wake up. Samantha, the girl with the British accent, sat listlessly on her bed and looked out through the dusty window, even though there was nothing to see. Cara stared at the floorboards. The only one who seemed at ease was Jen. She lay on her bunk, hands clasped behind her head, gazing at the ceiling. Wei-Lin had taken the bunk next to Pan. *So much for privacy*, thought Pan, though it also occurred to her it could have been worse. She liked Wei-Lin and certainly did not relish the notion of being next to the aggressive Jen or the depressed Cara.

'Okay,' said Wei-Lin. 'Tempting though it might be to soak up the luxury of our room, I need to show you the toilet and shower block and then get you to the canteen. If we are late, all the food will go, and believe me, we do not want that.'

The boys had already gathered by the time the girls emerged from their dorm. Nate was smiling faintly. When he saw Pan he gave a thumbs up and his grin broadened. She found herself smiling back. Wei-Lin took them to two shacks about fifty metres away from their dorm. They too were made of corrugated iron. The international signs for male and female toilets were painted on the doors. Wei-Lin popped her head around the door of the female toilets.

'Okay,' she said. 'No one here, so you boys can come in while I tell you how this works. The shower blocks are the same in both, apparently.'

'I believe I know how showers work,' said Nate.

'Not these showers,' Wei-Lin replied.

The interior was as comfortless and practical as the dormitories. Six or seven cubicles were ranged along one side of the wall. The toilets, presumably, though Pan noticed that two didn't have doors. *Great*, she thought. There was only one washbasin. Next to it was a large communal shower area, with four showerheads arranged evenly along the chipped and grimy wall tiles. A fifth shower head was set apart from the others. Each shower had a button at waist height.

'It's pretty simple,' said Wei-Lin. 'You hit this button on the wall and you get two minutes.' She laughed. 'Cold water. Salt water. Then you get under this shower head.' She pointed to the one separated from the others. 'You press this button and there's a further twenty seconds of cold water to rinse off. Fresh this time. Welcome to the Ritz hotel.' Wei-Lin punched the button to demonstrate. A thin trickle came from the head. Almost before it started, it dwindled and died.

'What's to stop us hitting the button again?' Sam asked. 'Get a decent rinse.'

Wei-Lin smiled.

'Nothing,' she said. 'But we don't do that. It's not fair. We have to conserve water. Taking more is just robbing someone else. And we are all in this together. You'll see how things work. A small tip. Most people bring along a container of some kind, a cup maybe, to collect as much water as possible. When salt water dries on you, it's not pleasant. Any questions?'

'Let me get this right,' said Karl. 'These two blocks are for all the students here? There are no other showers or toilets?'

'Apart from the Infirmary, this is it,' said Wei-Lin. 'For nearly four hundred students. So get in, get out. At least you boys have an advantage over us girls.'

'Yes?' said Karl.

'There is a big outside for you guys, depending upon what you need to do. Oh, by the way. Toilet paper. There's not much of it, so use it sparingly. Be considerate.'

'Fantastic,' said Nate. 'I can see how this place got its four stars.'

'Time for lunch,' said Wei-Lin. 'If you think this is bad, wait until you see the canteen.'

~~~

The canteen was considerably larger yet equally uninspiring. It was about a ten-minute walk from the dormitories. Plain wooden tables and basic benches were arranged in rows. Pan guessed it could probably seat about two hundred people, and when the group walked in, it was virtually full. A long counter dominated one side and a small kitchen could be seen behind it. Five or six young people stood behind the counter, ladling something into bowls. A long line of students waited to be served.

'Two shifts for each meal time,' said Wei-Lin. 'Breakfast at seven and seven-thirty. Lunch at twelve and twelve-thirty. Dinner at six-thirty and seven. This week, our group is on the earlier of those shifts. We alternate every week. Don't even think about going to the later session if you miss the first. People will know and it gets ugly. Similarly, eat and get out as quickly as possible. This is not a social meeting place. Think about it as a place to stock up on energy supplies, nothing more. Anyway, once you've tasted the food, believe me you'll want to get out of here. Let's go.'

She led the group to the end of the line. They picked up a bowl each and a spoon. At least it didn't take long to get served. They weren't offered a choice. Each student held out their bowl and something sloppy was ladled into it. At the end of the counter, a young boy handed out chunks of bread. He was probably ten years old or less and his face was covered in freckles. An untidy mop of red hair stuck out at strange angles. Pan smiled. Small boys, in her experience, didn't bother much with keeping their hair tidy unless there was stern parental supervision. The implications of her thought caused the smile to freeze. Immediately she thought about her brother and tried to push the image away.

'Thanks,' she said as the boy placed a ragged chunk of coarse bread onto her bowl. The boy looked up and Pan was struck by the fierce blue of his eyes.

'You're new, aren't you?' said the boy.

Pan smiled. 'Sure am,' she said. 'My name's Pan.'

'If you find any kind of meat in your food and you don't want it - you know, it doesn't matter if it's gristly, or anything, then can you save it for me? Please? Only meat, though. Nothin' else.'

Pan was as much puzzled by the intensity of the boy's stare as by his request, but she paused, despite the jostling of the queue behind her.

'Hungry, are you?' she said.

'Not me,' said the boy. 'Well, I am, of course. Everyone is. But it's not for me, it's for . . .'

'Tom?' Wei-Lin's voice came over Pan's shoulder. 'We would love to stay and chat but there's a whole bunch of people who need to eat here. Keep the line moving, will you?'

'Sorry,' said Tom. 'Don't forget the meat,' he whispered as Pan moved on.

'I can't believe our luck,' said Wei-Lin as they walked away from the counter. 'A hot lunch. Most times we just get bread and, if the stars are aligned, a piece of cheese. You guys are privileged.'

Wei-Lin led the group to a small table that was unoccupied and they sat and examined the contents of their bowls. A coarse and grainy stew in which meat played a bit part, if any part at all. Nate fished among the mess and finally produced a gristly lump from his serving.

'Do I get a prize?' he said, squinting at it.

'I think that *is* your prize,' Pan replied. 'Hey, if you don't want it, there's a kid who does.'

Nate didn't reply, but popped the lump into his mouth. He grimaced and swallowed. Pan couldn't find anything even resembling meat in her serving. They both mopped up the thin and tasteless gravy with a hard chunk of bread.

'This is pretty good,' said Wei-Lin.

'You're joking,' said Karl. 'Tell me you're joking.'

'Serious.'

'Oh God.' Karl scooped up another spoonful and put it to his mouth. His nose twitched and his mouth turned down. Eventually he swallowed, but it was an effort of will. 'Oh God,' he said again.

The students around them didn't appear to find anything strange about the food. They ate relentlessly, with a kind of grim determination, as if they weren't sure if this was going to be their last meal. *And maybe that is actually the case*, thought Pan. Maybe she should treat the meal as a bonus. She tried, but it didn't taste any better. She noticed that Cara didn't eat anything at all. She'd pushed the stew around a little then abandoned it. The New Zealand girl had remained obstinately silent as well. Pan couldn't remember when she had last said a word. She or that Indian boy. What was his name? Sanjit, or something similar.

Wei-Lin glanced up. 'You not eating that?' she asked.

Cara shook her head.

Wei-Lin took the bowl. 'Anyone want to share?'

No one did.

'You'll be sorry,' said Wei-Lin. 'Eat when you can, whatever you can. Number one rule in The School.' She shovelled the stew down and cleaned the inside of the bowl with the last of her bread. 'Compliments to the chef,' she said.

Nate laughed.

Wei-Lin glanced at her watch. 'Okay,' she said. 'We have ten minutes. Burning questions about The School. Any we don't get time to cover will be dealt with after our weapons-training session. So. Shoot.'

'How come the food's so crap?' said Karl.

'Good question,' replied Wei-Lin. 'Obvious answer. We eat only what we grow or what is brought in. It is early days, but not much progress has been made on growing vegetables in this climate. We have an animal husbandry program, but there aren't many chickens so far and nothing like cows or pigs. Get involved in agriculture and caring for livestock. Our stomachs will be grateful. There are no fast food outlets, so ringing for a pizza will get us nowhere. Next.'

'There must be huge amounts of food just lying around out there,' pointed out Nate. 'Why can't we stockpile tinned stuff?'

'We do,' said Wei-Lin. 'The problem is not so much with the availability of food, but with its transportation. We have one helicopter - and I can't tell you how lucky we are to have someone who can fly it. The odds must have been astronomical. But the helicopter's number one priority is finding survivors and bringing them back. The pilot does bring tinned food back, but it's limited. For the rest, we rely on the people in the village - the place on the other side of the wall.'

'There are people there?' asked Nate.

'Sure. Maybe a hundred, give or take a few. They are our supply route. Boats go out constantly, looking for food supplies and other essential items. But it all takes time and the boats are small. They can only bring back so much.'

'What's with the wall?' asked Pan. 'Why is it there?'

'No idea,' said Wei-Lin. 'This place was, at one time, a military installation. It must have existed for a long time BV.' She glanced at Nate. 'That's Before Virus, as I'm sure you guessed, Nate. Who knows why the military does what it does? Clearly this was intended as a secure place and I imagine the wall was something to do with that security, but no one here knows anything more than that.'

'So how did we get here, then, if this was a military base?' asked Sam. 'How did anyone know it was even here? Wherever *here* is.'

Wei-Lin shrugged. 'More speculation. The best guess is that governments had contingency plans in case of disaster. You know, like in the event of a nuclear war, there are supposedly all these shelters where the privileged, the chosen, were destined to be protected. Maybe they also earmarked sites like this in case of a worldwide pandemic. That makes sense.'

'So there are other places like The School?' said Pan. 'I mean, this area couldn't accommodate ten thousand.'

'That's the word. According to some of the staff, there are at least ten other places like The School dotted around the world. They call them "arks", the last vehicles for humanity in a sea of disease. In time, when we have the technology up and running, we should be able to establish contact with them. Pool our resources and ideas. In the meantime, we do what we can to make this place liveable and prepare for when we get back out into the world.'

'Speaking of which . . .'

Wei-Lin interrupted Nate. 'No time at the moment. We need to get cleared up here and off to our lesson. Get your bowls, and follow me.'

They took their bowls to the side of the hall where there were rows of basins filled with tepid water. Each student washed his or her spoon and bowl and stacked them to dry in racks along the wall. The water was oily and filled with a suspension of grainy food remnants. Pan doubted her bowl was any cleaner by the time she had finished scrubbing its surface. Nate grinned. He had a cute lopsided grin.

'Just gets better and better, doesn't it?' he said. 'We need to ask that helicopter pilot dude to pick up a serious industrial dishwasher on his travels.'

'Hey, Wei-Lin,' said a boy in front of Pan. 'Heard you'd left your old group. This your new bunch, huh?' He looked over the eight students and didn't appear impressed. His mouth narrowed into a sneer.

'Best group in The School, Mitch,' replied Wei-Lin. 'Kick your sorry arse any day.'

'Whoa, girl. Them's challenging words.'

'Any time, Mitch. Any time.'

The boy chuckled. 'I love pissing contests,' he said. 'Bring it on.'

'You in Gwynne's weapons class next up?'

'Sure.'

'Excellent. We're coming to watch. It's your chance to impress us, Mitch. Make sure you don't drop the weapon on your toe. I hate to see grown boys cry.'

'"Coming to watch"?' He feigned a shiver. 'What a tough bunch of guys. I'm crapping myself, Wei-Lin.'

Wei-Lin smiled before turning back to her group. 'Follow me,' she said. 'Gwynne's a hard task-master, but he knows his stuff.'

She led her team out into the pale sunshine, Cara and Sanjit trailing at the rear.

Chapter 5

Thirty students were assembled on a large rocky outcrop. The cold seemed to have intensified despite the weak sun, and Pan wondered if it was ever warm in this place. The instructor paced up and down in front of the class. He was a short, stocky man with a shaved head. His features appeared to have been forcefully rearranged a number of times in the past. His nose had clearly been badly broken and even more badly reset. He wiped at it constantly and sniffed.

'Right,' he barked. 'Beginners weapons-training. Range of weapons and how best to use them.'

Wei-Lin and her group stood off to one side. The instructor glanced in their direction and then ignored them. 'That's Gwynne. Ex-military,' whispered Wei-Lin. 'And with the sense of humour of an Uzi submachine gun.'

'Today, simple staff work,' the instructor continued. 'A staff. Oldest and noblest of weapons.' He strolled up and down in front of the students. 'And easy to find. Readily available. Later I'll show you how to make one. Wood, sharp knife. Result, lethal weapon.'

'Does he always talk like that?' whispered Pan.

Wei-Lin laughed. 'Oh, yes. Sometimes I think he looks on words as bullets. Quick sprays are best. Don't waste your ammunition.'

Gwynne picked up a length of gnarled wood from a pile behind him and shifted it in his hands.

'Balance is key. Not just staff, but also you. Weapon becomes extension of body. Practice. Very important. Objective is you don't know you're even carrying it. Okay. Basic techniques. Volunteer?'

No one moved. *I'm not surprised*, thought Pan. *This looks dangerous*. Gwynne glanced along the line of students.

'What? None of you chickenshits?' he said.

'I will.'

The voice came from Pan's right. She glanced around. Jen's hand was raised. *Of course*, thought Pan. *What had Jen said about her interests? Martial arts?*

Gwynne frowned. 'Haven't seen you before,' he said. 'New?'

'Yes. But I know something about Hapkido.'

Gwynne sniffed and wiped at his nose.

'Hapkido?' He smiled, but there was no warmth in it. '*I* call it stick-fighting. Hapkido. Interesting. Step forward.'

He tossed the staff to Jen, who caught it expertly and hefted it in her hands, testing the weight and balance.

'Right,' said the instructor, wiping once more at his nose. 'Now, basic moves - defence, blocks and counter-attacks. Avoid injury. Protective clothing. Put it on.' He indicated a pile of clothing next to the jumble of staffs. Jen pulled out a padded helmet. It was like a cyclist's helmet, but with extra panels built in to protect the ears and the neck. There were also arm and leg guards and a bulky vest. Jen placed the helmet on her head and fastened a buckle under her chin, cinching it tight. Then she took the protective gear, simple pieces of moulded heavy-duty padding that joined with Velcro strips. It took her only thirty seconds to be ready. Gwynne looked her up and down, nodded and then addressed the waiting students. He was clearly not quick to give praise or encouragement.

'Watch,' he said. 'We'll do this slowly. I will attack. She will employ basic defensive manoeuvres. We'll do this a few times. Then you lot, in pairs, go through the moves.' He moved closer to Jen and examined the position of her hands. He nodded again, but it seemed, to Pan at least, a grudging acknowledgement. 'Must have hands like this. Pay attention. See? This position allows you to move without changing grip. Changing grip, time-consuming, dangerous. Now watch. I bring staff over. Roundhouse blow to top of head. I connect, game over. Luckily, it's easy to block.'

He stepped forward and brought the staff in a very slow and lazy curve towards Jen's head, stopping as he reached the highest point of the arc.

'Now. Simple block.'

Jen immediately brought up her hands so the staff lay parallel to her shoulders, a metre or so in front of her face.

'Good,' said Gwynne. 'Note barrier protects head. Safe, even from solid blow.' He took a step back and then brought his staff down quickly. There was a resounding thud as Jen's staff met his and halted its downward movement.

'Excellent. Note how the new girl kept hands fluid. Easy to get knuckles rapped. This happens. Important not to drop staff when it does. Do not grip too hard. Staff must be able to move, slide between fingers. Note how the new girl moved hands wider, means more staff to block thrust. Again.'

They went through this routine half a dozen more times, the circle of students watching carefully. Jen blocked each attack with ease, her feet shifting to maintain balance. After the fifth time, Gwynne took a step back.

'Name, new girl?' he said.

'Jen.'

'I'm impressed, Jen. How much do you know about stick-fighting?'

Jen shrugged. 'Enough. But I'm always eager to learn more.'

Gwynne nodded. 'Good,' he said. 'The reason we are here. Right. Time for other manoeuvres, in slow motion. I will try to break Jen's defences, attack her side and legs. Legs are particularly important. Sweep away opponent's legs, you win. Almost certain. Difficult defending yourself from the ground. Watch.'

This time Gwynne moved his staff slightly quicker. He started with the same attack on Jen's head, but followed it immediately with a thrust to the side. Jen blocked both easily and fluently. When Gwynne went for her legs she skipped backwards and blocked that too. Gwynne stood with his legs slightly apart, the staff planted between his feet.

'Jen makes this seem easy. It isn't. Plenty of practice, plenty of bruises. Right. This time I will attack, full speed. My opponent defends, attacks if given chance. Okay, Jen?'

Jen stretched out her arms, the staff balanced on her palms, and bowed towards Gwynne. He smiled, but it appeared an unaccustomed action.

'Another world, young Jen,' he said. 'Advice. This is no longer a sport. No meaningless rituals. Think only of survival. Bow again and I'll hurt you while you're distracted.'

Jen smiled.

Gwynne rocked back and forth on the balls of his feet, took a couple of paces to the side, his eyes never leaving Jen's face. His attack was sudden and brutal. He feinted a blow to Jen's head, but then immediately moved his staff so that it traced an arc towards her feet. Jen skipped back and blocked, brought her own staff up towards Gwynne's head. He parried and performed a complex manoeuvre that managed to attack his opponent on a number of different levels, apparently simultaneously. His staff moved so quickly that it was a blur in the air. Jen took a couple of steps back under the pressure of the onslaught, but she blocked every attack. *It's in the feet*, Pan thought. This might look like a couple of people trying to smash each other with sticks, but it was also a balletic sequence in which balance, rhythm and timing were of paramount importance. There was something almost beautiful in it.

The ending happened so quickly that no one watching could quite understand how it occurred. One moment they were dancing around each other, the next Gwynne was on his knees and clutching his stomach. Pan had an unimpeded view of his face, which was screwed up in agony. For a moment she thought he was going to vomit.

Jen stood motionless, her staff pointed straight towards her opponent. It was clear she had connected with a straight jab to Gwynne's stomach, knocking the air out of him. *I'd have to watch that in slow motion*, thought Pan. *Maybe frame advance, it was so quick.*

Gwynne took a minute to get to his feet, his face ashen. He picked up his staff and straightened gingerly, taking in deep lungfuls of air. The silence was intense. Jen had returned to a position of rest, the staff balanced on her palms and parallel to the ground. Gwynne sniffed and rubbed at his nose with a sleeve.

'You know where you went wrong?' he asked finally. It was clear the words were a considerable effort. Jen cocked her head.

'I was on ground,' Gwynne continued. 'Should've finished me. A sharp blow. Back of the head. All over.'

'You didn't have protective gear on,' Jen replied.

'So? My mistake, your advantage. Should've capitalised. Now I am back up, ready to fight.' He coughed. 'Well, nearly ready.' There was a titter of nervous laughter among the audience. 'If I beat you next time, then your mistake may have cost your life. Never let an enemy get up. Never, understand?'

'I understand,' said Jen. 'But in this case, it doesn't make any difference.'

'Why?' asked Gwynne.

Jen smiled. 'Because I'd just beat you again.'

The knife appeared in Gwynne's right hand so quickly that it seemed as if it had always been there. He gripped the blade lightly between thumb and index finger. This time *he* cocked his head.

'You've a throwing knife in your neck, young lady,' he said. 'Game over. Take note. I didn't bow. I didn't pose. I didn't admire my own skill. Now I'm alive and you're dead. Maybe there's a lesson in that somewhere.'

Jen watched Gwynne and then slowly nodded.

'It won't happen again,' she said.

'Good. Anyway, next time I'm wearing protective clothing.' He smiled and this time there was some warmth in it. 'What's your skill set?'

'Skill set?'

'Talent or gift. You've been told about that? The School, identifies student strengths, develops them. Core part of curriculum.'

'Yeah,' said Jen. 'It was mentioned.'

'I want to work with you. Martial arts. We could learn from each other.'

'Okay,' said Jen.

'Excellent. Four-thirty to six-thirty, Monday to Saturday, you're mine. Meet me here, understand?'

'Including today?'

'Of course today,' said Gwynne. 'What else do you have on? A hairdressing appointment?'

'I'll be here.'

Gwynne nodded and turned back to his group.

'Right,' he said. 'Protective gear on, pair up. Doubtless, it amused you to see your instructor beaten. Enjoy it while you can. The next hour will be high on pain and low on chuckles. No joke.'

Wei-Lin rounded up the rest of the group, while Jen took off her helmet and pads. Wei-Lin moved towards the path, the group trailing behind, and on the way she tapped Mitch on the shoulder.

'Kick your sorry arse, Mitch,' she whispered. 'Told you. The best group in The School.'

Mitch smiled, but it came out twisted.

~~~

Wei-Lin's group sat in the same chairs they had occupied that morning. The mood was a little better, almost celebratory after Jen's performance at weapons-training. Nate congratulated her, as did Wei-Lin, Sam and Karl. Pan didn't join in and neither did Cara or Sanjit. *Those two are dysfunctional,* thought Pan. *They seem removed from everyone else. Maybe their demons refuse to be tamed. Not that anyone's memories can be tamed, I imagine. Perhaps the rest of us are better at containing them during waking hours.*

Jen didn't say much, but it was clear she was pleased with the attention and the acknowledgement of her skills. *I should congratulate her*, thought Pan, but she couldn't bring herself to do it. There was something feral within the beauty of Jen's dance and it scared her.

'Okay,' said Wei-Lin. 'Back to business, guys. I still have to go through the curriculum of The School with you and answer any further questions you might have. Should we start with the questions?'

Nate immediately jumped in.

'Seems our biggest problem is still the virus,' he said. 'Do we know what it is, whether it is still a threat to us and what it means to the world out there?'

Wei-Lin folded her legs beneath her and rested her chin on a hand.

'Excellent question,' she said. 'Actually *three* excellent questions, but I can only answer in part. Do we know what it is? According to Dr Macredie, there were a number of outbreaks about a decade ago of something that the media called bird-flu and the scientists called the H5N1 virus.' Wei-Lin smiled. 'She's been doing a lot of reading up on this. Basically, some birds, both wild and domestic, often from Asia, became infected with a virus that was easily passed from one individual to another. This influenza virus was well-known but it had undergone either a mutation or something happened that the scientists called reassortment, which is when genetic material is exchanged, giving rise to a new form of virus with different characteristics and abilities. Whatever happened, a number of people became infected with H5N1. Roughly half died. The only positive thing from all this was that the new virus strain didn't appear to have the ability to transmit itself from one human host to another. At least, not easily. There were a few cases of people infecting other people, but basically it was not able to spread. The worry was that further reassortment or mutation might take place within the virus, in which case we would not be so lucky.' Wei-Lin paused. 'Sorry, this is all a little technical. Are you following me so far?'

There was general nodding.

'Okay,' Wei-Lin continued. 'Dr Macredie thinks that's what happened. Reassortment, not mutation. Because mutation, by definition, takes time. This new virus was both highly infectious and deadly. It killed within hours. Whole cities died within a day. The rest of the people on the planet followed within another forty-eight hours. And there was no time to identify the virus. These things take years and years, and the scientists, I imagine, who were tasked with working on it are most likely dead now. It's probable we will never know.'

'So it's possible,' said Sam, 'that this virus is natural, but it's also possible that it's man-made, isn't it?' She turned to the rest of the group. 'I mean, you've all probably heard about governments putting big money into chemical and biological warfare. Isn't it just as likely that some military lab somewhere had an accident and let this bug out?'

Nate laughed. 'I love it,' he said. 'There's only a few of us left but conspiracy theory is still alive and flourishing.'

'It's possible,' said Sam. 'That's all I'm saying.'

'Distinctly possible,' said Wei-Lin. 'But I'm not sure it matters where it came from. It's out there, and for some reason we are immune. Which brings me to Nate's second and third questions. From what I remember of Biology in school, once you've had a disease you are normally resistant to it. So I would guess that it's unlikely the virus will hurt us again, though there are no guarantees. What it means for the world is that there are billions of bodies out there, decaying, polluting drinking water.' She shuddered and closed her eyes briefly as if fighting off unwelcome images. 'No way we can move them, burn them or bury them. So we wait, here in The School, until nature takes care of the problem. A year, maybe two. We'll have to see.'

'Why are we separated from the village beyond the wall?' Pan didn't fully understand why this question felt so important, but she couldn't help herself asking.

'This region has been divided into distinct sections,' said Wei-Lin. 'Possibly the existence of the wall dictated it in the first place. We are students, here in The School, preparing for when the world is ready for us to graduate. The others in the village are generally older and either not physically up to the regime we have in here, or they simply weren't interested in becoming staff or students. Instead, they go out to collect supplies, retrieve what is retrievable out there, and bring back food, animals and other items that The School believes are important to our survival. Generators, for example, and the fuel to run them.'

'Who decides what's needed?'

'School staff in consultation with the student representative council. Any one of us can put ourselves up for election, by the way. Similarly any of us can put in requests for items we need, but don't hold your breath that they will be delivered.' Wei-Lin smiled. 'I have asked for weeks for some decent arrows and a good quality bow, but that's not top of the list of priorities, apparently, because I am still waiting. So I wouldn't rush out and put in an order for a computer, Karl. Sorry.'

Cara put her hand up. It was a gesture both endearing and amusing. Surprising also. It hadn't been clear that she had been paying any attention whatsoever.

'Go ahead, Cara,' said Wei-Lin. 'And you don't have to put your hand up here.'

'Can I go to the village, then?' she said. Again, the members of the group had to lean forward on their chairs to catch her words. 'If I don't like it here in The School?'

Wei-Lin shook her head. 'Sorry, Cara. It was decided early on that we couldn't have people simply going from one place to another. Those in the village are making trips out into the world, and although we probably shouldn't be too concerned about the virus, we also don't know about other diseases they are being exposed to. It would be irresponsible if those of us who survived the worst pandemic in history should then get wiped out by cholera or tuberculosis or an uncommon cold. Like it or not, this is home from here on in.'

A silence greeted these words. Cara resumed the contemplation of the floor beneath her feet.

No one else had any questions so Wei-Lin moved onto the curriculum at The School and the way the days were organised. She explained that they operated a six-day week, with Sunday designated a rest day, though few students treated it as such. It was a time to wash clothes, and do various jobs they hadn't had time to do during the week. Most spent the majority of the day practising and honing their talent or gift. This was the day, Wei-Lin said, when she spent hours on her archery or making arrows out of whatever materials she could find. Others worked with the small number of animals they were raising, or toned their fitness or helped at the Infirmary. 'There is little rest here, even on a Sunday,' said Wei-Lin. 'But if you want to read a book on the day off, then we have a small library. That's something else you could volunteer for.'

Wei-Lin explained that most students got up around five-thirty and cleaned their dormitories and the shower blocks. After breakfast, there was a two-hour session of physical labour, often clearing the paths of rocks or renovating the buildings with the few supplies they had at their disposal.

The first formal lesson of the day was at nine-thirty and took place in a classroom similar to the ones they were familiar with from the 'real world'. These classes ranged from domestic science to agriculture for beginners and basic carpentry, among others. In addition there were more mainstream subjects such as mathematics and literature.

'That's Professor Goldberg,' said Wei-Lin. 'The oldest and weirdest member of staff. Actually, he's the only qualified teacher we have, but he was a university lecturer, so his classroom skills are a little . . .' She waved a hand in the air from side to side '. . . rusty, shall we say?' After lunch there was another prolonged session, focusing on fitness and survival. 'Weapons-training is one of those,' she said. 'For our sins, we have Gwynne the day after tomorrow.'

The two-hour block from four-thirty onward was for developing each individual's talent or gift. 'Jen has hers sorted out,' said Wei-Lin. 'I suggest the rest of you find your area of expertise quickly. Anyone caught wandering around aimlessly can find themselves cleaning out the septic tanks. *Not* a good option, trust me.'

After dinner it was free time until lights out at nine o'clock. Apparently, there *were* electric lights in the dormitories, but they were controlled remotely and were only on for two hours in the evening.

'I have copies of our group's timetable for the next two weeks,' said Wei-Lin. She passed a sheaf of papers to Pan, who took one and passed the rest to her left. Nate took his and handed on the remainder in his turn. 'Study it carefully and don't be late tomorrow to any of the classes. There's quite a bit of competition between groups and we have to think of ourselves as a team. A mistake from one person reflects badly on the group.'

Pan glanced at her timetable. They had English

Literature and Philosophy the next day at nine-thirty. The afternoon session was with someone called Miss Kingston and was entitled 'Personal Fitness'. *I don't think I will be looking forward to that one*, thought Pan. *Though I'm probably not dreading it as much as Cara.*

Wei-Lin glanced at her watch. 'Okay, guys,' she said. 'I suggest you explore the grounds, get yourselves orientated. Use the maps I gave you this morning and make sure you know where the classrooms and the meeting areas are for tomorrow. I'll see you back at the canteen for dinner. Remember, that's at six-thirty as we are rostered on the early shift.'

~~~

Pan studied the map and tried to find her bearings. She noted the Garden on Top of the World, which was clearly marked on the map. Even so, it was difficult. She turned the map upside down and squinted at it.

'Women turn maps upside down,' said a voice in her ear, 'but men don't. Something to do with gender differences in spatial awareness. Did you know that?'

Pan almost jumped. She also almost smiled.

'Thanks, Nate,' she replied. 'But I *had* heard that. Did *you* know that men who sneak up on unsuspecting women are generally considered dickheads?'

'Yeah, but the scientific research is still continuing.' He smiled. 'Why don't we pool our spatial awareness skills? Two heads are better than one when it comes to exploring unfamiliar territory, or so they say.'

'Sure,' said Pan.

The School was large in area, but it didn't take long to become familiar with its layout. The classrooms were fairly close to both the canteen and the dormitories while other specialist areas, like the weapons-training ground, occupied the periphery. There was also a large area, roughly the size and shape of a football ground, close to the cliff that rose to the Infirmary. It was deep in shadow and Pan felt the chill creep into her bones as they explored it.

'Physical fitness area,' said Nate. 'Where tomorrow we meet Miss Kingston. Looking forward to that, Pandora?'

'I'm not,' Pan replied. 'Too cold here. It wouldn't get much sun.'

'Probably why they chose to have it here,' said Nate. 'It's better to run in the cool than under the sun.'

'Better not to run at all.'

'Go wash your mouth out with soap and water,' said Nate. 'You're talking about something I love. I must admit, though, it's not the best running surface I've ever seen. Too many rocks.'

Pan spread her arms out to take in the surrounding mountain peaks.

'I wonder why?' she said.

Nate smiled. 'Perhaps we should put in an order for artificial turf. I can't see real grass getting a foothold here.'

'Great idea,' said Pan. 'The world has been destroyed and you want a good running surface. I'm sure that will go straight to the top of the list, right above antibiotics.'

Nate grimaced. 'You have a sharp tongue, Miss Pan,' he said. 'Maybe that's the talent you should be developing. Breaking guys' hearts with sharp-edged words.'

'I don't need to develop that talent,' said Pan. 'It's generally acknowledged that it's perfect already.' *We're flirting*, she thought. The idea was both shameful and exciting. Shameful because it was difficult to imagine a more inappropriate time for it. Yet, for all that, her skin tingled.

They wandered back towards the main collection of buildings. Nate stopped to check the map from time to time. He pointed out the buildings where carpentry and basic blacksmith lessons were conducted. Further off, close to the side of the mountains, he identified the staff quarters.

'They keep a distance from the students, then,' he said. 'Bet their quarters are significantly better than ours.'

Pan was about to reply when she heard a distant buzzing sound. She stopped and lifted her head to the sky. Grey clouds formed a canopy that stretched to the horizon and masked most of the mountain peaks towering above. The buzzing increased and Nate also lifted his eyes.

'Helicopter,' he said. 'Getting closer.'

It was the first time that Pan had heard a significant mechanical sound since she had been at The School. *How strange*, she thought, *that we can become so accustomed to silence when most of our lives have been dominated by the noise of civilisation.* She realised how difficult it was to find the position of a plane or helicopter by sound alone. The mountains, she imagined, distorted any sense of direction and added to the disorientation. The buzzing resolved itself into a drone and it appeared impossible that something so loud could remain unseen. It sounded as if it was just above their heads.

The helicopter appeared suddenly, a black shape that dipped through clouds shrouding the mountain above the Infirmary. It hovered for a moment, shimmied to the left, before descending rapidly towards The Garden on Top of the World. The noise of its engine echoed from the mountain walls and drowned out everything else. Pan and Nate watched in silence as it hovered briefly a few metres above the Garden and then landed. A small cloud of dust billowed and stilled. The blades continued to rotate for a minute or more before coming to rest. Silence returned. Pan glanced around her. Many students had appeared and were standing on paths or outside buildings, all of them staring at the black shape high above.

'Another survivor, you reckon?' said Nate.

'Who knows?' said Pan. 'Probably. I hope so.'

Another cargo of misery, she thought. *Another scrap of flotsam in a sea of destruction.*

It was too far to see what was being unloaded from the helicopter, and after a few minutes it seemed pointless to continue staring. They continued their walk back towards the canteen. It was close to six-fifteen and Pan's stomach was complaining, though the thought of The School's food did not fill her with enthusiasm.

'I guess if someone has been brought to the Infirmary,' said Nate, 'they'll be joining our group. I wonder who it is.'

'Someone damaged,' replied Pan. 'I can guarantee that.'

There was silence for a minute. 'Then they'll fit right in,' said Nate eventually.

Chapter 6

Pan lay on her bunk and gazed at the ceiling. Even though she had earphones in, she could still hear someone crying out in their sleep. It was probably Cara. Pan glanced at the luminous dial of her watch. 4 a.m. She felt confident she would get no more sleep that night. After her nightmares, that was almost a relief.

~~~

Dinner had been worse than lunch. Once again, the canteen had been full to bursting and all the students had eaten with a palpable sense of urgency, heads bent over bowls, shovelling food into their mouths. It was another kind of stew. Or maybe it was the leftovers from lunch with a few added vegetables. There was some kind of white tuber, cut into large chunks that bulked out the meal. It didn't taste of much and immediately sat heavy in her stomach, as if resisting digestion. Pan forced herself to eat all of it, and she noticed that again Cara ate virtually nothing. Wei-Lin polished off what she left.

In theory, after-dinner was given over to free time, but Pan noticed, as she took a stroll around the grounds, that few students took the opportunity to rest. Most attended extra lessons or developed their individual talents. Some focused on weapons-training, or fitness - lifting large rocks in lieu of weights. Some went running in a group, Nate included.

Wei-Lin worked outside the dormitory, fashioning a new arrow. She painstakingly whittled away at a piece of wood with a penknife, turning the shaft constantly to check if it was straight. She nodded a greeting as Pan walked past. Pan noticed, in the distance, Samantha and Karl going for a jog together. *Is there a romance blossoming there?* she thought. It was possible. The way they looked at each other appeared neutral, but she had a feeling about it. The plain English girl and the Kiwi computer nerd. It would probably never have happened in the old world, but circumstances had changed. Perhaps they could find comfort in each other's company.

Cara was the only one who didn't do anything. When Pan entered the dorm, she found her sitting on her bed, staring at the wall and biting her fingernails. Pan busied herself tidying her locker and remaking her bed - she felt embarrassed that she couldn't do it as neatly as most of the others, though not embarrassed enough to spend *too* much time at it. She considered trying to engage Cara in conversation, but sensed it wouldn't be welcome. Maybe in a few days. She knew there was a well of unhappiness in the girl - it was written on her face - but Pan had no idea how to lift her from it. *I'm not sure she is going to make it*, Pan thought, and then felt guilty for thinking it. It was almost a relief when Cara pulled a small notebook from her drawer and began writing. Her brow was scrunched in concentration and her pencil raced across the page. When a tear trickled down her cheek she seemed unaware and didn't brush it away.

Eventually, Pan gave up on her bed - it still looked as bad as ever - and went for another walk. Watching Cara write was as tedious as bed-making, and she had to do *something*. Dusk was blending into night. Some of the clouds had dissipated and she could see a few pale stars. She wandered without purpose, trying to ignore the chill that seeped through her clothes. *Maybe I will have to take up running*, she thought, *if only to stay warm*. The weariness in her limbs had lessened and she could feel strength returning. Maybe there *was* some nutritional benefit in The School's food, despite its appearance.

Her eye was caught by movement off to her left and she stopped. Nightfall made it difficult to see, but there had been a blur of something moving at tremendous speed. She walked closer. A boy stood in the middle of a clearing, his arm raised. Something was balanced on his hand, and as Pan approached she saw it move. Its silhouette was unsettled. Pan's foot slipped on a rock and the noise caused the boy to turn towards her. Even in the gathering dusk she could pick out the bright red of the boy's hair.

'Hello?' he said.

'Hi,' said Pan. 'Sorry to scare you. It's Tom, isn't it?'

The boy smiled.

'That's me,' he said. 'And you're the new girl. Hey, did you save me any meat?'

'Sorry,' said Pan. 'My meal turned out to be entirely vegetarian.'

'Pity,' said Tom. 'Kes here would've loved a snack.'

On the boy's hand was a large bird of prey, a kestrel or a falcon of some kind. Its hooked beak snatched at something the boy held in his gloved hand.

'Is that a falcon?' said Pan.

The boy beamed. 'Yes,' he said. 'Isn't she beautiful? Do you want to hold her?'

'Well, I'm not sure . . .'

'Go on. She won't hurt you.' Tom took a towel that had been tucked inside the waistband of his shorts and handed it to Pan. 'Wrap it around your left hand and up your arm. I haven't got another gauntlet, and I don't think mine would fit you. Too small. But the towel will work. Just make sure you don't leave any of your skin exposed.'

'Maybe . . .'

'Please,' said Tom. He was hopping from foot to foot in excitement. His enthusiasm was so infectious that Pan couldn't help smiling. She accepted the towel and wrapped it around her hand. Tom helped her arrange the towel so Pan's fingers were uncovered.

'You need to be able to hold the jesses,' he explained.

'Jesses?'

'These.' He showed her the leather cords attached to the bird's legs. 'Keep a tight grip on these and she can't fly anywhere. Put your arm out,' he said, 'and I'll pop her on your hand. Here we go. Careful. Don't spook her. And make sure the jesses are nice and secure between your fingers. That's it. There you go.'

The bird was much heavier than Pan had expected. It skittered a few paces along her hand and she felt the muscles in her arms bunch. Even through the thick bulk of the towel she could sense the power of the talons. The bird swivelled its head and preened a couple of feathers.

'You want to see her in flight,' said Tom. 'The way she stoops.'

'Stoops?'

'Dives to intercept her prey. Like a missile. Bang.'

'Is that why you keep the falcon, then? To hunt?'

'Of course. Falconry is one of the oldest hunting sports.' The boy took the bird back onto his hand, fished a hood from an inside pocket and deftly fastened it over the falcon's head. 'When I was rescued, I had Kes with me - we'd been doing some training - so I had this equipment as well. The jesses, the gauntlet and the hood. Luckily my rescuers knew how useful she'd be, and brought her along. I've put in an order for some extra equipment and another falcon - through the student representative council, you know? - but so far they haven't brought anything back...'

I wouldn't hold your breath, either, thought Pan.

'I want to breed them. Get a colony going. If we had six or seven falcons, then we could get plenty of meat. I've told them that, The School council. And I've explained that I could train other students how to handle them.'

'I'm sure you could,' said Pan.

'Let me show you,' said Tom. He dug a hand into his shorts pocket and produced a small dark object. Pan narrowed her eyes.

'A mouse,' he said proudly. 'Don't worry, it's dead.'

'Where do you get mice around here?'

'The chook yard. There aren't many, but I check every night. I put traps out at the edge of the forest as well. Get the odd shrew, or whatever. Kes doesn't care. So long as it's meat, she's cool with it. Here.'

He tucked the mouse into the gap in the towel where she had clasped the jesses. Pan suppressed a shudder as its limp tail brushed her fingers.

'What do I do?' she asked.

'I'll take Kes to the end of the clearing,' said Tom. 'When I take off her hood, hold your hand up and let the mouse dangle by its tail. She'll fly to you. Well, she'll fly to the mouse.'

'She'll be able to see it from that distance, in this light?'

The boy laughed. 'Oh yeah,' he said. 'From much further than that. Their eyesight is phenomenal. You'll see.'

'Er, Tom?' said Pan. 'I'm not sure I . . .'

'Don't worry.'

He marched away across the clearing and almost disappeared in the fading light. When he was about fifty metres away he turned to face her.

'Now. Hold your arm up. That's the way. And don't flinch when she lands. Let her have her food. Trust me, you don't want to come between her and that mouse.'

Tom removed the falcon's hood and raised his arm. Almost immediately the bird took off and speared through the air towards Pan. She barely had time to glimpse the graceful arrow of its flight before it thumped onto her arm and took the mouse in a single fluid movement. The impact made her stagger. The sharp hook of its beak ripped and tore. It was beautiful in a raw and elemental way. But it was also terrifying.

Tom ran over.

'Amazing, isn't she?'

Pan nodded. 'Beautiful,' she said.

'I could save one for you - you know, when I get the breeding program up and running. And then I could show you how to train it. Once you've trained a falcon, you get to love it.'

'And does it get to love you?'

'Nah. These birds don't love. It's not in their nature. But a bond? Yeah. You build up a bond. It's pretty special.'

Pan looked at the falcon. Most of the mouse had disappeared. *Like the rest of us*, she thought. *Eat to survive. Just get it down your throat.*

'That would be great, Tom,' said Pan. 'I'd very much like to learn from you. And if I ever discover any meat in my food I'll be sure to keep some for Kes.'

Tom beamed as he took the bird back onto his gauntlet. Just before he slipped the hood on, he looked into the falcon's eyes. Pan recognised love when she saw it.

~ ~ ~

By the time she returned to the dormitory it was eight-forty-five and Pan decided to brave the shower block. She hoped the rush would have subsided by now and she might be afforded some privacy. She opened the door. Four girls were in there, one of them Wei-Lin, standing under four shower heads that trickled dispiritedly. For a moment, Pan was embarrassed at their nakedness, but the girls didn't seem to care.

'Hey.' There was a chorus of yells. 'Close the door. Keep the warmth in.'

Pan shut the door. She shivered. She doubted that shutting the door would have any effect on the temperature inside the toilet block which appeared to be a couple of degrees below that outside. She shivered, reluctant to take her own clothes off. *Toughen up*, she thought.

There was a small bench and Pan sat there to wait for a shower to become free. It didn't take long. Wei-Lin stepped out from beneath the shower head and walked over to the rinsing head. She held a small plastic cup and collected as much of the fresh water as possible. When the trickle dried up she poured the water she had collected over her head and splashed it all over her body with both hands. Then she grabbed a towel from a nail on the wall and started towelling her hair dry. She stood in front of Pan, entirely unembarrassed at her nakedness, and smiled. *Mind you*, Pan thought, *if I had a body like that, I probably wouldn't care either*. Pan doubted her bony frame would ever have the athleticism of Wei-Lin's.

'Hey,' said Wei-Lin. 'You're cutting it fine. Most students get here a bit earlier to make sure they can see what they're doing. The lights go out at nine.'

If that was the only way to guarantee privacy, she'd consider having her showers after lights out every evening. But Wei-Lin had already seen her naked at the Infirmary. And it would have been even more embarrassing to leave.

She stripped off quickly. The other girls' bodies were hard and honed. Pan felt ashamed, not just of her nakedness, but of how her body seemed to signal that she was weaker, inferior. She stepped under the shower head vacated by Wei-Lin, picked up a cake of coarse soap from a dish on the wall and punched the button. An icy stream of water hit her head and she gasped. The rest of the girls laughed.

'Gets you good the first time, doesn't it?' said one.

'Don't worry. You get used to it,' said another.

'No, you don't,' said Wei-Lin. They all laughed.

~~~

After what passed as a shower, Pan lay on her bunk. She was watching Cara write in her book when the room was plunged abruptly into complete darkness. *The lights have gone out all over the world,* she thought. *This is the way it is for ninety-nine percent of humanity. The way it will be for the foreseeable future.*

The day had taken its toll. Her body was still recovering, and even though she had done no strenuous exercise, she felt weary to the bone. Almost immediately, she fell asleep and into a series of vivid dreams.

Pan walked down a curiously deserted street. Off to one side there was a park and a woman was sitting on a bench, watching a boy on a swing. There was something familiar about the woman, but Pan couldn't pin it down. She was distracted by another woman coming out of a shop on the other side of the street. She had a bundle of clothes over her arms, and she staggered slightly as if drunk. A void. Then a car hitting the woman. A crunch of bone on bitumen and a pool of blood.

A man grabbing her arm. He wore a police uniform and he was talking, but Pan couldn't understand what he was saying. Sunlight glinted off one gold tooth. There was something odd about that, the presence of the golden tooth, but she could make no sense of it. Even when he put a gun into his mouth and blew the back of his head off, she was bothered more by the tooth than the confetti of blood and bone.

There was a man, hanging from a bedroom window. He had knotted sheets around his neck and he swung slightly as if in a breeze. His face was livid and a swollen tongue poked from bruised lips. She started to run. She needed to get away from these images, but wherever she went she was surrounded by horrors. She ran faster.

Pan didn't see the car. She ran through a tunnel of her own vision, eyes fixed ahead and stinging from sweat. There was a screech of brakes to her left and an explosion of pain in her hip. The world flipped, sky and clouds a flickered image, replaced by the textured grey of asphalt. She got to her feet instantly, her conscious mind by-passed, her body moving to its own rhythm. Pan's right forearm, raw from friction, sweated beads of blood, but she ignored it.

The car. She had collided at the driver's-side wheel arch, spun across the bonnet, slid five metres on the other side. Pandora didn't register pain. She looked for pursuers, but there was no one in sight. Not yet. But she sensed she only had seconds.

The driver's door opened and a man's body eased out. She locked eyes with him for a moment. Over his right shoulder, she saw two men appear. They wore sunglasses, their suit jackets flying, flapping as they ran. Pan glanced back at the driver and saw something dark in his eyes. She backed away a few paces, grateful the car was between them. The man reached into his jacket pocket, but Pan was already turning away. She had lost time. For one brief, glorious moment, hitting the car had offered a chance of rescue. Now, she knew it had simply cut her lead. How did she know that? Rescued from what? Nothing came to mind. She broke into a run again. There was something wrong with her hip. A sharp splinter of pain jagged up the side of her body with each impact of foot on ground. She focused on pushing the awareness of pain back, concentrated on breathing in and out, finding the rhythm once more, the pumping of arms and legs.

Pandora Jones ran for her life. Even in her dream, she was acutely aware of that danger. Footsteps closed on her. And then the sound of ragged breathing, rising in volume. The skin on her neck itched with the anticipation of a hand closing, grasping, pulling her down. She lowered her head and reached for another store of energy. It was there, but ebbing fast. She tapped into what was left and picked up pace. Her heart raced and she tried to cry out.

~~~

Pan sat bolt upright in bed, the scream still fresh in her throat. For a moment she didn't know where she was, and then the sounds of the dormitory brought her back. The School. She clutched the blanket and tried to still the hammering in her chest. Her face was slick with sweat. A minute passed. Her cry had woken no one, but only because everyone was still wrapped in their own nightmares and had no time for hers. The groans and cries of restless sleep were all around. And sobbing. It was pitiful and filled with hopelessness.

Pan felt through the darkness and found the drawer in her bedside table. She groped blindly until she located the earplugs and put them in. The noise subdued, but she could still hear muffled moans and the thin tinnitus of despair. Pan lay down again, closed her eyes and feigned sleep. Dreams had claws. Instead, she reluctantly tried to recall the terrifying fragments of her nightmare, in the hope that examining them would dispel their terrors. But the more she thought, the more she became convinced that there was something odd about her dreams. They were absurd. After all, dreams have only a dislocated logic, but she felt there were clues in those dreams, if only she could decipher them. Her unconscious was telling her something, but the more she focused on what it might be, the more elusive it became. A gold tooth. There was something sinister in the gold tooth. More sinister than a woman hit by a car or a body hanging from a bedroom window. More disturbing, even, than a woman in a park and a child swinging and coughing, swinging and coughing. How could that be?

It was no use. Like a memory that slips and slides the more she tried to recall it, this feeling defied examination. Finally, Pan sighed and glanced at the luminous dial of her watch. A little after four in the morning. She slipped out of bed and dressed quickly, trying to control the shivering of her limbs. Goosebumps prickled her skin. What she needed was exercise, something to warm her body and distract her mind.

Pan padded down the centre of the dormitory and felt for the door handle. For about thirty seconds, she couldn't find it, and almost panicked. She had never been susceptible to claustrophobia, but the groans and moans at her back fed her imagination. She felt trapped in some kind of hell with no way out.

But then she found the handle, turned it and stumbled out into the clear, cold night air.

Chapter 7

A few stars shimmered in the frosty air. Pan hugged herself, but it made little difference. She sat on a rock outside the toilet block and tried to make herself small against the wind. The sky was smeared with the first blush of dawn. Far in the distance, towards the sea, she became aware of a series of flickering lights, and she fixed her eyes on them. They were too high to be part of The School. Then she realised. The wall. A series of lights spread evenly along the top of the wall. The watchtowers. Why would there be lights in the watchtowers? Who was up there and why were they watching?

Pan stood. The cold was numbing and she decided she needed to run. Her hip was still a little sore and her legs felt weak. All the walking of the previous day had made them ache. There was only one way to strengthen them and that was to push herself physically. Besides, it would warm her up. And the jumbled memories, the tormented dream fragments were pressing on her. She needed movement. Simple movement to flush her mind.

Her eyes adjusted to the dark, and the rough pathways threading through the grounds were faintly visible. Pan took off towards the wall. It dominated The School's landscape and she wanted a better view of those flickering watchtower lights. The first few hundred metres were hard going. Her muscles, wasted by months of inactivity, rebelled, and her lungs strained to draw in air. But soon she settled into a rhythm and the aches and pains in her joints soothed. Warmth seeped into her body and her breathing eased.

Pan kept her eyes fixed on her destination – the lights that danced above the barely visible grey expanse of stone stretching from distant mountain to distant mountain. Yet the wall didn't seem to be getting any closer. She tried to ignore the sensation that she was running along a conveyor belt. Moving, moving, but not making any progress. The dawn bled along the horizon. She kept running, even though her body ached all over.

It took twenty minutes before the wall loomed up, casting deep shadows, filling her vision. She stopped about five metres from its base, bent over, hands on knees, sucking in air. Only when she was able to draw in measured breaths did she look up at the towering expanse of stone.

The wall was about fifteen metres high and composed of massive blocks of stone, each taller than she was. It was still night in the shadow of the wall and she looked back at the landscape of The School behind her. Most was shrouded in dark, yet she could make out the high structure of the Infirmary and the sheer sides of the cliff that led up to The Garden on Top of the World. Above the building, the mountain was brushed with light. She took a step or two back from the wall and tried to take in its size and extent, but her mind had difficulty absorbing scale.

'Overkill, ya reckon?'

The voice made her jump. She spun around.

Nate was smiling at her.

'Yo, Pan. Sorry, kiddo. Didn't mean to scare you.'

'Yes, you did,' said Pan. 'What are you doing here, sneaking up on me like that? And how come I didn't hear you?'

Nate's smile broadened.

'I was running beside the wall. It's too dark to see me in the shadows,' he said. 'But you should have heard me. Tut, tut, Pandora. You need to hone your survival skills. I could have been a predator.'

Pan wiped the sweat from her face.

'Problems sleeping?' asked Nate.

'Not so much sleeping. It's my dreams.'

Nate nodded. 'Is your dormitory like mine? You wake up in the middle of the night and you can't hear yourself think for the weeping, wailing and groaning?'

'It's bad,' said Pan. She didn't admit that she made her own significant contribution to the night terrors.

'Running helps. And it's good for you, Pan.'

'What did you mean?' asked Pan. 'When you said "overkill".'

Nate's forehead scrunched, then he glanced up at the blank face of the wall and smiled. His face was dry and he breathed normally, Pan noticed.

'It's too big,' he said. 'This thing is meant to keep people out, right? Yet a fence would have done the same job. Bit of razor wire along the top. And the watchtowers. I mean, this is beyond top-level security.'

'But isn't it ex-military?' said Pan. 'Maybe they kept nuclear missiles here. That would explain why a fence and razor wire wouldn't cut it.'

Nate shook his head.

'I've seen missile sites,' he said. 'My dad was a big brass in the military. And this place isn't big enough. You need bunkers and the ground here is rock solid. Which begs the question: What went on here that needed this kind of security?'

'Does it matter?' asked Pan, but even as she asked she knew the answer. It did matter. It mattered enormously, though she couldn't understand why.

'Maybe not,' said Nate. 'But I don't like questions I can't find answers to, that's all. With the sea and the mountains this site is secure in terms of natural geography. Think about it. If you were going to attack this place, what would your chances be like? Coming in from the sea, you'd be spotted a mile off and the bay is easy to defend. Good luck with sending troops over those mountains. And - BV - any air attack would be detected by radar if this was a secure military base. So what's with the wall?'

Pan said nothing. The wall was blank and featureless. Sheer. Impenetrable. A fortress.

'And those watchtowers,' Nate continued. He was on a roll. 'The lights are on all night. Why?'

'There are people up there,' said Pan. She didn't know how she knew, but she knew. Pan could sense eyes watching. They were too close to the wall to be visible. But she knew that eyes roamed the landscape.

Nate examined her face. 'What makes you say that?'

Pan shrugged. 'No idea. Just a feeling.'

'That psychic thing?' This time Nate didn't smile. Pan shrugged again.

'Okay.' Nate spoke quietly. 'If that's so, it raises even more questions. Why put guards up there and keep the place illuminated?'

Pan shared his sense of wrongness, but she couldn't explain it.

'Maybe,' said Nate, his voice quiet and reflective, 'the wall is not designed to keep people out. Maybe it's designed to keep people *in*. Us, for example.'

'Why?'

'Well, that's the important question, isn't it?'

'Wei-Lin said we were segregated from the village to protect against disease.'

'Wei-Lin told us what Wei-Lin had been told. And anyway, the wall was here before the virus. So what was its original purpose?'

Not enough information, thought Pan.

Maybe Nate came to the same conclusion because he suddenly laughed.

'Time to run, Pandora,' he said. 'My body is telling me the mind has had too much stimulation. I'm not so good at thinking, but running? That's a different matter.'

Pan knew that Nate's mind was as fit and flexible as his body, but she didn't respond. Was he fishing for compliments? Let him fish. She wasn't taking the bait.

'So why did you come to the wall tonight?' she asked.

Nate smiled. 'Not stalking you, if that's what you think,' he said. 'Honest. Cross my heart and hope to die. I just needed to run and the wall seemed like a good destination.'

'Don't you ever stop running?'

'No. I run in my sleep. I'm serious.'

He indicated the sky, which was lightening. 'It's an early start in this place and I need a shower before first lesson. I'm a morning shower kind of guy. Prefer to stink at night when everyone's sleeping and doesn't notice anyway. Run with me?'

'You intend to find out what's on the other side of the wall, don't you?' said Pan. As soon as the idea popped into her head, she knew it was true.

Nate rubbed a hand through his hair. 'What makes you say that? It's a village. A port. Boats. Our supply route. Potentially diseased. Why would I risk my life when I've only just been saved?'

'Because the wall is stopping you,' Pan said. 'And you don't believe that stuff about diseases.'

He gazed at her for a moment or two and then burst out laughing.

'Psychic, huh? Boy, I'd better be careful with you, Pandora Jones. You have the distinct potential to totally freak me out.'

Pan said nothing, but she didn't take her eyes away from his.

'Run with me,' Nate repeated, and this time he didn't wait for an answer. He took off up the path and Pan had to sprint to catch up with him. They jogged for five minutes before he spoke.

'Let's just say I don't like being in prison.'

'Prison?' Pan had to gasp the word, because her lungs were burning once more. *I need to get fit*, she thought. *There is no alternative and this pain is a reminder of how far I must travel.*

'Sure. There are wide open spaces. We can go wherever we want. Trouble is, there's nowhere to go. There are different kinds of prisons, Pandora. I reckon this is one. And I'll tell you something else. Put me behind a door and I have to open it. Doesn't matter if there's nothing on the other side. I need to see for myself.' He glanced at her. 'Loosen your stride, your arm movements are all over the place, and don't get me started on the way you hold your head. I could help, if you like. I know squat about most things, but running is what I was born to do.' He accelerated smoothly.

She tried to keep up but it was hopeless. Even with a burst of speed she couldn't prevent his form shrinking ahead of her. She stopped, put her hands on her knees and waited for her breathing to slow.

'Take me with you,' she yelled after him. 'When you go.'

He didn't turn around. But she heard a faint tinkle of laughter drift towards her.

Chapter 8

Breakfast was a simple chunk of hard bread covered in a thin layer of something vaguely resembling butter. Pan nearly broke a tooth eating it, but she persevered. She was learning from Wei-Lin. Don't leave *anything* on your plate.

The two-hour session after breakfast was given over to physical activity. Pan joined a group of students working on clearing rocks from the paths leading to and from the canteen. Cara was one of them. There was no wheelbarrow available to shift the stones, so they piled them up along the edge of the paths, leaving a trail of packed earth and making the definition of the paths more obvious. Pan worked close to Cara and noticed the New Zealand girl chose only the smallest stones and took an age to carry them to the perimeter.

'Not exactly stimulating, is it?' said Pan, wiping sweat from her brow and smiling, but Cara merely averted her eyes and scoured the ground for a suitably small stone. Pan shrugged and picked up another rock. *It's going to take time*, she thought, *to win this girl's trust*.

Even in the chill of the morning it was sweaty work, and after an hour Pan was hot and flushed. She looked up to see how their work was progressing and found the small area they had cleared rather dispiriting. At this rate it would take years to have the paths totally free of rocks. Then again, time was something they had in abundance and she did feel some sense of accomplishment in the physical activity. It was almost as though she could feel her body growing stronger, despite her weariness.

At nine-fifteen they stopped and drank from a pail that another student had filled with cold, clear water. Pan noticed that everyone else – with the exception of Cara – had a cup attached to their fatigues by a short length of string, and she resolved to find one for herself. It was the same cup, she imagined, that they took to the showers.

Then it was time for the first formal classroom lesson of the day. She took out her timetable and checked the classroom number, though she'd found the place the previous day when she'd been walking with Nate. Hut 43. Literature and Philosophy with Professor Goldberg. She made her way there and joined a thin stream of students filing in. *Not just my group, then*, she thought. With over four hundred students at The School, she imagined, the classes, by necessity, had to be large. Nonetheless, she was pleased to note that Cara had followed her, albeit lagging a few metres behind.

The classroom was depressingly austere. Rows of battered and stained desks were lined up in front of an old-fashioned blackboard, a teacher's desk just off to the blackboard's right. There were probably sixty chairs. A man, by far the oldest she had yet seen at The School, sat at the front, his feet up on the teacher's desk and a dog-eared book in his left hand. He had to be in his seventies at least. He peered at the students over gold-rimmed glasses as they filed in and found a place. A few chose to stand at the back of the class, but Pan found a seat right on the front row. She smiled as Cara slid behind the desk next to her. Pan glanced over her shoulder. Despite the crowded room there were a number of unoccupied places in the front row. *The way of schools all over the world*, she thought. *The desks in the front row are always the last to be occupied.*

Her eyes suddenly filled with tears and a lump came to her throat. It was unexpected and almost absurd, she realised, that the sight of a classroom should ambush her emotions in that way. *Is it because this is a reminder of what has been lost*, she thought, *or an affirmation that human nature does not change, even in the most extreme of circumstances?* She forced the tears back and swallowed hard. There was danger in thinking too precisely about such things. It could open up a chasm through which one could easily fall.

When everyone was in place, the room fell silent. The teacher ran long, gnarled fingers through the tangled mat of his beard and spoke.

'Good morning,' he said. 'I notice that we are even more packed today than yesterday. Even to my admittedly feeble intellect - the product, I hasten to add, of advanced years rather than genetic predisposition - this can only mean one thing. We have new students joining us. A blessing, of course. I extend both my welcome and my sympathies to you, and implore you to embrace your studies - if for no other reason than to distract you from the horrors you have endured. The rest of the class must forgive me if I cover old ground for the benefit of our latest additions. My name is Menachim Goldberg and I am the Principal.' Then he laughed. It was a surprisingly youthful laugh and nearly infectious. Pan felt her lips twitch. 'Though one suspects that has little to do with my skills and education and all to do with my advanced years. Plus, I am the only qualified teacher at The School and I suppose that counts for something. As does being, perhaps, the oldest human being left on this planet. Even if I am not, when I look out at your metaphorical sea of youthful faces, I feel I must be. Call me Professor Goldberg, sea of youthful faces. Or Prof, if you prefer. Goodness, taste those fricatives. Prof if you prefer.'

He coughed a couple of times – thick, rheumy coughs. Images from Pan's dreams flashed through her mind, but she banished them with an effort of will. The Prof continued running his fingers through his beard. His eyes were watery and glistened in the dim light that infiltrated the small and filthy windows of the classroom.

'I am your teacher for Philosophy, Religion and Literature,' he said. 'An immense body of knowledge, whose size is matched only by the extent of my ignorance. However, we must make do, in this brave new world.' He coughed once more.

'New students,' he continued when he had the coughing fit under control. 'We are currently engaged in analysing one of the greatest works of literature – some have convincingly argued *the* greatest work of the imagination – in the history of humanity. I refer, of course, to *Hamlet* by William Shakespeare. Some of you may have heard of him. We are reading the text and discussing it. Or more accurately, I am reading it to the class, for we have only one copy. I have requested a full class set, but as yet it would appear that generators and drums of gasoline have taken priority over educational resources. 'Twas ever thus, my friends.'

The initial silence had given way to a low hubbub of conversation among the students. Even at the front, Pan had difficulty hearing what the Prof was saying. Maybe he couldn't hear that the students were talking. Maybe he didn't care. Whatever the reason, he proceeded as though he had their full attention.

'Unfortunately, I am unable to recap what has transpired in previous lessons. *Tempus fugit*, you see. I suggest you talk to fellow students, who will almost certainly be delighted to bring you up to date with the details of the Prince of Denmark's melancholic journey thus far. Splendid. Time to start our lesson. We have reached the point where Claudius and Gertrude are discussing Hamlet's apparent madness. Gertrude describes Hamlet's mental state as, "Mad as the sea and wind when each contends which is the mightier." An image, obviously. Could one call this pathetic fallacy? I leave that to you. But the important thing is that the turmoil within the mind is here being compared to elemental forces of nature. Destructive, certainly, but also - and this is the significant point, I think - part of natural flux. Even when our minds are dislocated, we are still a part of nature, subject to those forces, though we might suppose we are, somehow above such things ...'

Pan turned her head. Out the window, a grey sky, low cloud shrouding a mountain face, the moving specks of birds finding thermals. The scene was at once comforting, familiar and terribly alien. A piece of screwed up paper flew from somewhere at the back of the room and hit Cara on the neck. She flinched but didn't turn around, keeping her eyes fixed firmly on the Prof. The student sitting on the far side of Cara was asleep, head resting on splayed-out arms. In fact, as Pan glanced around, she saw that many students had fallen sleep. Others talked among themselves, while a tiny minority paid attention. Wei-Lin was one, and Pan was pleased to see her. She couldn't see Nate, though she imagined he was there somewhere. The Professor's voice droned on and after fifteen minutes Pan too was fighting the pull of sleep. She tried not to look at her watch, but after what seemed an eternity she couldn't resist. They still had an hour of the lesson left and they had only covered a few lines of dialogue. It might have been more interesting if they'd been able to follow in their own books, but as it was, it was difficult to focus.

Someone behind her loudly cleared their throat. The Prof didn't look up from his book.

'Hamlet, of course, is the diametric opposite of what we could call modern man, who acts without thinking, whereas our tragic hero, as we know, subsumes action beneath the cerebral. He . . .'

''Scuse me. Prof?' The voice was loud and harsh, unmistakable. Jen.

Pan was tempted to look over her shoulder, but forced herself to keep her eyes to the front. Out of her peripheral vision she saw Cara stiffen in her seat.

The teacher glanced up and raised a grey eyebrow. 'Did someone wish to make a point?'

'Yeah. Me.'

'Excellent. Pray do so.' He narrowed his eyes and squinted through his gold-rimmed lenses. 'I don't believe I know you, do I? Are you new?'

'Yeah.'

'Then welcome. Your point, new student?

'More of a question, really,' said Jen. Pan still didn't turn around. 'Why are we studying this crap?'

There was surprised laughter around the classroom. Professor Goldberg put the book on his desk, interlaced his fingers and rested his chin on the prongs of his thumbs.

'This is a question I have encountered before, new student. Many times.'

'Maybe so,' said Jen. 'But it's the first time I've asked it.'

'Perhaps you will allow me to answer your question with one of my own. Do you not feel that the study of Shakespeare, the greatest writer the world has ever known, is, in itself, a subject worthy of you?'

'No.'

'What if I argued that in the works of Shakespeare and, in particular, *Hamlet*, there is enormous insight into the human condition - the essence of being alive and human? An essence we must keenly understand if we are to survive and thrive. What would you say to that, new student?'

'I'd say you were talking bullshit.'

There was more laughter. Professor Goldberg sighed.

'Another familiar response, unfortunately.' He stood and grimaced. 'Leaving aside the intellectual poverty of your response,' he said, 'tell me: how would you prefer to spend your time?'

Jen stood and walked purposefully between the lines of desks. Even as she passed, Pan did not turn towards her. Cara, she noted, did the same. Jen sat on the teacher's desk, her back to him, and grinned at the rest of the class.

'No offence, Prof,' she said without turning to address him. 'But this is the kind of crap that belonged in the old world. It is not useful. Out there . . .' she waved vaguely towards the window, '. . . are the ruins of civilisation. What we need to know is how to survive among those ruins. How to be strong. How to hunt for food. How to protect ourselves from anyone or anything that tries to destroy us. What if, Prof, there are other survivors, people who have stocked up on guns and are prepared to defend their patch, their families? What are we gonna do, Prof, when we come up against a bunch of mercenaries out there in the real world? Guys with automatic rifles and no qualms about using them. Quote poetry? That's gonna help?'

'An interesting point, new student,' said Professor Goldberg. 'And you make it in a way that shows me you are more than just a collection of over-developed muscles.' Pan stifled a laugh. 'Is there anyone who would like to counter her point? Make an argument in favour of Shakespeare? Or are we all of the mind that he is dead and buried, both literally and metaphorically?'

There was silence. Jen's intervention had stopped the chattering. Pan turned and surveyed the room. Everyone was awake and paying attention. It was clear from the body language that most students agreed with Jen. Pan should have kept her mouth shut. She knew that. But her hand was up before she could think all the implications through. The Professor smiled.

'Ah, yes. Another new girl. You are another new girl, aren't you?'

'Yes, Prof. Pan.'

'Excellent. And your thoughts, new girl.'

'Prof, I ... I think there *is* more to survival than physical strength. Or fitness. We have to have fit minds, as well ...'

Jen got to her feet. She wasn't smiling now.

'I wasn't saying we shouldn't have fit minds, *Pandora*,' she said. She pronounced the name as if it left a toxic taste in her mouth. 'We just don't need this bullshit ... this *poetry*. Because it has no practical application. It's a waste of our time. We need real skills.'

'And I'm not saying we *don't* need practical skills,' Pan said. 'I'm suggesting there's room for both. Let's take your mercenaries scenario. Does it matter who wins? Us or them? If we are all intent on the destruction of human life, rather than the preservation of it, what kind of new world will it be?' Pan had not planned to say any of this, but her confidence was growing with each word. 'We've been through so much. This is a new beginning. But if we are to be the best we can be, then we also need to take with us those things that make life worth living. Otherwise the future is savagery. And we are not savages. At least, while we have the choice, we shouldn't be.'

Jen's face flushed. Her biceps clenched as her fingers gripped the sides of the desk. She opened her mouth to speak, but the Professor was on his feet.

'Bravo, new girl!' he cried. 'Bravo, indeed. Yes. Savagery versus humanity. Chaos versus civilisation. Excellent. Excellent.' He turned to Jen 'Think, new student. Think. Is it true that the pen is mightier than the sword?'

Jen stormed back to her seat, her eyes fixed on Pan. *Terrific*, thought Pan. *Just what I need. An enemy with muscles the size of punching bags.*

'Tell you what, Prof,' said Jen when she reached her seat. 'It would have to be a hell of a big pen.'

Most of the students laughed.

~~~

Wei-Lin was not pleased at lunch. Jen sat to her right and Pan sat opposite. They didn't so much as glance at each other.

'We are a team,' said Wei-Lin. 'Let's act like one. We have to be able to depend on each other.'

'Says who?' said Jen. 'I thought you were our mentor, not our superior?'

Wei-Lin sighed.

'I *am* only your mentor, Jen,' she said. 'I have no authority over you. And as your mentor I would advise you two to find some common ground.' She pushed her bowl to one side. Pan was surprised to notice there was still some pale soup left in it. Jen leaned over and took the bowl, emptied it into hers. Wei-Lin spread her hands. 'We need to get on with each other,' she said. 'Help each other. We need to work together.'

Jen pointed her spoon at Pan. 'She was the one arguing. Maybe *she* should have kept her mouth shut.'

'Maybe we should all shut our mouths,' said Nate. He turned his head slightly and gave a small private wink to Pan. 'Normally, as soon as I open mine, I stick my foot in it. I'd sooner put food there.' He grimaced. 'Even this food.'

Chapter 9

'Don't ever, ever, make the mistake of thinking I am your friend.'

The instructor, a woman in her mid-twenties, paced up and down in front of Pan's group. They were inside a large, windowless building close to the foot of the steps leading to the Infirmary. The only illumination came from the double doors, which had been left open to admit a pale curtain of sunlight. Pan stood with her hands behind her back and tried to relax, but a muscle twitched in her right leg. Memories of past physical education classes at her old school drifted through her head. They had rarely worked out well and she had no confidence that this session would be any different.

The instructor was dressed in running shorts and a singlet that showed off stringy, yet powerful, muscles. Her dark hair was swept back from her face, secured in a bun at the back of her head. Her voice was measured and she gazed at the floor as she paced.

'I understand you've paid a high price of admission to be in this School. We all have. But I cannot be your friend if I am to fulfil my duty to the students in my care. And what is that duty? To make you fit for survival in a hostile and unforgiving new world.' She glanced up and then returned her gaze to the floor. 'I am your instructor and this class is fitness and survival. You will call me Miss Kingston and you will obey my instructions. There are counsellors here who will listen to your problems, give advice, offer support. If you want warm and fuzzy, go to them. Do not bother me.'

She stopped in the centre of the line and raised her eyes. Slowly, she examined each student in turn, her hands clasped behind her back.

'I am not interested in your personal problems,' she continued in the same impersonal tone. 'I don't offer advice or support unless it concerns fitness and survival. I doubt you will find my methods pleasant. But you know what? That is something else I'm not interested in.'

'I think she's trying to win us over with her charm and humour,' whispered Nate who was standing next to Pan. She tried hard to suppress a giggle. She didn't think it would be wise to laugh.

'You,' said Miss Kingston, pointing at Nate. 'Step forward and state your name.'

Nate advanced a pace and snapped rigidly to attention.

'Nate Mitchell, sir,' he yelled. 'Reporting for duty. All present and correct.' He saluted. This time a few of the group giggled. Miss Kingston nodded a couple of times and resumed her pacing.

'Mr Mitchell,' she said. 'Very amusing, but my name is Miss Kingston and this is not a class for stand-up comedians. Now, this is your first day with me and I understand some of you may have adjustment issues.

Get over them. Quickly. The remainder of my class are doing a fitness test, so I could induct you newcomers properly. This is the last time we shall enjoy such a small number. Make the most of it.

'This is called a school but it is not like any school you have ever attended. Get that straight in your heads, particularly with regards to my classes. I do not give detention. I do not make you stand in a corner. I do not issue reports saying your attitude needs to improve. Nor do I ring your parents so we can all have a cosy chat about your progress. Can you tell me why I don't do any of those things, Mr Mitchell?'

'Because, despite your affable nature, you are not my friend?'

'Correct. But it is also because your parents are dead, Mr Mitchell. And all of those people who might have cared about you out there in the world? They're dead, too. Here is lesson number one. Commit it to memory. No one gives a shit about you, Mr Mitchell. Least of all me.'

Pan glanced along the line. She felt, rather than saw, Nate's back stiffen. But she did see Jen smile. *This is her kind of class*, thought Pan. *I can't see it being my kind of class.*

Miss Kingston nodded and stood in front of Nate, her eyes centimetres from his.

'Good. Lesson number two. You are alive. And if you want to stay that way, then you will toughen up. To die was easy. If you want proof, there are billions of examples out there in the world. To survive where so many failed will take all your strength. Do you understand, Mr Mitchell?'

'I think I'm making progress, Miss Kingston.'

'Excellent,' said Miss Kingston. 'Just to clarify things further, give me ten push-ups. Now, Mr Mitchell.'

'Sure thing.'

Nate dropped to the floor and started his push-ups. He clapped his hands in front of his chest after each one and counted. He did twenty.

'Problems with numeracy, Mr Mitchell? Obey without question. Another ten, if you please.'

He dropped to the ground again. When he had finished the series of push-ups, he wasn't even breathing hard. Pan was fairly sure she couldn't have managed five. She made a resolution not to annoy the fitness instructor. When Nate sprang to his feet, Miss Kingston flicked a finger, indicating he should get back into line. He winked at Pan as he took his place next to her, his eyes twinkling with amusement. The instructor resumed her pacing.

'We will start today with basic cardio-vascular work. Spread out in a circle around me, facing inwards. I will take us through some warm-ups and some stretching exercises. Then we will do a two-kilometre run, at the end of which I will make notes on each of you. Time, heart rate, blood pressure. This will provide a baseline to gauge your increasing levels of fitness. Right. Listen up and follow exactly what I do.'

Ten minutes later, Pan found herself jogging around the clearing at the base of the cliff on which the Infirmary was situated. Nate had been right about its unsuitability as a running track. The ground was generally level, but she had to be careful where she put her feet to avoid turning an ankle on one of the scattered rocks or stones. The sky was clear, but there was a bitter wind blowing into her face. Within a minute a stitch developed in her side and her breathing became ragged.

At least she wasn't as bad as some of the others. Nate was way out in front, of course. He moved with a natural elegance and covered the ground with ease. Jen was second. She didn't possess Nate's gift for running, but she was making up for it through sheer determination. Not far behind Jen was Wei-Lin, her lean physique ideal for this kind of exercise. Quite a way back was Sam.

Pan was fifth and losing ground on Sam. Sanjit and Karl were some way behind, but even so, they had lapped Cara, who was barely running at all. Pan hoped Miss Kingston would go easy on her. She didn't think Cara was resilient enough to cope with much, let alone public ridicule.

Pan concentrated on her breathing. In. Out. In. Out. Soon, her breathing regulated and the stitch eased. She glanced behind her. She had put extra distance between herself and the boys. Pan focused on the inhalation and exhalation of cold air. Before long, she had a rhythm going. It was only on her last lap that the rhythm deserted her. The first four members of the group had finished and were having their pulses checked. Blood pressure monitors were strapped to their arms. Pan lost concentration. Her legs cramped and weariness spread through her body. The last few metres were incredibly painful, and when she made it to the group, she crouched over, hands on knees while her lungs struggled to take in air.

After Miss Kingston had checked and recorded Pan's pulse and blood pressure, Cara finally struggled over the line. She had given up any pretence of running and even her walking was slow. Miss Kingston said nothing. She simply took the girl's pulse and attached a blood pressure monitor to her arm. When the last of the records had been written in her notebook, she gestured for everyone to follow her back inside the hut on the perimeter of the clearing.

The students sat in a circle on the cold concrete floor while Miss Kingston resumed her pacing. *Does she ever keep still?* wondered Pan. An image flashed through her mind of a woman jogging through a city, weaving between pedestrians, a dark V of perspiration staining the front of her T-shirt. Pan shook her head and the image vanished.

No one spoke for a minute, the only sound that of Cara's laboured breathing.

'Consider this,' said Miss Kingston eventually. 'What if that had been a real-life situation? Say that you, as a group, were running for your lives. From predators of some kind. Or hostile survivors. If one member of your group was lagging far behind, what would you do in that situation? Any ideas?'

Nate rocked back and placed both hands on the floor behind him.

'You mean should we leave her or should we go back and help her out?'

Miss Kingston shrugged.

'If you want to put it that way. All I'm asking is that if that had been an emergency, what would have happened to . . .' she leaned forward and examined the name in her notebook, 'Miss Cara Smith? Give me your thoughts.'

Jen immediately jumped in. *Why am I not surprised?* thought Pan.

'If that had been a life or death situation, then we wouldn't have had any option. We would have been forced to leave Cara behind. The risks of trying to save her would be too high. It would be a waste. Pointless. Why should *we* die because someone else is weak? Sorry, Cara, but that's just common sense.'

Pan tried to clench her mouth shut, but it didn't work. Instead she turned to Jen. 'And what about morality?' she asked. 'What about doing the right thing? Protecting those who can't protect themselves. Wouldn't that be the decent thing to do?'

'Oh, here we go again, Miss Bleeding Heart,' replied Jen. 'Stuff decent, okay? We're not about decent anymore. We're about survival. Morality doesn't play any part.'

Pan opened her mouth to argue again, but Miss Kingston held up her hand.

'You have both expressed the problem very well. And the options. This is something you need to consider in our new world. Are we "moral" as …' She glanced at her notebook again. '… Miss Pandora Jones expresses it? Or are we survivalists, as Miss Jennifer Maxwell would have it? Let's put it even more brutally, at the risk of offending Miss Jones's moral sensibilities. If Miss Smith proves to be too weak, should we actually sacrifice her to ensure that those who are strong have the best possible chance of survival?'

'Can we stop talking about her like she isn't here?' said Pan. 'She's not a "problem" or a hypothetical situation. Her name is Cara and she is a person with feelings.'

'And you think that matters?' said Miss Kingston.

Jen leaped in. 'What you don't get, Pandora, is that the world has changed. You didn't get it in the Prof's class either. Maybe in the past we would worry about hurting someone's feelings. Maybe we could afford to help those who couldn't help themselves. But now, we're fighting for survival. If we are not tough then we probably won't survive at all. Is that worth it, do you think? We all die, humanity becomes extinct, but at least we didn't hurt anyone's feelings?'

A burst of animated conversation broke out. Wei-Lin, Sam and Karl seemed to be arguing among themselves and their words merged into each other.

'. . . can't believe that you would . . .'

'Karl, that is a typically male thing to say. What about . . .'

'Hey, I'm not sexist, it's just . . .'

'Soon as anyone says they're not sexist, you know they *are* . . .'

'Guys, you're missing the point . . .'

Cara and Sanjit, as always, said nothing and simply stared at the floor. Eventually Miss Kingston raised a hand for quiet. In the ensuing silence she paced again.

'Mr Mitchell,' she said. 'You have been very quiet. Anything to add to this debate?'

'I think it's . . . complicated,' he said.

'Meaning?'

He sat forward and clasped his hands around his knees. Everyone waited. When he spoke, others listened. *He is a natural*, thought Pan. *He leads.*

'We appear to have a moral versus pragmatic divide here.' He looked around the other students and thought for a moment. It was clear that he read incomprehension in quite a few faces. 'What I mean is, at the extremes of the argument Pan believes morality is all-important, while Jen prioritises what is useful, what is practical. I'm suggesting that it is foolish to believe it *has* to be one or the other, that we are forced to make a choice, as if there is no alternative. I don't believe that.'

'Excellent, Mr Mitchell,' said Miss Kingston. 'I am sure you will score highly in the philosophy component of the curriculum. I'll pass on my recommendations to Professor Goldberg. But I am here to teach you about fitness and survival. So make a point, rather than showing off your cleverness. That doesn't have any practical importance in this class.'

'Okay,' said Nate. He took no offence at the instructor's words. 'Let's say we go the Jen option. Cara dies. The weak link has gone. We, the strong, run off and come to a place where there are a number of possible escape routes. But we don't know which is the best. Because it turns out we are good at running, but don't have much between our ears. It also turns out that Cara is a brilliant navigator and just happens to be a lousy runner. She would know how to escape, but she is dead. So by letting her die, we've decreased our own chances of survival. What do you reckon, Jen?'

Jen frowned, but she had no chance to respond. Miss Kingston clapped her hands together.

'I think that is an excellent place to leave our discussion. Think this through before we meet again. You see, not only do I administer physical torture to make you fit, but I also have to rid your minds of excess fat. Being fit is not the only factor involved in survival. I imagine most dinosaurs were very fit, but that didn't help them any.'

She glanced at her watch.

'We have forty-five minutes of the class left. This will be spent clearing rocks from our running track. Pile them up outside the perimeter. Let's move like we have a purpose, people.'

Pan felt tired, but she forced herself to get to her feet. Nate, of course, sprang up.

'Not you, Mr Mitchell,' said Miss Kingston. 'A word in your ear, if you please.'

~ ~ ~

Pan's muscles ached and she regretted having chosen rock-clearing as her physical activity that morning. Now here she was doing the same thing. She stopped and wiped at her forehead with a sleeve. At least it kept her warm.

Wei-Lin had stopped as well. 'Hey,' she said.

'Hi.'

'I wonder if you could do me a favour,' said Wei-Lin.

'Sure. If I can.'

'I've lost my watch,' said Wei-Lin. 'I mean, I had it on at lunch and I'm fairly sure it was still on my wrist when we came to fitness class, but . . .' She brought her arm up, displaying a watch-less wrist, as if for some reason Pan might doubt her word. 'Now it's gone.'

Pan noticed that the other members of the group had also stopped work and were watching her. Even without a gift of premonition, it wasn't difficult to work out what was going on.

'And I remember you saying,' Wei-Lin continued, 'that you were able to find things. So I was wondering . . .'

'This is a set-up, isn't it?' said Pan.

'I don't know what you mean.'

'Yes you do,' said Pan, but she smiled anyway. 'It's a test. You've planted your watch somewhere, just to see if I can find it. You must be as bored by rock-shifting as I am, Wei-Lin.'

Wei-Lin's eyes widened. 'How did you know that?' she said. 'Can you read minds?'

Pan laughed and gestured towards the onlookers. 'Get real, Wei-Lin,' she said.

'Okay, okay. But will you try?'

'It doesn't always work, you know. And I'm not comfortable setting myself up for failure just to provide everyone with a laugh.'

'We won't laugh. Honest.'

'Jen will,' Pan pointed out. Wei-Lin glanced over to the group.

'Okay. Jen will,' she admitted. 'But come on, Pan. It's a way of passing the time and some of us are curious, you know? As you just said, anything's better than carrying more bloody rocks. Please?'

Pan sighed. On the one hand, she didn't want to use her talent – if it *was* a talent and she was far from certain about that – for a cheap trick. On the other hand, it *would* be a distraction from the rocks. Pan wasn't convinced there weren't more of the damn things littering the track than there had been when they'd started.

'Give me your hand,' said Pan.

Wei-Lin held her arm out and Pan grasped her by the wrist and closed her eyes.

'What are you doing?' Wei-Lin asked.

'Sometimes it helps,' replied Pan. 'If I touch the

person who's lost something, I can occasionally locate stuff quicker.'

'How does that work?' Wei-Lin was almost whispering.

Pan laughed. 'I have no idea,' she said. 'To be honest, I'm not certain it works at all. Maybe I just get lucky. Though, after this build up, I dare say I'll have no clue where you've planted that watch and you can all have a good giggle. In fact, in some ways I hope that happens. Just so you don't all think I'm weird or something.'

'We won't,' said Wei-Lin.

Pan let go of her wrist. 'Okay,' she said. 'I'll give it a go. But please don't stand around staring at me.'

'Doesn't it work if you're being stared at?'

'It's not that. I just don't *like* being stared at.'

Pan closed her eyes again. It was true she had done this a number of times, and probably four times out of five she'd had success. It was also true she had no idea how it worked. All she knew was that if she cleared her mind and let her intuition have free rein, then she might get some sense of where the missing item might be. It was like that game she'd played as a kid, where someone would tell her whether she was 'hot' or 'cold', the closer or further away she got from a hidden item. In the case of her intuition, of course, there was no external voice guiding her, but something whispering within. She walked at random, back towards the hut where Nate was still presumably talking to Miss Kingston, but then she stopped. That was not the direction. It felt cold. She turned in a circle, but no particular direction seemed better than any other. She walked towards the cliff at the far end of the running track, but that also didn't feel right, so she abruptly turned left. Almost immediately, that felt warmer.

Pan left the running track and continued twenty or thirty metres into an area that was essentially a jumble of stones, possibly the result of a fall from the cliff that towered above her. The direction still felt right, but then she had an urge to change direction once more. She didn't question it, but simply obeyed. It would probably have been better if she had been able to close her eyes and follow some kind of mental path, but the terrain here was too rough to take the risk. She certainly didn't want to stumble over a rock, twist an ankle and make a clown of herself for the watching group.

Definitely hotter here, she thought. But not burning. Once again, Pan stopped and took her bearings. To her right, this time. Further away from the watching students. The rational part of her mind thought this was an unlikely location. Wei-Lin must have taken some time to find a good hiding place, but surely Pan would have seen her if she had come all this way out? Wasn't it more logical that she would have found a site closer to the running track? But all she could do was follow her feelings, and her feelings told her she was getting close.

It took another five minutes to pin down a specific location. It was strange. She had never felt so confident before, not when she had found lost keys or mobile phones in the past. Maybe her recent experiences had honed her skills. Or maybe there were fewer distractions. She'd think through the implications later. Pan moved a rock, but it wasn't there, so she moved the one next to it. The hard earth beneath had been scraped away. Pan dug her fingers into the dirt, felt a thin strap and pulled out the watch. Even at a considerable distance she heard applause from the members of her group. *Is it better to succeed and, in particular, thwart Jen's perception of me*, Pan thought, *or will this only mark me out as a freak?* It was too late to worry about that.

Wei-Lin was impressed and excited when Pan handed the watch over.

'Wow,' she said. 'There is *no* way you could have found that by chance. I mean, I hid it really carefully. Jeez, Pan.'

'Or maybe she saw you hiding it,' said Jen. She stood a few metres away, her hands on her hips. 'Wouldn't be too hard, then.'

'She didn't,' said Wei-Lin. 'I was watching. She didn't even look in my direction.'

'Yeah, right,' said Jen. 'Like you could have been watching her *all* the time. You had to take your eyes away at some point to hide the watch in the first place.'

'Maybe that's it,' said Pan. 'Just a trick, right Jen? Or Wei-Lin and I are in it together.'

Jen didn't take her eyes from Pan's.

'She said it.'

There was silence. Wei-Lin glanced from Pan to Jen and back again. A momentary break in the cloud cover caused the sun to wash over them. Somewhere, far off, a bird shrieked.

Then Nate appeared from the hut and jogged towards them. Everyone turned to wait for his arrival. *They are turning from confrontation*, thought Pan, *and that's okay with me.*

'Hey,' said Nate as he slowed and stopped before them. 'What's this guys? A time-out?' He looked around the running track and gave a theatrical sigh. 'Woeful progress, guys, if you don't mind me saying so. Really woeful.'

'What did Miss Kingston want with you?' asked Jen. 'Did she rip you a new one?'

Nate grinned.

'Nah. She's a pussy cat. Actually, if you really want to know, she persuaded me to team up with her for my elective. The skill training.' He winked. 'But if you want my opinion, I think that's just a ruse. The woman is hot for me and who can blame her?'

'So what's the skill?' asked Karl? 'Sexual magnetism?'

'Well, she said she detected leadership skills in me, but I reckon you're right, Karl, old buddy.' His grin broadened. 'It radiates from me, doesn't it? I give it less than a day before she tries to jump my bones.'

Jen snorted and turned away. The rest laughed. Even Sanjit laughed. Cara gave a thin smile, and that too was progress. *Maybe we* can *bond as a group*, thought Pan. *If I can just mend this rift with Jen.*

Nate looked from face to face.

'So what's going on here?'

Wei-Lin explained how Pan had found her watch. Nate whistled.

'Thanks a bunch, guys. As soon as my back is turned, freaky shit happens and I miss it. Couldn't you have waited until I got back?' He turned to Pan and spread his arms. 'I want to see this. Will you do it again for me?'

'There *is* something you've misplaced, Nate,' said Pan, 'but I'm afraid there's no chance I'll be able to find it.'

'Oh, yeah? And what might that be?'

'Your sexual magnetism.'

This time, even Cara laughed.

Chapter 10

At four-thirty, Jen, Nate and Wei-Lin prepared to go to their personal development sessions.

'You are the newest of the student body,' Wei-Lin said to the rest of them, 'so that will give you some leeway. But I can't stress enough that you need to find something within the next day or so. Remember, the septic tanks await if you don't.'

'What do you do?' asked Sam.

'Me?' Wei-Lin smiled. 'Archery, of course. Actually, I run a group that has shown some ability in that area.'

'An instructor, huh?'

'Yeah. I'm *so* important. Anyway. Cara, maybe you should go to the canteen and offer your services. Sam and Karl . . . hell, I don't know. Find something, okay? You too, Pan and Sanjit. I'm serious.'

But Pan couldn't think of anything. Karl and Sam set off together to explore what courses were on offer and Pan thought about asking if she could tag along. *A fifth wheel*, she thought. Karl and Sam deserved privacy. Pan didn't want to spoil any chance of a romance before it had time to develop. Cara wandered off listlessly. Sanjit walked away without a word and Pan was left on her own.

She ran through options in her head. Sure, she had intuition, but that wasn't an activity she could easily practise. She couldn't fight and she certainly wasn't gifted in any kind of physical activity. Pan wasn't sure if there were any academic activities that she could become involved in. Maybe Professor Goldberg could help. Then again, Professor Goldberg didn't strike her as the kind of person from whom she could get a straight answer. Maybe the septic tanks would have to do. How difficult could it be? Mindless physical labour, true. And extremely smelly. Perhaps that wasn't such a great idea.

Her thoughts turned to Tom and the falcon. Was that even a program, or something he simply did in his spare time? Pan wasn't sure, but she had nothing else to do, so she went searching. She retraced her steps to the clearing where he had been practising the previous night, but there was no sign of him. In the distance she could see groups of students pairing up for weapons practice. Everyone appeared to have a purpose - everyone apart from her. It made her feel useless.

To hell with it, she thought. *The septic tanks must be better than feeling like this.*

The voice shouting her name was so distant it took her a moment to realise she was being called. Pan stopped and turned.

It was Nate, running effortlessly towards her. She waited, aware that her heart was beating faster than normal. Or was that simply her imagination? Nate was physically attractive, there was no doubt about that. And he was very self-assured. But there was something else.

'Yo, Pan,' said Nate as he drew alongside her.

What are you hiding? she thought. The question surprised her.

'Now I *know* you're stalking me,' she said. 'Miss Kingston is about to jump your bones and yet you're running after me.'

'She's playing hard to get,' Nate replied. 'Anyway, I have a message for you.'

'For me?'

'Yup.' He offered her a piece of paper, neatly folded. 'So, you see, I'm simply a messenger boy. Miss Kingston was thrilled. "Get back here in five minutes," she said. "Think you can run that fast, Mr Mitchell?" I love a challenge. So, here it is.' He looked at his watch. 'I have slightly less than two minutes to make it back. I'd hate to give her the satisfaction of being late.' He looked at his watch again. 'One minute, fifty seconds, and counting.'

Pan opened the slip of paper.

Please come and see me in the Infirmary at your earliest possible convenience. Best wishes, Dr Morgan.

'What is it?' Nate was bouncing up and down on his toes. Pan would swear that his muscles were protesting at the lack of action, demanding movement.

'It's a note from Dr Morgan,' said Pan. 'He wants to see me.'

'Okay,' said Nate. 'I'll run with you. Come on.'

'What, now?'

'As our fearless weapons instructor might say, "What are you waiting for? Do you have an appointment at the hairdresser?"'

'You only have one minute to get back to Miss Kingston,' Pan pointed out. 'You'll be late.'

'Actually, fifty-five seconds, so I'm going to be late anyway. Hey. Pandora Jones, enough already. Let's run.'

He took off without waiting for a reply. Pan watched his back for a moment, sighed and started running after him. Almost immediately, her breathing became laboured and she knew she couldn't begin to match his speed.

'Not so fast, Nate,' she called.

Nate laughed. 'This is not fast, Pandora. This is tortoise pace. Come on. You can do it.'

'I can't.'

'Save your breath,' Nate called over his shoulder. 'You'll need it for those steps.'

Oh, God, thought Pan. *The steps to the Infirmary.*

'I'll pace you,' Nate added. 'Keep focused on your breathing. Get that right, and the muscles will follow. You'll get through the lactic acid build-up. Provided you don't stop, that is.'

It did become easier. Nate ran a few metres in front of her and she matched her rhythm to his. Within moments, the nagging stitch in her side eased. Her breathing became more regular. It was still hard, but now the cliff face was getting appreciably nearer. Pan kept her eyes fixed on the side of the cliff, where she knew the steps to the summit started.

When they got there, Pan wanted to rest, perhaps lie down for a few minutes before starting the ascent. Her body was aching and her legs felt like they had heavy weights attached to them.

'Don't stop,' warned Nate. 'Go straight up. Keep your breathing rhythm. Push through the pain. I have to go.' He looked at his watch and laughed. 'I'm going to be *so* late and the Princess will be pissed. I'll have to plumb the deepest recesses of my charm.'

Pan had no breath for thanks. She was aware of him wheeling around and heading back down the path. The steps loomed in front of her, carved out of the cliff side. They seemed impossibly steep and an image flashed through her mind of getting halfway up the steps and then tumbling off the side. She didn't want to die just trying to keep an appointment.

Pan pushed the thoughts aside, and started up the steps.

~~~

Dr Morgan was waiting in Reception. There was a twinkle in his eye as Pan pushed open the doors and staggered the last few steps.

'Looks like The School has been pushing you hard, Pandora,' he said with a grin. Pan couldn't answer. Her lungs were on fire. She crouched over, hands on knees, and fought the urge to vomit.

'You need to do your warm-down exercises, my dear,' the doctor added. 'I'm sure the redoubtable Miss Kingston has shown you how. Come on, stretch and pull those muscles before they seize up. This is the clinician in me speaking.' He chuckled.

It was almost as much agony to do the exercises, but after a few minutes, Pan at least felt partly in control of her body. Dr Morgan brought her a large glass of water. When she'd finally recovered enough to walk without her legs giving way, she followed him back to the same conference room they had talked in only a few days before.

Pan sat and sipped at her water.

'Thank you for responding so promptly to my request for a meeting.' He glanced at the clock on the wall. 'It's nearly five-thirty. Halfway through the personal development session. Now, a little bird told me you haven't yet chosen your skill area to develop. Is that correct, my dear?'

Pan nodded. 'I don't think I have a gift to develop, Doctor,' she said. 'Though I've been reminded that they are always looking for someone to clear out the septic tanks.'

'How appalling,' Morgan said. 'To my mind that would be a waste, if you'll forgive the pun. In fact, I'd go so far as to say you'd be simply going through the motions.' He laughed at his own joke. Pan smiled and drummed her fingers on the side of the chair. The doctor put his own hands flat on the table.

'I have a proposal for you, Pan,' he said, leaning forward. 'I would like to work with you on a skill that I have reason to believe you possess. It's also a field I have a personal interest in. Something I worked on, purely as an amateur, you understand, before the virus. It would be tremendously satisfying for me to take up my studies again in that area. If you agree, of course.' He tilted his head to one side and smiled.

'I don't know what you mean.'

'I'm talking about your gift of intuition,' said Morgan. 'I understand you gave a very impressive demonstration of it this very afternoon.'

Had he been watching? thought Pan. *Or did someone tell him?*

'How did you know about that?' she asked.

Morgan tapped the side of his nose with an index finger.

'I have my ways,' he chuckled. 'You'll learn that very little goes on in The School that I don't find out about. I have my finger on the pulse in more ways than one, my dear.'

'I'm afraid you might be disappointed, Doctor,' said Pan. 'And I suspect I'm better employed at the septic tanks.'

Morgan continued as if Pan hadn't spoken.

'I would need a commitment of two hours a day and I would like to conduct a series of tests, first of all to determine whether you actually *do* have some intuitive gift. Should that prove to be the case, then I have some ideas as to how we could improve and hone that skill.' He smiled. 'To be honest, I'm excited at the prospects, Pan. Enormously excited.'

'Look, Dr Morgan, I can understand that you might be enthusiastic if this has been a hobby of yours, but don't you think we might both use our time better? Something more ... practical?'

'No, no. Listen to me, Pandora.' Morgan was very earnest. 'This could be of enormous benefit to The School. And not just The School. In the long term, the very future of humanity.'

Pan laughed. 'Forgive me, but that seems ludicrous. I can find stuff that's been lost, Dr Morgan. Sometimes. If it's a skill at all, it's a very modest one.'

'I disagree. Think about it, Pan. You talk about finding "stuff", but if you have the ability to do that, then it's reasonable to assume that locating lost items is only one application of your ability. Who knows what you might be capable of? And as far as the future of humanity is concerned, whether you like it or not, you are now part of a very restricted gene pool. Can such gifts be passed on to the next generation? My research suggests that this is a distinct possibility. What if, in succeeding generations, clairvoyance becomes a natural ability? A whole world that could communicate through thought transference, for example. A world that, at the very least, uses much more of its brain than, unfortunately, we do at the moment. You could be the next step in our evolution, Pan. I'm serious, my dear. From *Homo sapiens* to . . . well, whatever follows.'

'You're suggesting I could be a breeding machine for super people?' Pan said. 'Do you have any idea how creepy, how *insane* that sounds? If it was possible, which of course it isn't.'

Morgan smiled. 'You misunderstand. Anyway, this is all academic until we've proved that this gift exists. What do you say, Pandora Jones? The bottom line is it's better than shovelling shit, wouldn't you say?' He laughed so hard he had to wipe tears from his eyes.

Pan waited until he'd finished and then shrugged.

'What do you have in mind, Doctor?'

'Oh, just a few basic experiments to begin with.' Morgan stood and moved to a cupboard on the wall. He opened it and brought out a strange machine and then placed it on the polished table opposite Pan.

'Let me introduce you to a continuous shuffling machine. I put in a requisition and a colleague across the wall was resourceful enough to get it for me. What we will be doing today, my dear, is a little experiment. The machine will randomly select cards and slide them face-down in front of you. You simply have to guess whether the card is red or black.'

'Why can't you shuffle them?'

'I could, but this machine holds five decks which would be a challenge for me to handle.' Dr Morgan smiled. 'Plus, it removes the human element, which is important in studies like this. Neither of us will know what card is dealt until after you have made your guess. Basic scientific methodology, my dear.' He put both elbows on the table and fixed Pan with twinkling eyes. 'Shall we give it a go? What do you say?'

'You want to start right now?'

'Why not? We have forty-five minutes of the session left.'

'Okay. I guess so.'

'Excellent,' said Morgan, rubbing his hands. 'This should be fun.' He pressed a button on the side of the machine. There was a brief whirring sound and a card slid out onto the table in front of Pan. She looked at it.

'What am I supposed to do?' she said. 'Put my fingers on the side of my head, focus on the pattern, try to "see" through it? I mean, how do I do this?'

'I've no idea,' replied Dr Morgan. 'Just tell me if you think this is a red card or a black card. Have a guess.'

Pandora gave a small laugh. She looked at the back of the card, waited to see if anything floated into her mind. It didn't. The back of the card obstinately refused to give her any information whatsoever.

'Red,' she said eventually.

Dr Morgan turned the card over. It was the four of clubs.

Pandora laughed again. 'Good start,' she said.

'Don't worry about it,' said Dr Morgan. 'Relax. You can't tell anything from one card. You can't really tell from a hundred cards. If we are to discover anything, it will be in the statistics, and that will take thousands of repeats. The more we do, the more accurate the data.'

'By chance, random guessing, I should get fifty percent right, shouldn't I?'

'Exactly. Right now, you're a hundred percent wrong. But do this ten thousand times and anyone will hit really close to five thousand right and five thousand wrong. The interesting thing would be if you got eight thousand right. That would be very interesting, statistically.'

'And if I got two thousand right?'

Morgan laughed. 'Equally interesting, my dear. We'd be able to say that you have an uncanny instinct to get things wrong. I think that would be very useful. Anyway, let's press on.'

This time, he did not flip the card to reveal its colour. He simply glanced at it before putting it back into the machine and making an annotation in a notebook. Fifteen minutes later, Pan asked how she was doing. Dr Morgan squinted at his notebook and totted up the totals.

'Fifty-eight correct, forty-seven incorrect. Statistically insignificant. But try something for me, Pan. At the moment, I think you are concentrating too hard. You are forcing yourself. Don't even think about the card. Don't look at it. The first colour that springs to mind. No second guessing. No agonising.'

'Can I touch the back of the card?'

Morgan frowned. 'Does that help?'

'It might. When I find things, I generally like to touch the person who's lost something. It's probably nothing, but it makes me feel more confident.'

'Then go ahead, by all means.'

Pan found it a lot easier after that. She took the doctor's advice about not thinking too hard. She kept her eyes fixed on her glass of water and watched as the beads of condensation rolled down the sides. At the periphery of her vision she noticed the cards come down and she reached out her left hand to barely brush their backs. Then she simply said the first colour that came to mind.

Pan was surprised when Morgan abruptly put the machine away. She looked at the clock and saw it was six-twenty.

'Definitely enough for today's session,' said Dr Morgan. 'Especially as you are on the early dinner shift.'

'So what's the verdict, Doctor?'

'We are a very, very long way from reaching a verdict, my dear. Come on, I'll walk you to the steps.'

Pan groaned.

'It's a lot easier going down, trust me,' Morgan added.

'What's the point of having a hospital in the most inaccessible place?' asked Pan as they walked along the corridor. 'Isn't it inconvenient?'

'Not for me,' chuckled the doctor. 'I like to be away from the hustle and bustle of The School proper. And the view is fantastic.'

'But if anyone gets hurt, they have to be brought up those steps. That can't be efficient.'

'You sound like The School Council. No. It's not efficient. But this is the way it was set up when we arrived. Beds and equipment already here. Maybe the military had their reasons for having a hospital in such an inaccessible place, but there's no one to ask anymore. And don't forget we have some exceptionally fit stretcher-bearers among the student body. You'd be surprised at how quickly they can get a patient here.'

He pushed open the swing doors. The Garden on Top of the World was to their right, shrouded in twilight. The first of the stone steps could just be seen off to their left. The cold had intensified now. The sky was dotted with hard pricks of light. They were too far from the edge of the cliff to see anything of The School below. But Pan could just make out the sea in the far distance. Lights flickered in the village that nestled on the shore. The wall separating it from The School was a wedge of darkness, though in the towers along its length bright lights burned.

'Answer me one question before I go, Doc,' said Pan.

'Of course, my dear.'

'The most basic resources are missing in this place. From what I can see, we need energy, food, educational material, tools, livestock. A whole bunch of stuff that would make life here much easier.'

'Correct,' said Morgan. 'We are desperately short of almost everything. But, as I'm sure has been explained, we have limited means of transporting things here. We try to build things up slowly, while the number one priority is still searching for survivors.'

'Yes, I was told that. So my question is how did you get a shuffling machine?'

Pan felt, rather than saw, Morgan stiffen in surprise. There was silence for a long time and then he laughed.

'You've caught me out, my dear,' he said. 'You're absolutely right. I should never have got such a thing. But . . . let's say I know one or two of the people who go out on their boats to get supplies. And let's say also that one or two of them owe me a favour. It's reprehensible, my dear, and I would be grateful if you didn't spread this around. But it's the way the world has always operated. I scratch someone's back and they scratch mine.'

Pan nodded, but inside she was shaking her head. The answer was wrong. Not the basic idea that he might have persuaded someone to do a favour and source something outside the official requisition lists. But who in their right mind would want a shuffling machine, of all things? Pan hadn't had time to think all of the implications through, but she knew two things. Dr Morgan had secrets and she didn't trust him. *He wants to learn about me in these personal development sessions*, she thought, *but they will also give me the chance to learn more about him and The School. If I do have intuitive gifts he may find that they could rebound on him.*

'One other thing,' she said. 'How is the survivor doing? We saw the helicopter land here yesterday. We assumed someone had been brought in.'

Morgan sighed.

'Indeed. A boy, not in good shape, I'm afraid. In fact, at the moment it's looking unlikely he will make it. But we do our best with what we have at our disposal. Trust me, we are working hard to get him through.'

'The virus?'

'Maybe. In part.' Morgan spread his hands. 'Though our main concern is to do with something altogether more basic. I'm afraid he suffered a serious bullet wound to the chest.'

'He was shot?'

'The pilot spotted him a few days back,' said Morgan, 'and because there wasn't enough room to land in that particular location, we sent out a team of students to locate him, bring him back. That happens, Pandora, when circumstances dictate. When they got there, they found he had been badly wounded.'

'How did that happen?'

'If he recovers, he may be able to give us the full story. But we do know that there are some survivors who ... how can I put this? ... have reverted to a state of barbarism.' Morgan rubbed at his forehead. 'It is sad, but a part of human nature. Though now, more than ever, there is enough for everyone, some will always not want to share and will protect what they consider their property by any means at their disposal. When law and order breaks down entirely and life and death is at stake ... well, there are dangerous people out there, my dear.' He patted Pan's shoulder. 'That's another thing The School is meant to prepare you for.'

Pan would have asked more, but her attention was drawn to a flickering light that appeared at the top of the steps leading down to The School. The light resolved itself into a flaming torch, its fire dancing in the breeze. Shadows swarmed over the silhouette of the person holding it. Then the torch was lowered to illuminate the figure's face.

'Nate,' said Pan.

'I will see you tomorrow, Pandora. Four-thirty sharp,' said Dr Morgan, and he was gone before she had a chance to respond.

Nate stepped forward a few paces.

'Hey,' he said.

'Hi,' said Pan. 'What are you doing here?'

His face was wreathed in dancing patterns from the torch.

'Oh, you know. Had some time to kill.' He laughed. 'Thought it might help if I brought some light for your journey down. The flame torch that Wei-Lin mentioned. I love them. So medieval.'

Pan smiled.

'Well, thank you. I must admit, light will be a comfort. At least it'll make it easier to avoid thinking about the drop.'

'You afraid of heights?'

'Terrified.'

'In that case, I'll go first. Should make it easier for you to see. Just keep on my heels, though I'd appreciate it if you didn't tread on them.'

They set off down the steps. This time there was no great rush, so Pan could choose her path carefully. True, they were going to be late for dinner, but provided they got there before the second sitting there would be time to eat. The canteen was not a place where people lingered, and it didn't take more than ten minutes to be served and finish your dinner.

The steps themselves were broad, and they kept to the cliff side. After a few minutes, Pan almost forgot about the drop to her left. Almost. Nate threw remarks over his shoulder.

'So what were you doing with the Doc?'

'He wants to team up with me for personal development,' she replied. 'It seems that just as you were head-hunted by Miss Kingston, Dr Morgan wants to work with me.'

'Ah, it's good to feel wanted,' he said. 'So what is it then? Don't tell me. You've always had a burning ambition to be a surgeon.'

'Not quite. Apparently, he wants to test whether I have psychic ability.' She felt embarrassed just mentioning it.

'Seriously?' Nate stopped and Pan almost trod on his heels. He turned to face her. 'That is so cool. Like that thing you did today, finding Wei-Lin's watch? Wish I'd been there, Pan. That is serious *X-Files* shit.'

'Did you mention it to Dr Morgan? Or anyone else?'

'Me? No. I wasn't even there, remember. Why would I mention it?'

'He knew about it. So either someone told him, or . . .'

'If you're psychic, you should already know.'

'Ha, ha. Funny guy.'

Nate smiled and turned back to the steps. Pan thought they must almost be at the bottom but the light from the torch, although illuminating a small area, had the effect of making the darkness close in around them. She continued to take one step after another.

'How did your session with Kingston go?' she asked.

'"People listen to you, Nate, and are prepared to follow." What a crock. But part of the program is improving my fitness levels, so that's okay. I don't mind that. We had a race.' He laughed. 'A two-hundred metre sprint and she kicked my butt. That'll change, trust me. I cannot allow someone ten years my senior to beat me at running. It's unacceptable.'

They completed the rest of the descent in silence. At the base of the cliff, The School was spread out before them, shrouded in darkness, but pinpointed with moving sparks of light as students returned from the canteen to their dormitories. Despite the cold, it lent warmth to the scene, the reflection from the flickering torches giving the buildings a fairy-tale quality.

'We're late for dinner,' said Nate, holding the torch up to his watch. 'If we stand any chance of eating we are going to have to run.'

Pan groaned. Her legs were so tired and the last thing she felt like was yet more exercise. But she was also starving. They set off running, side by side, down the path towards the canteen.

Chapter 11

During dinner, everyone denied saying anything to Dr Morgan about Pan finding Wei-Lin's watch. It was difficult to tell who might be lying, but the group's puzzled looks seemed to indicate a genuine innocence. The only member of the group not at their table was Cara, who was serving food behind the counter. But given that Cara had barely said two words to anyone at all in the last couple of days, the odds of her being the informant were low.

I do not know who to trust, thought Pan. *And that means I can trust no one.*

She bent her head to her bowl. It might simply have been her imagination, but the food this evening tasted better. Not good, but better. Maybe Cara was making a difference in the kitchen.

~~~

The dream took up where it had left off.

Pan entered the alleyway five metres ahead of the chasing men. She dimly understood that this was an alleyway she had already run down. And with that realisation, the first fear returned. That the space ahead, the mouth of the tunnel seventy, eighty metres ahead, would fill. A man in a dark suit. A man with sunglasses. Blocking her exit. And as the image filled her head, so it happened.

Had he stepped out ten seconds later, Pan would have run straight into him. As it was, she barely broke stride. She veered to the side and, throwing her right hand onto the top of the wooden fence that bordered the alley, leaped as high as she could. Her school skirt ripped as her right hip snagged painfully on the fence. The pain blossomed so that, for a moment, it filled the entire world. She almost passed out as she fell onto her side. But she had cleared the fence. Pan hobbled to her feet again and looked around. Someone's back garden. A Hills Hoist, underwear fluttering. A garden shed. A kid's sand tray. No one around. No place to hide. She heard footsteps on the other side of the fence. She didn't wait for hands to appear at the top of the railings. She ran to the low fence bordering the next garden. This was easier to get over. Easier for those following, too. A small dog yapped at her, made darts for her ankles. She screamed for help.

Pan made it to the third garden before looking back. The men, three of them, were jumping into the second. One aimed a kick at the yapping dog, which yelped and cowered. Pan ran round the side of the house towards the front garden. Where was everyone? How could an entire neighbourhood be so deserted? All she needed was for someone, anyone, to come out of their house to find out what all the noise was about. Just one person. This thought was running through her head as she came around the side of the house and ran straight into a fourth man. A man with a suit and sunglasses. The collision staggered both of them.

She tried to run. But he grabbed hold of her shirt, pinned her to him. One arm clamped around her waist, a *hand smothering her mouth and nostrils. She couldn't catch her breath and panic surged. Pan kicked back at the man's ankles, felt the satisfying clunk of shoe against bone. But his grip tightened and he dragged her back towards the garden, away from the road. Her lungs ached to take in air, but there wasn't any.*

Pan fumbled in the waistband of her torn skirt. She wrenched a canister from her hidden pocket, almost lost her grip, found it again. Her fingers fumbled for the nozzle. He had her leaning backwards now. Her shoes were dragging against the ground, vision filled with tumbling images of sky, and brickwork to her left. She brought her hand up to her shoulder, pressed the button and sprayed. She couldn't aim. All she had was instinct.

The man let out a thin scream and his arms relaxed. Pan twisted, regained her footing and kicked back once more. This time his grip fell away and she spun to face him. His sunglasses were askew, one arm dangling from his ear. He was rubbing at his left eye with the palm of a hand. Pan stepped in closer and sprayed his right eye. He screamed again, crumpled to his knees. She didn't hesitate. Already she could hear footsteps approaching. Pan turned and ran to the gate, pushed through it, stumbled again, but her feet fell into the rhythm of running once more. Pan turned right down the road, and ran along the centre line.

The police car swung left onto the road about a hundred metres ahead, its lights flashing, sirens silent. It sped towards her. Pan couldn't quite believe it. She tried to blink away the sweat from her eyes, get the car in focus. It swam towards her, misty with refracted light. She ran faster, straight into its path. She wasn't aware of waving her arms over her head, didn't

*stop until the car slewed to a halt right in front of her, didn't
stop screaming even when a police officer took her in his arms.
All the strength left her, then. She slumped and a realisation of
pain flooded in.*

'It's okay, love. You're safe now.'

*The words seemed to come from an enormous distance.
Pan struggled to control her legs, which felt rubbery and like
they belonged to someone else. She wiped the tears from her
eyes. The officer was tall. He had a handlebar moustache. It
reminded her, bizarrely, of a main lead in an old American
TV series. She couldn't remember what it was called. His
arms felt reassuringly strong. She concentrated on her ragged
breathing, calming herself consciously, feeling the air draw
in, controlling the exhalation. She fought for power over her
body and gradually won.*

~~~

Pan sat up in bed, her face slick with sweat. For a moment,
the dream was so real that she had difficulty dissociating
from it and realising where she was. Then the night
sounds returned, the muffled sobs and cries that filled
the dormitory, even through her earplugs. She rubbed
at her eyes and took deep breaths. Her hands came away
wet. *Breathe*, she thought. *The night is filled with terrors,
but they can't be real. Can they?*

She took out her earplugs and scrambled around in
the bedside drawer for her torch. She hadn't used it last
night and she vividly remembered the sense of horror
when she couldn't find her way out of the dormitory. This
time she would take whatever help she could find. And,
judging by the cries of her fellow students, it would be a
relief if the light woke them. She found the switch and

turned it on briefly to get her bearings. The beam lit up Cara's bed. It was unoccupied, the sheets crumpled and thrown back.

Pan found the door easily this time, using the torch sparingly. The night was cold, the sky clear and fretted with stars. She shivered. 'Cara?' she whispered. 'Are you out here?' The only reply was the faint whistle of the wind. Pan turned on her torch once more and explored the immediate surroundings of the dormitory but there was no sign of the girl. She might have come out for fresh air, but it wasn't likely she would wander far, not at night when the absence of flickering torches lent The School such a sinister atmosphere. Pan turned off the torch again and spotted a thin band of light coming from the shower block. She walked towards the door, picking her steps carefully. She put her ear against the shower door and heard the faint hiss of running water. The light beneath the door must have been a torch beam.

Pan waited. She sat on a rock about ten metres from the toilet block. She hadn't knocked on the door for fear of frightening Cara and she turned the torch on for the same reason. Pan considered returning to her bed, but sleep was terrifying. Perhaps she could have a conversation with the quiet girl. Reassure her. Reassure each other. So she sat and waited and tried to ignore the night chill.

Cara stiffened when she opened the shower door and saw the pool of light around Pan's feet.

'It's okay, Cara,' said Pan. 'It's only me.'

Cara's eyes darted away and she pulled her camouflage jacket closer to her, an instinctive act of protection. She didn't say anything.

'Late for a shower,' Pan remarked.

'It's quiet.' Cara spoke so quietly that Pan had to strain to hear her.

'I guess.'

Cara lifted her head and met Pan's eyes.

'I like my privacy,' she explained. 'It's too crowded at any other time.'

Every student in The School is in hell, thought Pan *but those who are sensitive and insular suffer the worst.*

'Fair enough,' Pan replied.

Cara said nothing. She shifted from one foot to another, looking like a child who was waiting for permission to be excused.

'Feel like talking?' Pan asked.

'What about?'

'Anything at all. Just talking. You know, like girls do.'

Cara remained silent, but she walked over and sat on another rock about two metres to Pan's right. She shivered and hugged herself tighter.

'You're a quiet one,' said Pan.

'There's not much to say.'

'Sometimes it's good to talk even when you haven't got anything to say. Nate does that, have you noticed? Just talks for the sake of it.'

Cara shrugged. There was silence for a minute.

'You're not alone in your pain, Cara,' said Pan. 'You must know that.'

'Yes I am,' said Cara. 'We are all of us alone in our pain.'

'I thought the food was better at dinner tonight,' said Pan. *She will not respond to anything directly. I need to build this slowly.*

Cara seemed to relax slightly. 'They have no idea about spices,' she said. 'It's amazing how something basically tasteless can be made better with a sprinkle of pepper and some salt.'

'Keep teaching them,' said Pan. 'Please.'

Cara turned her eyes to the stars. 'It's peaceful out here,' she said. 'I like this time of night. Just watching the sky, feeling the night air on my skin. It's calm.'

'Whereas in there it's anything but calm,' said Pan. 'No one can find refuge in sleep; dreams wait for all of us. Nightmares. The monsters from our past.'

'Do you know the worst thing about my nightmares?' said Cara. 'It's not the horrors, the bodies in the streets. They seem . . . distant to me, somehow. What I can't cope with is the other dreams, the nightmares that make more sense.'

'What do you mean?'

Cara got to her feet. 'I'm going back to bed, now, Pan,' she said. 'I know you mean well, but I just need to be alone.'

'I want to be your friend, Cara.'

The girl smiled then, but it was pale and lifeless. 'Can you have friendship without trust?' she said, as if to herself. 'I don't even trust my memories, Pan, so I'm not ready to trust people. But I thank you anyway.'

Pan stayed another hour outside on that rock, watching the night sky. *What I can't cope with is the other dreams, the nightmares that make more sense. I don't even trust my memories . . .*

The words struck her with the force of truth. What was wrong with her dreams and what did they really signify?

~ ~ ~

'Right,' said Gwynne. 'Get into protective gear, pair up. I'll go through basic attacking manoeuvres again, how to counter them. Then you practise on each other. Questions?' He sniffed and wiped at his nose.

There were none.

Pan struggled into the bulky clothing and she welcomed some warmth. Nate winked at her as she fastened her helmet.

'What do you say, Pandora?' he said. 'Want to partner up with me?'

Jen stepped in front of him.

'I think that would be unfair, Nate,' she said. 'Girl on girl is much better. How about it, Pan? You and me?'

Pan's first instinct was to refuse. But she thought that showing weakness towards Jen was not wise. Plus, Gwynne was supervising and no real harm could come to her. Could it?

'Sure,' she said with as much confidence as she could muster.

Jen smiled and picked up a staff. Nate leaned close to Pan.

'I'd watch out if I was you. Jen *is* tough and we both know she's not the founding member of your fan club. Be careful, okay?'

Pan nodded. She watched as Jen did warm-up exercises, twirling her staff in complicated geometric patterns. She was strong and light on her feet, and the air sang. Pan picked up a staff. It felt heavy and cumbersome in her hands. Gwynne called the group to order.

'Listen up. Watch carefully. Attacking manoeuvres

and how to defend them. We'll do this very slowly. Jen and partner. Step forward.'

Pan and Jen stepped into the circle of students. Gwynne sniffed.

'Okay. The basics. Watch as Jen brings the staff over. A roundhouse arc towards the top of the head.'

Jen took one pace forward and brought the staff in a curve towards Pan's head, stopping as she reached the highest point of the trajectory. The instructor brought Pan's hands up so that her staff lay parallel to her shoulders.

'Remember? The barrier protects the head. Even a solid blow shouldn't get close.' He nodded to Jen, who brought the staff down quickly. A jolt of pain lanced through Pan's left hand. She nearly dropped her staff, but held on. Jen's blow had glanced across her knuckles before meeting the barrier of the wood. She bit hard on her lip and fought back tears. Her hand pulsed with fire.

'Remember I warned about this? Jen's partner wasn't listening. Keep your hands fluid. Again.'

This time, Pan moved her hands and Jen's thrust hit the centre of her staff with a satisfying clunk.

'Better,' said Gwynne. 'Now watch other attacking options and ways to counter them.'

They went through methods of blocking blows aimed at the sides. Despite the cold air, Pan was sweating freely and the staff shifted in her clammy hands. Finally, they did a couple of multiple manoeuvres - blows aimed at the head followed immediately by attacks to the side. Even though it was all done in slow motion, Pan had to concentrate hard to ensure that Jen's blows didn't get through.

'Okay,' said Gwynne. 'Pair up, go through those routines. I will be watching. Carefully.'

'What do you say, Pandora?' said Jen when the other students were lined up and going through the slow-motion roundhouse attack and defence. 'We've done this loads. Think you're ready for a few multiple blocks?'

Pan *wasn't* ready. She didn't trust Jen. But she simply nodded and hefted her staff in her hands, flexed her knees and stood, feet slightly apart. She concentrated upon keeping a good balance, both of her body and the heavy staff, which felt like lead.

The first attack came quickly. Jen went for an overhead blow, but it was a feint. The staff twirled in her hands and as Pan brought her staff up to block, the weapon smacked into the protective padding of her vest. The breath was punched from her lungs.

'You okay?' said Jen in a tone of voice curiously devoid of care. 'Should have seen that coming. It's important to react quickly. In battle, you can't expect an opponent to follow the rules of a drill. Gwynne taught me that. Go again?'

She didn't wait for a reply. This time, she skipped forward, her staff a blur. Pan had no time to react. She half-blocked a thrust to her side, but couldn't recover before her helmet took a sharp blow just above her right ear. This time she staggered back, her head ringing with pain. *I will not fall*, she thought. *Whatever she dishes out, I will not fall.* But she was wrong. The next attack swept her legs from underneath her and she landed on the rocky ground. A jagged stone punched into her right thigh. Pan got to her feet immediately, but her leg felt dead. She could hardly move it and the next attack hit her square on the injury. She gasped with pain.

'Want to stop?' said Jen. 'Take a breather?'

Pan shook her head. *This shouldn't be happening,* she thought. *Gwynne should see that Jen is trying to hurt me and he should stop it.* But the instructor was down the line, helping to correct Sanjit's grip on the staff. *Toughen up. That was the key. Take it, then take some more. Get hard.*

Pan tried to ignore the pain. She crouched and balanced the staff. *Watch her eyes,* she thought. *The eyes are the key. Don't watch the staff. Empty your mind. Don't try to anticipate. Concentrate on your breathing. Watch her eyes.*

When the next attack came, Pan allowed her arms to react instinctively. She didn't take her gaze away from Jen's eyes, which bored into her own. Pan brought her arms up for the overhead, but then swung the staff down to block a side attack. The thud of wood on wood told her that blow would have hurt. Jen's eyes widened in surprise, but then narrowed again. Pan shifted her weight slightly, brought her staff round to block another blow and then another. She stepped in, made her own feint and cracked her staff against Jen's right knee. Jen gasped. Pan took a few paces back. She was dimly aware that the others had stopped their routines and had gathered in a circle again. But she didn't allow her gaze to shift from her opponent's.

Jen's eyes told Pan that she was hurt. But it was more a blow to her ego than anything physical. Her eyes hardened again and she readjusted her grip on the staff. The next attack would be serious. *Just react,* she thought. *Use your instincts.*

There was something almost beautiful in surrendering herself. She didn't focus on where her feet were placed or how they moved. She didn't think about the staff or altering her grip or even where the attack was coming from. She simply allowed her body full control, to react as it saw fit, to move to its own pattern. Pan was conscious of the movement of her hands, the blur as staffs sliced through air, the shifting of her feet, the impact of wood on wood. She danced backwards under the frenzy of the assault. Each block appeared to enrage Jen more. Anger was dangerous. Anger clouded the mind. She let the blows rain in on her, twisting the staff, blocking, skipping on the balls of her feet. When the opening arrived, she was scarcely aware of delivering the blow. Her staff swept under Jen's guard and she felt the solid and jarring impact. Jen's feet were swept from beneath her and she hit the ground hard, her head cracking on a rock. Instantly, Pan brought her staff round with devastating force. She saw Jen's eyes widen as the staff swung towards her head.

It stopped centimetres from its target.

There was silence and then Pan dropped her staff and crouched down in front of her opponent.

'Oh, God,' she said. 'I'm so sorry. Are you okay?'

Jen's eyes were flooded with pain. And something more. Fear. Pan flinched from the raw emotion.

'Okay, step aside,' said the instructor. He didn't seem particularly bothered. He helped Jen to her feet, removed her helmet and looked into her eyes. 'Mild concussion, maybe,' he said, matter-of-factly. 'Careless, Jen. Very careless.'

'A lucky shot,' replied Jen through gritted teeth.

Gwynne sniffed and wiped at his nose.

'No,' he said. 'It wasn't. Infirmary, Jen. Get yourself checked.'

'I'm okay,' said Jen.

'Not open for debate,' replied Gwynne. 'An order. The rest of you, put away equipment. Lesson's over for today.' He looked up and down at Pan, wiped his nose. Then he grunted and turned away to supervise the packing away of equipment.

~~~

'What the hell were you doing?' asked Nate. He walked with Pan as they made their way to their respective personal development sessions.

'Making an enemy even more of an enemy,' replied Pan.

'Not sure I'd want *you* as an enemy. Where did you learn to do that? It was ... like ... awesome. Ninja Pan.' He laughed.

Pan glared at him. 'I never learned stuff like that. That was the first fight I've ever been in. I think.'

'Looks like you've got a gift for it, then. Tough chick, huh?'

'No,' said Pan. 'Not tough at all.'

'If you say so.' He held his hands up in front of his face. 'Tellya. I'm not arguing with ninja Pan.'

She stopped and put her hands on her hips.

'This is not funny,' she said, 'I've hurt someone. I nearly killed her, for God's sake. I am not proud of that. And I'm not in the mood for stupid jokes. Grow up, Nate.'

He was silent for a while as they continued walking. Pan wasn't looking forward to a session with Dr Morgan. After what had just happened, the thought of guessing the colours of cards struck her as monumentally pointless. At least she would be able to ask after Jen when she got there.

'I wouldn't worry about her,' said Nate. 'I was watching. I think she would have killed you if she had half a chance. You did what you had to do.'

'I'm not worried about her,' replied Pan. 'I'm worried about me and what I might become.'

When Pan returned to the dormitory for free time, she found Jen doing pull-ups from a ceiling beam. She grunted as she brought her chin up to the beam and lowered herself gently before repeating. Pan heard her counting. Forty-four. Forty-five.

'Jen,' said Pan after a minute. 'Can I have a word?'

Jen didn't reply at first. She made it to fifty pull ups and then dropped lightly to the floor. She started stretching.

'So talk,' she said without glancing at Pan.

'I want to apologise for what happened this afternoon. I didn't mean to hurt you. I . . . I don't really know what happened. But I didn't mean to cause you pain. It's important you know that.'

'Why?'

'Why what?'

'Why didn't you mean to cause me pain?'

'As if you need to ask. We're in this together. We're on the same side. I have no desire to hurt you or anyone else.'

'Then you're a fool.' Jen stopped stretching and met Pan's eyes. 'We were in battle. I was trying to hurt you.

If I'd got through your defences, then it would have been you on the floor, counting stars. I didn't. You did. End of story.'

'Then you're not mad at me?'

'Why should I be mad at someone who beat me? I'm mad at myself. It won't happen again. I promise you that. It won't happen again.'

Pan nodded, but she still felt uneasy. There was nothing in Jen's tone that suggested forgiveness. There was nothing in Jen's tone. Maybe it was as simple as that. She saw Pan as a test she had failed. No resentment, just a determination to improve, correct a fault Pan had exposed. Nothing personal. But as Pan turned to her own bunk she found it hard to believe it was going to end as simply as that.

~~~

A week passed in a breathless tumble of routine. Running with Miss Kingston, the Professor's classes, which had moved on to comparative religions. Woodwork and basic metalwork. Pan was looking forward to Sunday, but when it arrived it was as busy as any other day. She took her dirty clothes to the building that served as a laundry and had to queue for nearly two hours before she could dunk her uniform in a large barrel filled with dirty, cold water. She kneaded her clothes as best she could, wrung them out and draped them over a rock to dry. The pale sun didn't fill her with confidence that they would be dry for a considerable number of hours. Even so, the change of clothing made her feel better, almost fresh, though she knew that in a day or two they would be stiff with sweat and stained with dirt.

The sessions with Dr Morgan continued, though he gave her little feedback about how she was performing. For the most part, they continued with the card guessing and Dr Morgan relentlessly took down statistics. Occasionally, they would try something else. Once Dr Morgan drew on a piece of paper, put the sheet into an envelope and then asked Pan to recreate what he had drawn. Pan held the envelope and drew a picture of a sea with two boats and a flock of seagulls. The drawing was child-like, the boats simple geometric shapes and the seagulls a series of wavy lines. Morgan looked at her drawing, but his expression didn't give anything away. Another time, he hid his keys and asked Pan to find them, which she did within two minutes. The sessions were boring, but climbing the steps to the Infirmary wasn't as onerous as it had been at first. Pan was becoming physically stronger.

Her nights were still broken by strange, disturbing dreams, and by the cries of others as they went through their own. But time passed.

At dinner on Monday, Nate leaned and whispered in Pan's ear. 'What you doing this evening?'

Pan almost laughed.

'Oh, I don't know, Nate. Let me think. Maybe take in a movie, go to a restaurant, check out a club.'

He frowned.

'Pity. If you hadn't been otherwise engaged I was going to ask you out.' He shrugged. 'Still, if you change your mind I'll be outside the dormitory at eleven o'clock. Maybe you'll give the club a miss and join me.'

Pan glanced around the table, but no one was paying attention. Even so, she bent and whispered in his ear.

'You're going over the wall?'

Nate shrugged again. 'I seem to remember you asked me to let you know. Hey, are you going to finish that soup?'

'This is soup?'

'Closest description I can make.'

'Yes, I'm finishing it. And, yes, I'll give the club a miss. You know what nightclubs are like. They get boring after a while.'

~ ~ ~

The lights went out at nine o'clock, as always. Pan lay under her scratchy blanket and coiled herself into the smallest shape she could manage. The cold was constant. She'd thought she'd get used to it, but she hadn't. She tried to conserve her body warmth, use the blanket as a cocoon to keep the night's chill at bay. Wei-Lin and Sam talked for five minutes before they fell silent. Within minutes Pan could hear faint snuffling and the occasional rustle as someone shifted in sleep. The moans and cries would come later.

Two hours until she could meet Nate. It had been a hard day and her body was crying out for rest. She felt her eyelids droop towards sleep and forced them open. Finally, she pulled the blanket away from her body. The cold would have to be her sentinel. There was no way anyone could sleep in the freezing night air. She watched the faint luminescence of her watch. Her breath fogged the glass. The minute hand moved unnaturally slowly.

Finally, at ten-forty-five, she swung her legs out of bed, collected the camouflage jacket from her cupboard and made her way gingerly down the line of bunks. She kept on the tips of her toes past the huddled forms of sleeping bodies. Some of the girls were stirring restlessly and an occasional moan broke the silence. Pan cracked open the door of the dormitory and slipped out into the night.

There was a thin sliver of moon and a frosting of stars. They made the landscape colder, bathed faintly in silver. Pan shivered and pulled on her jacket. She walked to the path that connected her dormitory to the rest of The School. No sign of Nate. She stamped her feet against the cold and hugged herself.

'You make too much noise.'

She jumped. Nate seemed to morph out of the rocks, like a shadow magically infused with life. Pan put her hands on her hips.

'Thanks a bunch, Nate,' she whispered. 'Trying to give me a heart attack, or what?'

When he grinned she caught a flash of white. His face was black, only the whites of his eyes visible. She looked him up and down. Even his hands had been daubed with something dark. No wonder he appeared part of the night.

'What have you done to yourself?' she said. 'You loser. I don't know. Boys! Always playing games. Bet you feel all macho in that get up, huh? What's your last name again? Bond?'

He grinned again. It was faintly alarming, the flash of white in the dark.

'Licensed to thrill, that's me,' he said. 'Anyway, this is no game. We want to get over the wall, this is the best way to do it without being seen. Come on, Pan. Get with the program, girlfriend.' He took something from his pocket and pressed it into her hand. A cold container. 'Shoe polish,' he explained. 'Smear it all over.'

'You're serious, aren't you?' said Pan.

'Absolutely. Look, Wei-Lin said that there was to be no contact between The School and those people on the other side of the wall, though how they manage to get supplies to us *without* contact strikes me as impossible. If we're going to check out what's over there, we don't want to be seen.'

Pan wanted to argue but Nate had a point. She opened the can and dipped her fingers into it. The sludge felt thick and slimy, but she spread it over her face as best she could. Nate helped to cover those parts she missed. When he was satisfied, he put the container back into his pocket and then lifted up a backpack from the shadows at his feet.

'Where'd you get that polish?'

'I borrowed it from Miss Kingston's stores.'

'Borrowed?'

'Okay, stole. Satisfied? Let's get going.'

He didn't wait for a response but ran into a night that swallowed him in seconds. Pan sighed and followed. The pale disc of the moon hovered above the dark bulk of the wall and they headed towards it.

~ ~ ~

Nate ran his hands along the stonework.

'Smooth,' he said over his shoulder. 'No hand holds. Nothing to get a grip on. Strike you as suspicious?'

'It's a wall, Nate. A stone wall built a long time ago.'

'Yeah. Maybe.'

They had headed towards one of the six towers

spaced evenly along the length of the wall. The glow of a torch burned within, though they couldn't make out any movement in the window slits. Nate had insisted they wait and observe, to establish the level of security. 'First rule of leadership,' he'd said. 'Assess all risks.'

'A Miss Kingston saying?'

'Nope. Made it up all by myself.'

They waited in the shadow of the wall for twenty minutes, but there was no sign of guards patrolling, no voices. The wall and the tower that erupted from it like a dark and swollen tooth remained blank, featureless and eerily silent. Finally, they walked along the base until they were roughly halfway between one watchtower and another. The moon was obscured by the wall and Pan could barely see Nate, though he stood only a metre or so from her. The night pressed in on them. It was a perfect place to begin their ascent. If they could find a way over.

'So what now?' whispered Pan. Her words sounded unnaturally loud and she felt sure they would carry for a considerable distance. Pan barely breathed out her remaining words. 'Find a secret panel? Dig our way under?'

'You work on that if it makes you feel better, while I try something else. You see, I've come prepared,' replied Nate, digging into his backpack. 'That's my second rule.' He pulled something out, but Pan couldn't see what it was. She moved closer.

'Crossbow,' said Nate. 'And a grappling hook. Length of mountaineering rope. Another few items I borrowed from Miss Kingston's supplies.'

'Borrowed?'

'Okay, stole. Just using my initiative, Pandora.'

'Third rule?'

'You got it.'

'What's she doing with this stuff? I mean, a crossbow? We can't get decent supplies of toilet paper.'

'Who knows? Maybe it was already here. Anyway, keep quiet.'

Pan heard the hard metallic click of a mechanism locking. Nate took a few paces back. It was still too dark to make out exactly what he was doing, but she heard the whirr of the crossbow's release. High above, a second sound filtered through the night – a clank of metal hitting stone. Nate cursed as something landed a few metres to his left.

'Angle's wrong,' he muttered as he gathered up the coils of rope.

He got it right on the second attempt. This time there was a thin scraping sound as the grappling hook scratched its way up the other side of the wall, engaged at the top and held. Nate leaned backwards, put one foot on the wall and placed his full weight on the rope.

'Grab hold, Pan,' he said. 'We don't want this puppy slipping off halfway up.'

Pan took a length of rope curling behind Nate and added her own body weight. The rope didn't budge.

'This'll take our weight, then?' she said.

'Us and another four people,' replied Nate. 'At least. But we aren't going up together. I'll go first, since I reckon I've got more upper-body strength than you. Then, when I'm on the top of the wall, I can help you. When we're both up there, we can let the rope down the other side. Easy.'

'Easy' didn't seem the right word to Pan. She could

just make out the top of the wall, fifteen metres above. It was a wedge of darkness against the star-dusted sky. It looked a long way to climb. An even longer way to fall. Nate sensed her anxiety.

'I know. Scared of heights. I'll make a cinch knot around your waist before I go up,' he said. 'That way, if you slip, you won't hit the ground. Safe as houses, Pan. Trust me.'

He certainly seemed to know what he was doing. He made the knot with practised ease.

'When I get to the top, I'll give a couple of sharp tugs on the rope,' he said. 'That's your cue to start climbing. Put your feet against the wall as you go up. Try to walk up it. I'll be taking the weight from the top. Ready?'

Pan nodded. She wasn't ready, but she took a deep breath and watched as Nate took hold of the rope, pulled on it one more time and then climbed, hand-over-hand, into the darkness. He made it seem easy. He barely put a foot on the smooth surface of the wall, using instead the strength in his arms to support his weight. Pan squinted up into the night sky, kept the rope taut and waited. Fifteen metres was a long way, but the tugs on the rope came much sooner than she expected. A dark shape, a shadow against shadows, moved and squirmed against the sky. He had made it. Pan took a deep breath and started.

Within a minute, the muscles in her arms and legs shrieked in pain. She placed her feet against the wall, but it was so smooth that she slipped almost immediately. So she pulled herself up by the arms, clasping the trailing rope between her feet. Pull up a metre or so. Step on the trailing rope. Rest. Pull up again. At least she couldn't see the ground and that was a comfort. It was as though she were climbing in a vacuum. No way of knowing the drop. But no way of knowing how far to go either.

Toughen up, she thought. It was embarrassing that Nate could swarm up this rope like a monkey and she was taking an age. Pull up. Rest. And then the moon silvered her face and Nate grasped her wrist. She made one final effort and flopped onto the top of the wall, her heart hammering. Pan clutched at the cold masonry and waited for her breathing to slow. At least the top of the wall was broad – about two metres in width. She rested her face against the cool surface. Nate stood and looked out towards the sea, but Pan wasn't getting to her feet. She wanted to keep as much of her body as possible pressed to the security of that two-metre plane.

'Whose idea was this?' she gasped.

'Not sure,' said Nate. 'I think we came up with it together. Look, Pan. It's amazing up here.'

Pan got carefully onto her knees, trying not to consider the drop that lurked on both sides. She sat in the very centre. Nate paced up and down. Did he have no fear at all? Only when she was convinced she couldn't fall did she look out over the village spread before her.

It was bigger than it had looked from the Garden on Top of the World. And, judging by the number of lights sprinkled along the streets and in the buildings, much busier and more heavily populated than it appeared from The School. It must have been midnight, yet there were plenty of signs of movement down there. Many places were in darkness, true, but there were also buildings brightly lit. The faint murmur of voices, the occasional burst of laughter. Ships bobbed on the moonlight-dappled water and many of these had lights swaying against the darkness.

'All of this,' whispered Nate. 'Just to supply The School? I don't think so, Pan.'

Pan didn't think so either. There was something wrong about the village. Nothing she could put into words, but a cold feeling in her gut. She was learning to trust those feelings.

'Okay,' said Nate. 'No point being up here longer than necessary. Time to get down and do some exploring.'

He disengaged the grappling hook and attached it firmly to the other side of the wall. Its barbs dug into the masonry but it still looked a precarious hold against gravity. And Nate wasn't able to test it by applying any weight. He uncoiled the rope and let it fall down the side of the wall into the village. It snaked and disappeared into shadows.

'I go first again,' he said, slipping his body over the side. 'Feel the rope. When it goes slack, I'm down. You'll find it easier this way.'

It took only a minute. Then the rope felt slack against her hand and she took a firm grip and edged her body over the side. It wasn't easier. This time, all her weight tried to take her down faster than she wanted. She coiled the rope around her legs and slithered down. Despite the cold, her face was slick with sweat. Her hands were damp and the nylon rope was slipping and burning against her palms. She had to balance the desire to descend as quickly as possible with the caution that one slip would be her last.

Pan felt Nate's arms around her waist and then her feet touched ground. Her knees nearly buckled, but she remained upright, leaning against the smoothness of the wall. The cool night air made her flushed face tingle. Nate pressed his lips against her ear and she shivered. On this side of the wall, there was a greater chance of being overheard. He kept his whispers low.

'We leave the rope here. Keep together at all times. We stick to the shadows, suss out what we can but don't take any chances. No talking, okay?'

Pan nodded and he pressed her hand. Nate took one pace towards the village.

The light struck like a fist, pushed them back against the wall. Pan brought her hand up to her eyes instinctively. And then there were shouts.

'Down. On the ground. Now.'

'Hands behind your head. GET DOWN!'

A scuffle of footsteps. Pan brought her hand away for a moment, but the light was too intense. It brought tears to her eyes. Shapes moved at the edges of the light, men bearing down on them. She caught a glimpse of guns, uniforms. Then someone grabbed her by the hair, pushed her to the ground. The shouts increased in volume. Everyone was yelling. She felt her hands being wrenched behind her back and the cold circle of a gun barrel burning against the nape of her neck. More men were at her feet. She felt cord biting into her ankles and wrists. Then a hood blotted out the light. Hands were all over her now, searching her pockets. Within moments, the noise diminished. She felt herself being lifted, carried. The only sound was the occasional barked order.

Then the prick of a needle in her arm.

After that, there was nothing.

Chapter 13

When Pan woke, her head was pounding and she squinted against pale light. For a moment she couldn't remember what had happened, but then her memories flooded back. She groaned and rolled onto her side, closed her eyes again. The wall. The village. Men, soldiers, a needle. She shuddered as she recalled the pressure of the syringe against her arm. When she opened her eyes again she forced them to remain open.

Slowly, she took in her surroundings. She was in a room, similar to one of the huts where classes took place. But this was considerably smaller and had no furnishings other than the small bed on which she lay. There was only one window, a tiny rectangle of dusty glass just visible through sturdy bars. Her legs felt unsteady, but she staggered to the door and tried the handle. Locked. There was a small panel in the door - a peephole, she imagined - but there was no way to open it from her side. She turned back and surveyed the room. No way out. Not unless she smashed through the walls. Possibly use the bed frame as a tool. She sat on the bed and waited.

Slightly less than an hour later, the panel in the door slid open and a shaft of light painted the floor. Pan could see motes of dust dancing in the beam, but they were abruptly shut off as the panel slid across once more. There was a rustling of keys and the door opened. Pan blinked against the light and stood.

Gwynne stood there with a student she didn't know by name, though she'd seen him in the canteen. He was tall, muscled and unsmiling. *He's the security*, Pan thought.

Gwynne sniffed.

'Come,' he said.

'Where are we going?'

'You'll see.'

Pan shrugged. She didn't have a choice. Her legs still felt trembly, but she managed to walk as if she had purpose. This was not a time to show weakness.

Gwynne and the student flanked her as she left the room. Her hut was situated on the extreme edge of The School, in a block of four or five similar buildings. The wall stretched out across the horizon, dark and inscrutable. Her escort marched her to the closest building, a hut somewhat bigger than the one she had occupied. There were no markings on the outside. Gwynne opened the door and Pan walked inside.

Four chairs were set in a line on the far side of a battered desk. Two of them were occupied by Professor Goldberg and Dr Macredie. A single chair was on her side of the desk. Gwynne and the boy took their seats. Pan stood beside the chair. *Exert any power you can*, she thought. *Don't sit. Let them look up at me.*

Dr Macredie glanced at a sheet of paper in front of her.

'This is a special session of The School Council,'

she said in little more than a whisper. Pan noticed for the first time that the doctor's voice carried a hint of a Scottish accent. 'And the matter before us is an episode of trespassing by Pandora Jones.' She met Pan's eyes and smiled. 'Please sit down, Pan.'

'I prefer to stand.'

Dr Macredie shrugged. 'As you wish.' She paused for a long moment. 'Would you care to explain your actions?' she said finally.

'They need explanation?'

'You entered a forbidden zone. I think that justifies giving a reason.'

'A "forbidden zone"?' said Pan. 'Strange. I didn't see any signs.'

'But you *were* told that students in The School are not allowed to visit the village. That is true, isn't it?'

'I'm sorry,' said Pan. 'Can you speak up?'

Macredie pushed a strand of red hair back from her eyes and repeated the question, though the volume was not noticeably greater.

'Yes,' admitted Pan.

Gwynne chipped in.

'You knew you weren't allowed, but went anyway? Wearing gunk on your face. So the question remains. Why?'

'I wanted to see what was on the other side.'

Gwynne sighed, but Professor Goldberg chuckled. Gwynne rubbed at his eyes with one knuckle and glanced down at the desk as if summoning a reserve of patience and unsure if he would find it. He picked up a pencil and tapped it against the stained wood.

'You've been told what's on the other side of the wall,' he said. 'Supply route. Potential disease. Why did you scale the wall?'

'Because I needed to see with my own eyes.'

Gwynne threw his pencil down. It bounced, rolled off the desk and clattered to the floor. No one picked it up. Dr Macredie held up a hand towards the weapons instructor and then leaned towards Pan. She smiled.

'Pan,' she said. 'We must protect all of our students. It is a solemn duty. We hold the future of the human race, the continued existence of humanity, in our hands. We must not fail. The stakes could not be higher. You must see that. You must understand that.'

'I understand I have been assaulted, drugged and imprisoned,' Pan replied. 'Now I find myself in front of what looks suspiciously like a court, without any idea of my rights and without anyone appointed to defend me. It is difficult, under these circumstances, to see any of you as protectors. You must understand that.'

Gwynne sniffed yet again and wiped his misshapen nose.

'"Rights"? Let me explain. None of us have rights. All this rubbish. Assault, imprisonment, the right to a defence. That was then. This is now. This is our only hope. For the future. We cannot allow anyone to jeopardise that.'

'And that gives you the right to put a gun against my head and inject me with God knows what?'

'Under the circumstances, yes. Absolutely. Reasonable force.'

'Sounds like you've established a cosy little dictatorship here.'

'A benevolent dictatorship, Pan,' said Dr Macredie.

'That's what all dictators say.'

Gwynne shook his head.

'No point in this conversation,' he said. 'Brendan, put Miss Jones back. Then return. Discuss appropriate punishment.'

The tall student got to his feet and came around the side of the desk. He was huge. *Probably a rugby player in the old world*, thought Pan. *But he's scared.* He took her by the arm. Pan shook him off and left the room without a backward glance.

~~~

Less than twenty minutes after being locked back in her cell, the door opened and Dr Macredie came in. She left the door open behind her.

'So the jury's come to a decision then,' said Pan. 'What is it? Death by firing squad?'

Dr Macredie offered a wry smile and put a hand to her head. She suddenly looked very tired. She gestured towards the bed. 'Do you mind if I sit?'

'Be my guest.'

'Actually, it's a week of lost free time. You and Nate will be spending quality time together cleaning out the septic tanks.'

'How wonderful. I think I prefer the firing squad.'

'Were you always so hostile, Pan?' said Dr Macredie. 'I'm curious.'

Pan regarded her carefully.

'I'm told you're not actually a doctor at all. Is that true?'

'Absolutely correct. I was a nurse. First of all in my native Aberdeen in Scotland. When I emigrated to

Australia I worked in a number of hospitals in Sydney. But I was always interested in psychology and at the time of the virus I was finishing my Bachelor's degree. I like to think it was only a matter of time before I got my doctorate.'

'Psychology?' said Pan. 'So do you really need to ask why I am so hostile? Everyone I loved is dead. Everyone I ever met is dead, I'm haunted by horrific dreams and I've just been assaulted, threatened and forcibly injected with drugs. What do you want me to do? Audition for the next school musical? Put myself up for Head Girl? Maybe I'm entitled to be hostile.'

Dr Macredie sighed.

'Ay, maybe you are. But you must understand that we are all in the same situation, here at The School. And that our only hope is to stick together.' She ran a hand through her hair. 'You talk about dreams. Okay. Let me share something. Every night I watch my husband die again. Suddenly, and in great pain. Then my ten-year-old daughter. I hold her in my arms and wipe blood from her face and watch her . . . go. If I'm lucky, that doesn't rewind and I move on to the bodies in the streets. Everywhere panic and death. If I imagine what Hell might be like, I think it would involve reliving all that, night after night. Does this sound familiar, Pan?'

Pan didn't say anything.

'I'm not saying I had it worse than you, Pan, or anyone else here. We are all damaged. But maybe it's because I've had longer to adjust than you. Now I see life as the greatest gift ever.' She smiled. 'I always said that. Before the virus. It was an intellectual point of view. Now I *know* it. I believe that you see The School as ugly and cheerless and bleak and cold - a place of misery. I see people living here - living, not dying - and it is the most beautiful place in the world. I hope you will come to that view yourself one day.'

Pan thought. Like Dr Macredie, she knew others were going through private anguish, but no one talked about it. Everyone pretended it hadn't happened and got on with the daily routine. It was only at night that the monsters emerged. She felt somehow petty, as if she had been behaving like a spoilt child.

'What was your daughter's name?' she asked finally.

Dr Macredie smiled and gazed off through the dusty window. For a moment, Pan thought she wasn't going to reply.

'Hope,' she said, her voice even fainter than normal. 'How's that for irony? The death of Hope. But it wasn't, Pan. Hope can't die. I'm sure of it.'

A shadow appeared at the door frame and Pan narrowed her eyes to see who it was.

'Hey, Pandora,' said Nate. 'Ready to shovel some shit, girlfriend?'

Dr Macredie laughed. 'Go on, get out of here, the two of you. Just take some friendly advice. Do not try to get over the wall again. I can't promise The School will be so lenient next time.'

Pan walked over to Nate and put a hand on his arm. She turned back to the woman on the bed.

'Tell me, Dr Macredie,' she said. 'All that overreaction - and it *was* overreaction, despite what you say - what does it signify? What is on the other side of the wall?'

When Macredie's reply came, it was so low that Pan could barely make out the words.

'There is evil on the other side of the wall, Pan,' she whispered. 'Danger lives there.'

~ ~ ~

Pan laughed when she saw that Nate still had the shoe polish on his face.

'You cut a dashing figure, Mr Mitchell,' she said. She ran a finger across his brow and then showed him the blackness on its tip. Nate laughed and brushed Pan's cheek. She shivered.

'Thus speaks someone who cannot see her own face,' he replied. 'Maybe we should keep this on. It'll protect our skin from the joys of the septic tank.'

'And it'll be useful the next time we go over the wall,' said Pan.

Nate smiled. 'I had a feeling you were going to say that.'

The sun, pale though it was, felt good against their blackened faces. Pan checked her watch. Close to eleven. They'd missed most of the class on agricultural methods, which suited Pan fine. She'd found it difficult to become enthused about ploughing techniques in the absence of heavy machinery.

'That's strange,' said Nate.

'What?'

He pointed towards The School buildings. It was the middle of class time, yet the paths were swarming with students. 'Something's going on,' he said.

They walked quicker. Within a couple of minutes, they saw a figure break free from a knot of students and come running towards them. A few seconds later Pan recognised the willowy frame of Wei-Lin. She was running flat out. Pan felt a chill run down her spine. She and Nate ran towards her.

'It's Cara,' gasped Wei-Lin when she finally came to a stop beside the couple. 'She's missing.'

Chapter 14

'Cara disappeared sometime last night,' said Dr Morgan. He paused and gazed over the assembled students. It was the first time Pan had seen all of The School's students gathered together in one place, the running track at the base of the Garden on Top of the World. It was a surprisingly large crowd. Dr Morgan brushed a strand of hair back in place and continued. 'Her bunk has been slept in, but it's clear she disappeared while everyone else was asleep. We have no idea when. Staff have conducted a quick search but drew a blank. We are all concerned for her wellbeing. As a result, normal classes are suspended today while we organise search parties. Miss Kingston is in charge of the organisation. She will allocate specific areas for each group to search. Cara's group - a word in private, please.'

Pan's group waited while the other students rushed over to where Kingston stood with a clipboard in her hands. She could see her own fears and guilt reflected in the faces of her group. Wei-Lin was on the verge of tears.

'You know Cara better than anyone else,' said Dr Morgan after they had formed a horseshoe around him. His tone was unusually grave. 'It follows, therefore, that you might have some insights into her whereabouts. So, any ideas?'

There was silence for nearly a minute.

'I'm afraid none of us know Cara well,' said Wei-Lin. 'She is very... private. Keeps herself to herself, you know.'

Dr Morgan shrugged.

'I see,' he said. 'In that case, report to Miss Kingston. Let's get this search started.'

'Except...' said Wei-Lin. She looked at her feet.

'Yes?'

'I think Pandora Jones might be able to find her.' She gave Pan an apologetic glance. 'It's just that... Pan can find things. Lost things. So I thought... maybe she could find a person who's lost. I don't know. Thought it might be worth mentioning, that's all.'

Jen snorted and Dr Morgan looked at her briefly before replying.

'Of course,' he said. 'I have worked with Pan in personal development sessions and I know she has had success locating things.' He turned to Pan. 'Think you could help, my dear?'

Pan laughed, but there was no humour in it.

'I've found watches,' she said. 'Articles, personal possessions. Sometimes. And Cara is a person. It's not the same thing at all.'

'Why not?'

'It just isn't. All that other stuff. It's a game, really. It would be wasting time.'

Dr Morgan twisted his mouth.

'We'll have four hundred students searching. I think we can spare one person. I mean, it wouldn't hurt, would it? If you just gave it a go. If you can't locate her, you can't. Nothing lost, but maybe, just maybe, something gained.'

Pan glanced along the row of faces as if for support. She found none. Jen wore impatience on hers, and as her eyes met Pan's, she abruptly broke from the line.

'Do what you like,' she said over her shoulder. 'I'm getting instructions from Kingston.'

One by one, the rest of the group joined Jen, though Nate squeezed Pan's arm before he left. Eventually, only Pan, Wei-Lin and Morgan remained.

'Please, Pan,' said Wei-Lin. 'As Dr Morgan said, there's nothing to lose by trying.'

'But I wouldn't have any idea where to start. When I found your watch I touched you. It gave me a sense of ... connection.'

'Maybe it'll work the other way round,' said Wei-Lin. 'If you touch something that belongs to Cara, you might get that connection in reverse.'

'We're clutching at straws.'

'Like I said,' put in Morgan. 'There are plenty of others doing the leg work. We can afford for you to clutch at a straw.'

Pan sighed. 'Okay,' she said finally. 'I'll give it a go, but I don't hold out much hope.'

Wei-Lin smiled. 'Let's go to the dorm,' she said. 'Find something that belongs to her.'

~ ~ ~

Cara's bed was dishevelled. Maybe it was Pan's imagination, but she thought she could see the faint outline of Cara's body on the bottom sheet. She put her hand on the bed but felt nothing, not a trace of dissipating warmth and certainly no kind of connective charge. Wei-Lin opened Cara's bedside drawer.

'That's strange,' she said.

'What?'

'Her watch is in here. Why would she take off her watch? I never take mine off, not even in the shower. And Cara always wears hers, too.'

Pan sat on the bed and took the watch in her right hand. She closed her eyes and tried to empty her mind. But her mind refused to empty. Wei-Lin was right. Leaving the watch was strange, particularly since Cara must have made a conscious decision to do so. A thought tingled at the back of Pan's mind that maybe Cara had left the watch because she knew she would never need it again. The implications of that thought were too dark to pursue, so Pan blocked it and attempted to relax her mind. She sat for five minutes, but all that fluttered at the back of her brain was a vague sense of wrongness.

'It's no good,' she said, putting the watch back on the bedside cabinet.

'Try this,' said Wei-Lin. It was Cara's journal. Pan had seen her writing in it almost every night, an obsessive outpouring. *Why hadn't she talked more to Cara?* Pan vowed she would be a better friend in the future. She would try, at least, to *be* a friend.

Pan took the book in her hand. Almost immediately she felt the weight of despair contained within it. It almost took her breath away and she felt a strong urge to drop it on the bed. But she forced her hands to keep a tight grip.

'I don't want to read this,' she whispered. 'This is her personal diary.'

'We are probably beyond respecting privacy,' responded Wei-Lin. 'Cara's life may be in danger, Pan, and there could be clues in there.' She put a hand on Pan's shoulder. 'Look, I'll leave you to it, okay? Do what you think is right. That's all you can do.'

Pan closed her eyes again and didn't see or hear Wei-Lin leave the dormitory.

~~~

Pan closed the journal and dropped it on the bed. She wasn't even aware how much time had passed.

The diary had been powerful reading. It wasn't that Cara was a good writer. Far from it. But somehow, the poor quality of the writing made it more compelling as an expression of feelings. The first part of the diary had concerned her life in Christchurch, New Zealand. Even then, Cara had been unhappy, a loner. She'd lived with her mother, who had not been around much. The subtext indicated she'd been more interested in drinking than looking after her daughter. Then came her memories of the virus and its aftermath.

Cara hadn't seen her mother that day and when it became clear that death was all around she went looking for her. The description of what Cara saw as she walked through the streets was the most moving part of the whole journal. Pan read of bodies hanging from trees in parks; a family in a four-wheel drive on one of the main streets, still strapped into their seat belts as if on a family day out; a five-year old girl playing with a doll beside the body of her mother. The girl coughed continuously, her white dress stained with blood. Pan had had to put the journal down at this point and calm the hammering of her blood because the images summoned her own experiences so vividly. Only when she felt more in control, could she pick up the diary and continue reading.

Cara wrote of the day-to-day routine at The School, how she had no friends, how she had been made to feel expendable. Pan was pleased, yet saddened, that there was a brief entry concerning Pan's defence of her during Miss Kingston's class. But that could not banish the conviction that she could have done so much more. Cara also mentioned her dreams and how they haunted her each night. Most recounts dealt with the same images of death, but she also wrote about other dreams, strange dreams in which she was pursued by a menacing figure. Pan read those lines over and over. She found it disturbing that they had shared a similar dream. What was it Cara had said that night when she had come out of the shower? *I don't even trust my memories . . . What I can't cope with is the other dreams, the nightmares that make more sense.* Why did that strike such a nerve? Pan had forced herself to read on.

Most of the final entries contained nothing extraordinary. There was no sign that Cara was more depressed than anyone else, no indication that she was thinking of attempting an escape or, worse, taking her own life. What had possessed her to get up in the middle of the night and leave for an unknown destination? There was no reference to anyone she might conceivably meet, no indication of a place she favoured where she could be by herself. But the final sentence *was* interesting. *The watches are wrong*, she had written. Yet the watch she had left behind was keeping perfect time.

There are puzzles within puzzles here, thought Pan. *Why can I not even see them clearly?*

She rubbed her eyes, put the journal carefully back into the drawer and left the dorm. Pan stood and gazed out over The School and its surroundings. The afternoon was drawing towards dusk. People were out there, searching. But soon the search would have to stop for the night. Torches of the kind she and Nate had used to climb the steps to the Infirmary would be no use. They illuminated a circle only a metre in diameter. Soon it would be impossible to find Cara if she didn't want to be found.

Pan sat down on the rock she had sat on when talking to Cara that night. She suddenly felt weary. She closed her eyes and thought about Cara. What she had read in the journal, what she remembered of their infrequent conversations. Then she found herself thinking about the young boy, Tom, and in particular, his falcon. The bird of prey that had swooped straight to her despite the gloom, and torn a mouse to pieces. Pan had almost forgotten the episode. So much had happened since and there seemed no good reason to be thinking about it now. But she couldn't wrench her mind away from the bird's flight path as it carved through the air onto her hand. She felt again the thud as its body impacted on her arm. She saw the bird's eye as it tore and ripped at flesh.

Something strange was happening. Pan knew it. And as soon as she thought about the strangeness of it, the images faded. She cleared her mind as best she could and there was the bird's eye again, wide, unblinking, focused. The eye expanded, filled her vision until the eye was all there was. It seemed to suck her in. For a moment or two there was a battle within Pan's mind. Part of her resisted. But another part welcomed it.

And then she was inside the bird.

Pan gasped. She could feel her back arch and the shock almost wrenched her free. But she fought against it. Fought to stay where she was. The panic inside faded, and slowly she lost all sense of where she was, there on a small rock outside a deserted dormitory. She opened her eyes and looked around.

Her vision was breathtakingly clear. Nothing in the surrounding landscape escaped her attention. She could see the minutest details at the greatest distance. Down on the plain, she saw search parties returning home. She saw Nate in absolute clarity, down to the mole on his right cheek, close to his ear. He was grim-faced and tired. His group had found nothing, though what they were looking for she had forgotten. Her mind was in a different place entirely. A place where the concerns of these creatures were unimportant. Pan scanned the rest of the landscape. She saw other people in startling detail. Then, before she was aware of it, she moved. She felt the rush of air against her body as she moved at phenomenal pace towards the looming mass of a grey, heavy cloud. Pan had no time to react. She simply allowed herself to be taken.

The ground swept under her. Then she looked down and there was a dizzying drop. Not dizzying, exhilarating. She rejoiced in flight. She was the master of space and her eye ruled the universe. She could feel the air beneath her wings. She soared higher, banked, and swept in a fast arc towards the wall and the sea. Within moments she had cleared the thin band of wall. The village below was bustling with movement. People. Children. Animals. None took any notice of her. She took no notice of them. Instead, she passed over sailing boats, wheeled out to sea, then banked and floated on air currents.

The landscape was clear. Her eyes searched out all movement. Nothing escaped her attention. She didn't know what she was looking for. Pan performed an arc and headed back to land. This time she went higher. The ground rushed away from her, but her eyes still ruled over everything. She soared over white peaks and picked up a movement a thousand metres below, a dark streak across the white. Food. A rodent. She ignored it, though instinctively she wanted to swoop. She glided further into the white, spotted something else, stooped to get a clearer view. It was what she had been looking for, though she had no idea how she knew this. The shape below meant little to her. Pan banked to her right. The white plain swept by beneath her, was replaced by rocks, buildings. She flew towards a nondescript building. She picked up speed.

Pandora Jones's body jerked and her eyes snapped open. For a moment she was still drunk with flight. But then the solidity of her body, clumsy and earth-bound, pulled her back to reality. She rose unsteadily to her feet, was overcome with dizziness and had to sit down again.

She waited while the pulsing in her blood calmed. What had she just experienced? An illusion? A dream? That was the only possible explanation. She must have fallen asleep.

Whatever the explanation, she couldn't ignore what

had happened. She got to her feet again. This time, her legs were able to support her weight. A girl was moving towards her across the grounds, and for a moment Pan lamented the poverty of her eyesight. Then she walked towards Wei-Lin.

Chapter 15

'If you want me to be frank,' said Miss Kingston, 'I think this whole thing is nonsense and I am only going because Dr Morgan specifically asked me to. As for the rest of you, apart from Miss Jones who *has* to join me, I would advise you to stay here. Trust me, that mountain is dangerous if you don't know what you're doing.'

The group stood inside the large hangar where Miss Kingston conducted her theory classes. The instructor was packing mountaineering ropes and tackle into a large backpack. Nate was doing likewise. The rest of Pan's group stood, waiting. They were dressed in survival gear - thick mountain boots and fleece-lined jackets - and looked strange out of their normal school outfits.

'We've talked it over, Miss Kingston,' said Nate. 'And we're all going.'

Miss Kingston glanced up and sniffed before continuing with her packing.

'How noble,' she said. 'Group bonding, is that it? Look, we don't need more than two for this particular wild goose chase.' She glanced at Sanjit and her mouth turned down. 'I do not relish having to take responsibility for people who are ill-suited to physical exercise, let alone the demands of mountain climbing.'

'We're going,' Nate repeated. 'And we take responsibility for ourselves.'

'So you say.'

The clothing was warm. After a few moments Pan felt sweat trickle down her stomach, though she knew she'd be grateful for the insulation once they started climbing. Nate came over and adjusted her jacket for her.

'Take no notice of Miss Kingston,' he whispered. 'She's always grumpy. In fact, I don't think I've ever seen her smile.'

'She's right, though,' replied Pan. 'I'm not equipped for this. None of us are, apart from you and probably Jen. I've never climbed a mountain in my life. I just hope we aren't a burden to you.' She didn't add that the whole reason for them going was because of her intuition and that she felt the responsibility keenly.

'Nah. She's not right. Only the lead climber needs to be highly skilled, and she is. She'll free climb up the face and then put in a bolt or a piton. The rest of us following will be on belay devices attached to the bolt, so there's no chance of falling. Trust me, Pan. It's hard work, but it's not dangerous.'

'Even if you're scared of heights?'

Nate laughed. 'It's not an advantage, I must confess. But I'll look after you and you'll be fine.'

Pan shrugged as she pulled her bootlaces tight and knotted them. Nate looked her up and down and nodded, a small smile on his face. They joined the rest of the group in a line, facing Miss Kingston who paced up and down.

'Right,' she said. 'We do this quickly and we do this safely. I will lead. Mr Mitchell, you will bring up the rear. Take a backpack each and check the equipment in it. You should all have extra rope as well as karabiners, crampons and an ice-pick. Then we'll get our muscles loose by running to the ascent point. I'll set the pace and I expect you to keep up.'

The pace Miss Kingston set was fierce and the group had difficulty matching it. Pan felt her boots as leaden weights and her skin crawled with sweat. She glanced over at Nate. He looked infuriatingly cool and dry. Then she fixed her gaze on the mountains a kilometre away. They loomed ominously, cold and forbidding. Her mind was brushed with a tingle of menace.

~~~

The first part of the climb was easy enough. Where the mountain range met the plain, the land was covered with large rocks that meant footholds and handholds were easy to find. For the first fifteen minutes it was more like an energetic hike.

But then the ascent became steeper. Pan had to hook her fingers into crevices and pull herself up. Sweat ran into her eyes but she didn't dare take her aching fingers off the rocks to wipe them. So she blinked through the stinging and hauled herself up. Nate climbed behind her, helped her find the easiest route.

'You're doing fine, kiddo,' he said. 'Just a few more metres and we hit a plateau.'

Pan scrambled onto a flat rock plain and lay on her back, gasping. Overhead was a pale blue sky dusted with wispy clouds. She waited until her breathing slowed, then rolled onto her side. The remainder of her group was resting also, though none appeared as tired as her, not even Sanjit. Pan noticed that Karl had lost weight and his skin was much clearer. *The School is transforming us*, Pan thought. Miss Kingston stood, her face turned upwards. She had flipped her snow goggles onto her forehead and was using her hand as a makeshift visor against the snow's glare. Pan unscrewed her water bottle and took a few sips. Then she got to her feet. Her muscles were starting to cramp and she knew she needed to keep moving. Miss Kingston walked towards her.

'Where to now?' she asked.

Pan pointed.

'Pretty much directly up. Maybe a hundred metres. Then a little to the left. Ten or twenty metres, maybe.'

Miss Kingston quickly scanned the ascent and then turned her eyes to Pan's.

'What makes you so sure?'

Jen didn't give her the chance to answer. ''Cos she's the hot-shit psychic, Miss Kingston.'

Pan tried to ignore her, but any answer to Kingston's question would only validate Jen's sarcasm, so she kept quiet.

Miss Kingston sighed. 'This is crazy,' she said. She scratched her head. 'You do know, don't you, that there is no way Cara could have made this climb by herself? She was not ... physically capable. There are probably only four or five students in the entire School who could have done this without equipment and Cara was definitely not one of them.'

Pan shrugged, but a part of her noted that this was the first time she had heard the instructor call a student by her first name. *She has feelings.* The thought flashed through her mind. *Even if she tries hard to conceal them.*

'She can't be up there,' Miss Kingston continued. She shook her head. 'Wherever she is, I can guarantee it's nowhere near here. But . . . let's get this done. I want us off this mountain before anyone gets injured.' She mumbled something and Pan caught the word 'insane'. Then the instructor pushed her snow goggles down and clapped her hands. 'All right. Listen up. I will free climb the next hundred metres while you wait here. I will put in pitons wherever possible. When I tug the rope, you will follow. Do it safe. Do it right.'

Most members of the group nodded but no one said anything. Miss Kingston checked her equipment belt, tugged at it and moved to the rock face. She scanned the surface, found a small crevice at head height and inserted her fingers. Then she was away. Pan watched as she moved upwards, surely, swiftly and confidently. Once or twice Miss Kingston stopped and hammered metal pegs into the rock face. Then she was climbing upwards again, a dark figure against the white backdrop. Pan turned away and looked out over the plateau. The School was spread before her. She had never seen it from such a height, at least not in her own body. Even the Garden on Top of the World was far below. It all seemed so tiny set against the forbidding mountains and the wide expanse of sea. She shuddered and backed up against the rock face. Nate put an arm around her shoulders.

'Vertigo, huh?' he asked.

Pan nodded.

'You're doing great, Pan,' he said. He paused for a

moment and scanned the peaks above them. 'You really reckon she's up there?' he added.

'I think so.'

'That'll raise more questions than answers,' he said.

'I know.'

'Well, one thing at a time. Let's see if she's there first.' He laughed. 'I tell you, I don't know whether to hope you're right or pray you're wrong. If you're right, at least you won't appear delusional. Then again, if you're wrong . . .'

'I hope I'm wrong, Nate. I really do.'

'Time to find out,' said Nate. 'Miss Kingston's up there already. Jeez, she must be half mountain goat. Anyway. Showtime, kiddo.'

Pan and Nate watched as the others followed the route Miss Kingston had marked out. They weren't as quick as her, but appeared to climb without undue difficulty. Sanjit, she noticed, didn't find it easy but he kept going.

'Have you talked to Sanjit at all, Nate?' Pan said.

'Yeah, from time to time. Mainly at night, just after lights out. He's not a great talker. But he's a cool kid when you get to know him.'

Pan was pleased that Nate had spoken to the quiet Indian boy. She and Nate had formed a bond, Sam and Karl were clearly wrapped up in each other and Wei-Lin was friendly to everyone. Jen had no need of anyone and made that very plain. Only Cara and Sanjit were outsiders. There was a danger in being outside. It could be painfully lonely, and in this terror-stricken world, painfully lonely was dangerous.

Pan glanced up the rock face. The last of the group had made it and finally it was their turn.

'You go first,' said Nate. 'I'll be right on your heels.'

The cliff face was almost sheer, but Pan found there were plenty of handholds. She hooked her rope into each piton, limiting any fall to a survivable distance. Her fingers were cramped and her thigh muscles complained, but she took it one step at a time. *Find a crevice for your hands, find a foothold. Lift, raise. One hand at a time. Don't look down. Whatever you do, don't look down.*

It was over in a surprisingly short time. Maybe the concentration helped. A hand grasped her wrist and she scrambled the last couple of metres onto another small plateau. This one was narrower than the first and with most of the group already assembled it was very crowded. Nate hauled himself up a few seconds after Pan. She wanted to rest and stretch, to get the lactic acid out of her muscles, but Miss Kingston was determined to press on.

'Move, guys,' she said. 'Single file. Do not lose concentration. Miss Jones is of the opinion we are nearly there. Let's see if she's right.'

A ledge, maybe two metres wide, snaked around the curve of the mountain. The sun reflected slivers of light from the path, glisters of ice that betrayed the treacherousness of the path. Miss Kingston took the lead. She kept close to the mountainside and chose her steps carefully. Then she was around the bend and out of sight. The others followed. Once again, Pan and Nate brought up the rear, and once again he insisted she go before him. If she slipped, at least he would have a chance to grab her. Pan held onto a small crag jutting from the cliff and slid one foot forward, then another. She felt self-conscious at the slowness of her progress - the others hadn't exactly skipped around the ledge, but they also hadn't inched along, petrified by fear. Despite the cold, she felt beads of sweat stand out on her forehead.

'I wouldn't call *you* half mountain goat,' said Nate behind her.

'The way I'm sweating, I probably smell like one.'

Nate chuckled. 'Take it easy. The important thing is to stay safe.'

'I am taking it easy.'

'Good.'

Pan inched around the bend. She kept her eyes fixed firmly on the path and did not look up, even when the path broadened. *One step at a time*, she told herself. *One step at a time. Keep safe.*

'You can stop clinging to the mountain now,' said Nate. 'Look up, kiddo. The hard part's over.'

Pan did. The path had widened dramatically once it had skirted the mountain side. The edge was at least five metres to her left. The rest of the group had formed a tight circle in a clearing six or seven metres ahead. Their heads were lowered. No one spoke. Pan wiped at her forehead with one gloved hand and walked cautiously over to them. She pushed between the knot of backs to see. But she knew what was there.

Cara sat upright, her back against the mountainside. It was as though she were taking a rest, admiring the view. Her arms rested at her side, hands against the snow-slick ground, knees slightly bent. She was wearing her School clothes, the camouflage jacket pitifully inadequate for the conditions. There was a slight smile on her lips as if what she saw was pleasing. Her eyes were bright and clear but there was nothing behind them. Pan's eyes welled with tears. She choked a sob at the back of her throat.

Miss Kingston knelt beside the body. She removed her gloves and put two fingers against Cara's neck. Pan knew it was useless. No one could have survived up here. Not for a day and a night. Miss Kingston kept her fingers there for longer than was necessary. When she removed them, she brushed Cara's cheek. It was a strangely tender gesture. Miss Kingston stood.

'She's dead,' she said. She pulled her gloves back on. 'I'm sorry. There's nothing we can do for her. I suggest we get moving again.' She pointed to Sanjit and Jen. 'You guys, attach a rope to Cara. Make it secure. We'll take her back around this path and then lower her down the way we came up. I'll climb down first to take her body on each stage. Move it, people. I want to see purpose and I want to see discipline.'

The group shuddered as if waking from some kind of nightmare. Wei-Lin and Sam bent down and tried to move Cara's body away from the cliff face. Pan noticed that both were crying, though neither made a sound. Jen uncurled a length of mountaineering rope, and although she tried to hide it, there were tears on her face as well. Cara's body resisted, stuck to the mountain. Eventually, her jacket gave way and ripped. Even then they couldn't move her. Her body was frozen in place. Hands, legs, each part of her body that was in contact with the mountain stayed fused. The two looked up at Miss Kingston.

'She's dead,' said Miss Kingston again. 'You can't hurt her, whatever you do. Use your ice axes, if you must, but get her free and get her roped up. Do you understand?'

She was back to icy efficiency. Pan wondered if she had imagined that tender gesture. She was aware that Nate's hand was resting on her shoulder. She couldn't remember when he had put it there, but she wanted it to stay there forever. She had the feeling that if he removed it, her will would crumble and she would surrender to grief. But he did remove it and Pan shuddered but kept control.

The climb down wasn't as bad as the ascent. Even negotiating the narrow path was something Pan accomplished without too much fear. The worst was watching Cara's body as it was lowered from one stage of the descent to the next. Pan winced whenever the rope swayed and Cara's body bounced against the mountainside. She knew it was absurd, that Cara was beyond feeling pain, but it was an undignified process. It was almost a relief when it was Pan's turn to descend. She was in no danger - the ropes and the system of karabiners meant it was impossible for her to fall far. And staring at the rock wall rather than Cara's body was a welcome diversion.

Their progress had clearly been monitored from The School, and when they finally reached the ground, most of the students and staff were waiting. A couple of students rushed forward and put Cara's body on a stretcher, covered it with a blanket and carried it off towards the Infirmary. The crowd parted silently to allow them past. Miss Kingston pushed her goggles up on her forehead and removed her gloves. She looked tired, drained. Pan realised that she was, too.

'Right,' Miss Kingston said. 'Back to base. All the equipment needs to be checked in and stored.' She strode off without waiting for a response. After a few moments,

Pan and the rest of the group followed. The tiredness that they'd been forced to keep at bay swamped them. They all walked, heads down, saying nothing. Even Nate was quiet, as if exploring the inside of his head. At the hangar, they stripped off their gear and stowed it away. Miss Kingston oversaw the return of equipment and ticked off each item as it was returned. Eventually, they were done. The group stood in a ragged line, hands behind backs.

'Right,' said Miss Kingston. 'You are dismissed. The rest of today's program is cancelled and you have free time. The canteen, I have been informed, is open. Get a hot meal and then get some rest.'

'What will happen to Cara?'

Pan was surprised that it was Sanjit who asked. She couldn't remember the last time she had heard him speak. Miss Kingston sagged almost imperceptibly, then straightened.

'There's no precedent for this situation,' she said, her voice brisk, 'but I suspect her body will be taken out for burial at sea. I will let you know about any arrangements so that you can say . . . goodbye. For what it's worth, I am very sorry. That will be all.'

The line broke and the students shuffled towards the exit. Miss Kingston's voice followed them. 'You did well, guys. I'm proud of you.'

No one said anything.

Chapter 16

'Want to talk?' asked Nate.

Pan and Nate sat outside as dusk fell. The group had gone to the canteen, but no one had eaten much, despite their hunger. Sam and Karl sat very close together, their hands entwined. Most of the group avoided meeting Pan's eyes. *Are they scared of me?* she thought. *Or do they suspect me of somehow being involved in Cara's death?*

'About what?' Pan replied. 'How Cara managed to climb a mountain with no equipment in the middle of the night? Why she sat down and waited for death? Or how I knew where to find her body?'

Nate shrugged. 'I don't know. All of the above? Or maybe just about Cara. She's dead and I don't know why or how, but she was one of us. Perhaps we simply need to mourn her and worry about the rest later.'

Tears sprang into Pan's eyes, but she blinked them back. *I read her journal*, she thought. *Her private thoughts and feelings. I probably knew her better than anyone here. But it's too late to do anything with that knowledge.* She felt the full impact of her use of the past tense and it made her shudder.

'I had nothing to do with her disappearance, Nate.'

'I know.'

'I just used my . . . 'gift', whatever it is, to find her. The same way I found Wei-Lin's watch.' She considered telling Nate about her experience inside the falcon, but quickly dismissed the idea. It was too absurd and she didn't think she could bear to see ridicule in his eyes.

'I believe you,' said Nate.

Pan got to her feet and looked out over The School.

'It's wrong,' she said, almost to herself. 'All of this is wrong.' *The watches are wrong.*

'What do you mean?'

Pan almost laughed. 'I have no idea, Nate,' she said. 'Not a clue.' *No, that's not true. There are plenty of clues. You just haven't figured out what they mean yet.* 'But this place . . .' She lifted her arms as if to embrace the whole environment. 'There's something fundamentally . . .'

'Wrong?' Nate got to his feet also. 'I need to run, Pan. I *always* need to run, but now more than ever. Want to come with me? There's something I need to show you.'

'I'm exhausted, Nate.'

'All the more reason to run. Come on.'

Pan wanted to resist, but she was too tired to even do that.

~~~

The early evening air was crisp, but Pan was sweating after a few minutes. The muscles in her legs cramped and she developed a stitch within half a kilometre. She concentrated on her breathing and establishing a rhythm. After about a kilometre, she felt better. Not good. But better.

Nate, as always, loped along easily. It was clear he was running at well below his normal pace. He didn't say anything, which suited Pan. She wasn't sure she had the breath to hold a conversation and she knew she didn't have the inclination.

Nate led her away from the main paths to The School's buildings, off towards the left where the mountains started. Pan had never been to this part of The School before. She remembered how it had appeared from the Garden on Top of the World. A forest, showing that even in this barren landscape nature could thrive. Pan focused again on her breathing. Her steps had found a rhythm and the stitch in her side had eased. They were heading straight towards the forest which was much larger than she had thought. Gradually, the rocky terrain became softer. High above, the mountains loomed. A waterfall off to her left cascaded from a plateau maybe sixty metres above. The thunder of the falls drummed in her ears, became louder with each pace she took. The air was filled with water vapour. Where the dying sun caught it, small rainbows formed and reformed, glimmered and glistened.

Nate entered the forest ahead of her. There were a number of paths, but Pan couldn't tell if they had been constructed or were simply the trails of animals that lived in the cool shade of the trees. Nate took one path without hesitation. *He knows these woods*, Pan thought. She wondered how often he had been here. And for what purpose. It was much cooler in the forest, but Pan felt her spirits lift anyway. She glanced over her shoulder and could see nothing of The School. Trees curtained it from view. This was a different world. Something purer. Something softer. Peace lived here.

Nate picked up pace and followed the path around a corner. Pan cursed him, but kept her own rhythm. The sound of pounding water filled the world and she could hear nothing above it, not even the rasping of her own breath or the thud of boots against the ground. The air smelled of mulch, of trees, of life. She breathed it deeply into her lungs. She ran around the corner and stopped in her tracks.

They were in a large clearing. A clearing filled with mist. Her eyes lifted automatically to the source of the deafening sound. The waterfall was visible for only a few metres above the ground. A solid sheet of water pounded down and the earth trembled beneath her feet. Already she was coated in fine droplets. Nate stood with his back to her, gazing at the curtain of water. His hair was jewelled and rainbows played around his body. Pan walked to his side. He didn't glance at her.

'Melt water,' he yelled. Even though he shouted at the top of his voice and Pan was standing right next to him, she had to concentrate to hear. He pointed upwards. 'Season changing. Snow melting. Feeds this river. Even in the last couple of days, this waterfall has become stronger. The river runs to the sea. Beyond the wall.'

Pan nodded. She didn't think he would hear her if she spoke anyway. It was so beautiful. She understood why Nate would feel compelled to come here and she was pleased that he wanted to share it with her. She could almost forget what lay outside the clearing. The sound of pounding water and the mist-shrouded air washed away the ugliness of her memories. In particular, the vision of a girl frozen to a mountainside, her eyes fixed and unseeing. She touched Nate's arm and he turned his face to her. He was glazed in beads of water that shone on his eyelashes, sparkled on the down of his cheeks. *I could fall in love with him*, thought Pan. *Maybe I am falling in love with him.* She pushed the thought away. There was no room inside her for love.

'Thank you for bringing me here,' she said.

Nate smiled. Even his lips were wet with dew.

'It's a good place to come. When you're feeling bad. When you want to forget for an hour or so. Thought you'd like it.'

'I'm glad I came.'

'Hey. This isn't the main thing I wanted to show you, Pan.'

'It isn't?'

'Nah. We've got more running ahead of us. You up to it?'

Pan smiled. She couldn't remember the last time she'd smiled and meant it.

'No,' she said. 'But let's go anyway.'

~ ~ ~

Once again, Nate took the lead. He followed another path through the forest, keeping the river to his left. Before long, the trees thinned and The School came into view. The roaring of the waterfall faded and was replaced by the sound of rushing river water. They left the trees behind and Pan glanced around to get her bearings.

They were following the course of the river, running along the bank. It was good to feel grass beneath her feet, rather than hard, uneven stone. She didn't miss the jolt along her spine that accompanied each footstep on that rough terrain. Far off, the wall lay directly ahead. To Pan's right was The School. It seemed a separate world somehow, as the buildings blended into the dusk.

The river gushed and frothed. Pan imagined the almost endless supply of snow coming from distant mountain peaks, feeding it. She looked up to see if she could detect any difference in the snow fields, but the light was fading and the mountains loomed only as malevolent blocks of shadow.

It took ten minutes before they arrived at the buildings. A series of cabins scattered along the sides of the river. The staff quarters. They appeared considerably more comfortable than the dormitories the students used. But they remained functional. Almost austere. No gardens were planted. No chairs or hammocks stretched out along the small verandahs. No distinguishing characteristics. Nothing that indicated anyone had tried to impose their own personality on their home. Although the surroundings were pretty and it was peaceful, the atmosphere was the same as that which enveloped the rest of The School. Bleak.

Nate said nothing as they passed the houses, nor did he appear to pay them any attention. Two minutes later, they left the buildings behind. No staff appeared to question them. No curtains twitched. It was like a ghost town.

Pan was tired. Her legs were heavy and her breath was becoming ragged. But she didn't complain about the pace Nate set. Nor did she complain when it became clear that their destination, again, was the wall. The river ran straight towards it. A watchtower was directly ahead, where the wall and the river intersected. It swelled in Pan's sight as their steps took them closer.

She was relieved when they finally stopped under the ominous bulk of the watchtower. The wall blocked their progress. Implacable. Mysterious. It snaked away to their right where she knew it joined up with the mountain range on the other side of the plain that housed The School. To their left, the wall continued for a hundred metres to where it butted up against the solid mountain range that flanked them on this side. The blocks of stone had been carved to fit the terrain perfectly. There were no gaps between the wall and the mountainside, no way for anyone to scramble or slip through.

Pan flopped down onto the grass and put her head between her knees. She focused on regulating her breathing. Nate sat next to her, his breathing annoyingly regular. They sat in silence for a couple of minutes until Pan could trust her voice.

'So this is what you had to show me, Nate? The wall? I hate to disappoint you, but I've already seen it. More than enough of it, to be honest.'

He laughed.

'Not the wall itself, Pan. Something in the wall. You ready? Got your breath back?'

She groaned and got to her feet. Nate took her by the hand and led her towards the river. The flow was less rapid here as the ground had levelled out, but the current was still strong. The breadth of the river was about ten metres.

'There,' said Nate, pointing downstream. Pan followed his arm.

The river appeared to go straight through the wall. She took a few steps to get a closer look. Set into the base of the wall was a broad sluice gate. An interlocking metal lattice allowed the water through. Pan could see only darkness where the water disappeared. The water frothed against the gate, two or three metres from its top.

'Fascinating, Nate,' said Pan. 'So you brought me here to show me a minor engineering feature?'

'No,' replied Nate. 'To show you a way through the wall.'

Pan pushed her hair back from her forehead.

'We've been beyond the wall, Nate,' she said in as even a tone as she could manage. 'And we were assaulted, drugged and imprisoned. Why would you want to try again?'

'For the same reasons you want to, Pan. Answers. You say there's something wrong with The School. If that's true, I believe there's a good chance of finding out exactly what. But only on the other side of the wall where, it seems, they are desperate to stop us going.'

Pan said nothing for a minute.

'Let's just say that I would be interested in going back,' she said. 'Hypothetically, I mean. We can't get through here.'

'Wrong, Pandora. We can get through. Come see.'

Nate walked right up to the gate. Pan sighed and followed him.

'There,' said Nate, pointing.

The gap was difficult to see at first. Pan had to strain her eyes against the fading light. Then she noticed that one of the crossbars on a section of lattice had come loose.

It was still attached, but hung at a slight angle from the others. If the gate had been here for some time - and the structure certainly didn't look new - then the surge of water from the river, over a period of years, must have wrought some damage. Even so, the gap afforded by the loose metal strip was small. Perhaps it was possible for someone to squeeze through, but it would be tight. And dangerous.

'That's it, is it, Nate?' said Pan. 'That tiny gap? Even if we could get through, there's no guarantee there would be a way through on the other side, assuming there's a similar lattice on the village side.'

'Ah,' said Nate. 'I've thought about that. It's likely that the water has damaged that side as well. A simple matter of taking boltcutters with us. Finding the most vulnerable point. Snip, snip. Out the other side.'

'Assuming we could get hold of boltcutters. Assuming we could do that right under the nose of a watchtower and, presumably, a guard. Assuming, also, we don't drown while we're trying to get through. That water must be freezing. And we could end up under that wall. In short, the idea is nothing short of suicidal.'

'I know,' said Nate. He grinned. 'Cool, isn't it?'

'When are you going?'

'Soon. The night after next, I reckon. I've been checking the phases of the moon. With luck, there'll be plenty of cloud cover as well. So. Interested?'

Pan sat on the ground and started stretching. The muscles in her calves were beginning to cramp. Nate watched her, his hands on his hips.

'I'm jogging back, now,' said Pan when her muscles had stopped complaining. 'It will be dark soon.'

'Never jog,' said Nate. 'Jogging is for losers. Run with me.'

'I'm jogging. But don't let me hold you back.'

He shrugged. 'Okay. If you're sure. See you later, Pandora.'

'Nate?'

He turned back.

'Let me know when you go, okay?' she said.

He grinned and gave her a thumbs up before setting off into the thickening night. Within a minute Pan had lost sight of him.

Chapter 17

'I apologise for bringing you all here again,' said Dr Morgan. 'But this is a sombre occasion and I felt . . . *we* felt . . . that you deserved some information on today's . . . extraordinary events.'

The running field was shrouded in darkness, punctuated only by the pools of light made by the flame torches. There were probably fifty or so spread around the field and they gave a curious sense of celebration, as if this was a gathering for a night-time fete or festival. But the mood was far from celebratory. Not a sound could be heard as Morgan addressed the assembled School. He stood on a small, portable dais - a large box, really - surrounded by other staff members. Dr Macredie was there, to Dr Morgan's left, as were Miss Kingston, Professor Goldberg and Gwynne. They formed a line, hands behind their backs, as if asserting their role as protectors. Dr Morgan lowered his head for a moment and then spoke again. His voice carried across the plain.

'First of all, thank you all for your contributions today,' he said. 'It is a credit to The School that no-one - I repeat, *no-one* - did not involve themselves in the search for Cara Smith. I am proud of you all.' He glanced down and locked the fingers of his hands together. 'I only wish that your endeavours had resulted in a happier outcome.'

Professor Goldberg moved towards Dr Morgan, who bent to listen. A silence ensued and then Dr Morgan raised his head to the assembled students once more.

'I am certain that all of you are aware by now that Cara was found and that, tragically, her rescuers were not able to . . . save her.'

There was never a chance of saving her, thought Pan. Nate stood at her shoulder, a number of rows from the front of the assembly. *Cara had been dead for many hours. Are we going to be blamed for what happened?* But Pan remained silent.

'This is the first time in the short history of The School,' Dr Morgan continued, 'that we have lost a student, and I know that we are all suffering from shock, maybe a sense of . . . disbelief. Dr Macredie has asked me to remind you that if anyone needs to discuss their feelings, then she is available to offer counselling. Confidentiality is, of course, assured. If you wish to take up this opportunity then please make an appointment at the Infirmary . . .'

'What happened, Doc?' The voice was male and came from somewhere in the throng, though Pan didn't recognise the voice. The question rang through the cold night.

'We're not sure,' he said. 'Cara had not yet integrated herself emotionally into the social network of The School. I believe she was depressed – a state of mind that many, if not all of you, can certainly identify with. Whether that had anything to do with her unfortunate fate . . . well, I don't believe that such speculation is fruitful.' He rubbed his nose. 'In the course of my professional duties, I examined Cara and could find nothing that might indicate anything other than natural causes for her death.'

Pan couldn't help herself. The words issued before she was even aware of the impulse. 'So how did she get halfway up a mountain?'

Morgan tilted his head to one side as if considering all the implications of the question. The silence was profound.

'I know there are many questions you might have,' he said eventually, 'but I suspect we will never have the answers to most of them. All I can say is that, under extreme circumstances, people are capable of extraordinary achievements.' He paused for a few beats, and Pan couldn't help but think it was partly - maybe totally - for effect. 'Sadly, it's my personal opinion that Cara was depressed to the point of being suicidal. I think she believed there was nothing worth living for. I think she deliberately scaled that mountainside, difficult though that might be to believe for some of us, and . . .' He rubbed at his eyes as if to wipe away tears. Pan felt anger rise. It was bitter and all-consuming. *I knew her better than any of you*, she thought. *I don't believe she did this to herself. How could she possibly have climbed the mountain without equipment?* '. . . and lay down. As simple as that. It is tragic. Unbelievably tragic. But . . .' Dr Morgan raised his eyes and scanned the students. 'There is a lesson here for all of us. We must fight despair, challenging though that might be. The future of humanity is in our hands and that is a tremendous burden to bear. But it is also a sacred burden. We must work to ensure

Cara did not die in vain. If she has a legacy it is this: do not let the darkness overwhelm you. Fight. Fight for life. It is precious. Especially now.' Dr Morgan almost slumped on the podium. Dr Macredie moved towards him, but he waved her away and lifted his head. Pan felt like applauding the quality of his performance.

'Go now,' said Dr Morgan. His voice was strong, yet tinged with weariness. 'You need rest. Remember Cara. Remember also your responsibility. There are so few of us. Do not let her death be in vain. Rather, let it spur you on to greater efforts. For Cara's sake. Thank you.'

The crowd dispersed, murmurs of conversation muted. Pan headed for the dorm, her pace brisk, almost frantic. There was a pulse beating in her temple and she felt as if her head would explode. She was unaware of Nate's presence until he spoke.

'Talk to me, Pan,' he said.

She stopped and took a deep breath to calm herself. Around her, students were melting into the darkness, the lights from the flame torches spreading and dissolving. The night air was chill, but the coldness in her bones had nothing to do with external temperature.

'What do you want me to say, Nate?' she said.

'Anything.'

'Okay.' Pan tapped into her anger, found comfort in resolve. 'Here's the only thing I will agree with Morgan about. I won't forget Cara. That's a promise and you can bear witness. I *won't* forget. And I'll find the answers for her. You can take that to the bank.'

She walked away and felt Nate's eyes watching until she disappeared into the darkness.

Chapter 18

The dream morphed, as it always did, from images of bloodshed, deserted streets and the death throes of a city into another narrative altogether.

~ ~ ~

The memories of pursuit filled her with panic. She looked up into the eyes of the police officer with the broad moustache.

'What happened, love?'

She pointed, her arm trembling.

'Man. Attacked me. In the garden.'

There was another officer. Pan hadn't noticed her before. The cop with the moustache nodded to her and the woman came around the front of the car. He tried to ease his arms away from Pan but she held on tighter.

'Hey, love. It's okay. This is Laura. She'll look after you. You're safe. Trust me. But I have to get the bad guy. You hear me? You want to get the bad guy, don't you?'

Pan nodded.

'Then you'll have to let me go, okay?'

He gently untangled himself from her grip. The female police officer – what was her name again? – put a hand on Pan's shoulder and smiled. Pan leaned against the bonnet of the police car. The pain in her hip was growing. And other pains. Her arm, scraped and bleeding. How did that happen? She couldn't remember. Her right foot pulsed.

Pan lifted her head and looked down the street. People were out of their houses now. At least six of them, by their gates or standing outside their front doors. Where had they come from? And what had taken them so long?

'You're a brave girl,' said the female cop. 'We'll get him, don't worry. He can't have gone far. Spraying his eyes was a smart move, by the way. What was it? Deodorant?'

'What about the others?' said Pan.

'What?'

'There were other men. At least three. Probably four.'

'Okay. Let's worry about this guy first. Get him and I dare say the others will follow. Come on, let's get you in the car. You're about ready to fall down.'

She took Pan by the arm and helped her into the back of the police car. Even sitting was painful. And then the trembling began. It was as if she was having a seizure. Every part of her trembled, nerves and muscles twitching. Pan kept her eyes fixed on the road ahead, fought the sobs rising in her throat.

The officer with the moustache had disappeared. The street scene seemed unreal. So normal. Like nothing had happened in it, or would ever happen. It was hard to believe that trees still swayed in the breeze, that the sun still shone as if nothing at all had occurred. Nonetheless, terror threatened to overwhelm her.

The officer appeared again. He had his hand on the arm of a man dressed in a dark suit. The man stumbled and Pan could see his hands were handcuffed behind his back. The *officer jerked him forward towards the waiting car. Fear, sharp as a knife, cut across Pan.*

~~~

She jerked up in bed, panting, a cry building in her throat. A light shone into her eyes, which she shielded with the back of one hand. There was a dark form looming over her, but the light was too bright for her to make out who it was. For a moment she wondered whether the dream had followed her into the waking world, so strong was the sense of danger.

'Who is it?' she gasped.

'Pandora Jones,' said a male voice. 'Get dressed. Be ready to leave in two minutes. We meet outside.'

The light snapped off and Pan was plunged into darkness again. She heard footsteps receding into the distance, a door opening and closing. She could also hear sounds of girls stirring in their sleep, but there were other noises as well. Some students were getting out of bed. She heard the scrape of feet on floor and vaguely, in the darkness, shapes resolved themselves. Her visitor had not come for her alone, it seemed.

Pan groaned and swung her legs out of bed. The cold hit like a physical blow. Shivering, she dressed quickly and headed down the narrow corridor between the rows of bunks. When her eyes adjusted she could see that Jen, Wei-Lin and Sam were not in their beds. *My group*, she thought. *My group has been summoned.* As she got closer to the door she saw one girl, whose name she didn't know, sitting up in bed, her blanket rucked against her chin. Pan could feel eyes following her progress.

Outside, the night was cold, clear and dark. She hugged herself against the thin, biting wind. Four shapes detached themselves and moved forward. The girls from her dormitory and the unknown visitor. She recognised the bulk of Jen and the slender form of Wei-Lin.

'Okay,' said the man. 'That's it. Let's move it, people.'

'Where are we going?' asked Wei-Lin.

'No questions. No talking. Just move. And on the double.'

The shadow shifted and turned, ran down the almost invisible path. Pan sighed and followed. At least running would warm her up. It was strange running at night. The sky was dotted with stars but there was no moon. After a few minutes she had no idea where she was – there were no reference points to guide her. She suspected they were running towards the wall, but couldn't be entirely sure. There were no sounds apart from the ragged breathing of her companions and the thump of boots on ground. Within five minutes she found her own rhythm and her breathing became easier. Within ten minutes she saw a cluster of dancing lights in the distance, four or five that merged together and then separated. Flame torches. They ran towards the flickering yellow flames which seemed to beckon with the promise of warmth. *That's probably what moths think*, thought Pan, *just before they shrivel in the candle's flame.*

Sanjit and Karl were there, and so was Nate. Pan felt a surge of relief. She saw him first, his face down-lit by a flame torch. The flames made his face quicken with shadows and light. It lent him a sinister aspect. But then he saw her, smiled and the image softened. Pan relaxed. Whatever was happening, she was glad he was part of it, and judging by his smile, he felt glad she was here too.

They came to a halt. The man accompanying Pan's group picked up a flame torch and turned to face them. As the light flooded his features, Pan recognised him. It wasn't a man, but the student who had been present at her meeting with The School Council following her capture in the village. Once again, she was struck by his sheer size.

'Fall in behind me and keep up my pace,' he said. 'And there's still no talking.'

Immediately, he was gone, running along a rough track. The torch in his hand jerked as he held it aloft, the flames bending and swaying in the wind. The group followed and Nate fell in beside her.

'What's this about?' Pan asked.

'No idea. I was woken from a very deep sleep. No explanations. Just the order to follow. You?'

'The same.'

'If I wasn't so curious, I'd be angry,' he said. 'It was the first night in a long time I wasn't having bad dreams.'

I wish that was true for me, thought Pan.

'Can you tell where we're heading?' she asked.

'Yup. I've done a lot of running at night. This path leads to the wall.'

'Interesting.'

'Exceptionally. The way I see it, there's no point going to the wall just to run along the side of it. That would be ludicrous, even if this was just a night-time hike. You know, keeping the troops in order. Keep them disorientated. Make them follow orders without thinking. Nah. I think we must be going through it.'

'Why?'

Nate turned towards her and smiled.

'Well, that's the big question, kiddo. And I have absolutely no idea. I guess we'll just have to wait and see.'

'You at the back,' came a voice through the night. 'Silence.'

The group jogged for about fifteen minutes before the dark bulk of the wall became visible. As far as Pan could tell, they were roughly in the middle of The School, heading for the wall's central point. *There is a gate*, she thought. *Where the supplies from the outside world are brought into The School.* Pan concentrated on her breathing and kept her eyes on the head of the person in front of her.

Someone was waiting for them at the wall. A single spark of light hung a couple of metres from the ground. It cast a small halo on the stone. The group slowed and stopped. Without another word, the student who had roused them from sleep turned and ran away back towards The School. There was silence for a few moments and then a loud sniff. The single flame moved towards them.

Gwynne, thought Pan.

The man lowered his torch and the misshapen features of the weapons instructor were illuminated. The flames distorted his face even further. Shadows played across his shaved head.

'Line up,' he said and wiped at his nose. The group obeyed. Gwynne walked slowly down the line and then back again, stopping opposite Jen. He didn't acknowledge her directly but spoke to the group.

'Soon the door behind me will open.'

Pan looked behind him but couldn't detect any signs of a door. The stone wall was featureless. 'I'll lead you through, you follow. Single file. Do not deviate from the path. Do not look to either side. Complete silence. Understand?'

'No,' said Nate. 'I don't. What are we doing here?'

Gwynne stepped up to Nate, held his torch close as if to get a better look at Nate's face. He sniffed and again wiped his nose with the back of a hand.

'Follow instructions. All you need to know. Is that clear?'

Nate smiled and shrugged.

'Clear,' he said.

No one else said anything. Gwynne turned towards the wall, raised the torch and waved it to and fro in a couple of lazy arcs. Almost immediately there was a grating sound and a section of the wall started to swing back. Pan strained her eyes to see any evidence of hinges or locks or handles, but there was still insufficient light. It was as if the wall was folding back on itself. What lay beyond was black as pitch. Gwynne turned, made his way into the darkness, and one by one the rest of the group followed.

Pan was prepared to follow most of Gwynne's instructions, but there was no way she was going to follow the third once she was on the other side of the wall.

It didn't do much good. She looked to either side of the stone path they followed. But even with her eyes well-adapted to the dark there was little to see. The shapes of houses or shops could be vaguely glimpsed, but no details discerned. There were no lights on anywhere. The village was uniformly blank. *That's strange*, she thought. *No lights at all.* It was yet another fact to file away with all the other jigsaw pieces in her mind. There was a pattern or a picture, she was sure, but she couldn't fit it all together. Yet.

It became clear that Gwynne was leading them in a straight line at ninety degrees to the wall. That also was significant. There was only one thing that lay in that direction. The sea. Pan lifted her head, sniffed, and there it was. The salty scent of the ocean. After five or six minutes, Gwynne veered off to his left down a boardwalk. The wood gave beneath their feet, and Pan heard the gentle lap of waves. Looking to her right she saw the silhouettes of masts against the sky. *We are leaving The School*, she thought. *We are being taken on a boat. For Cara. And something else.*

Gwynne stopped at the end of the boardwalk and the group halted behind him. Sanjit and Karl were breathing raggedly.

'Down the steps,' said Gwynne, gesturing to his left. 'Single file. Into the boat, sit on the benches. Keep spaced out. Remain silent. Go.'

Wei-Lin was the first, Nate and Pan last. Gwynne descended the steps behind her, his sniffing loud in her ears. At the bottom was the dark bulk of a boat. It was low to the water and not much more than a small fishing vessel. There was no cabin, just a broad expanse of deck, most of it covered with a tarpaulin. Wei-Lin, Jen, Karl, Sanjit and Sam were already seated. Nate skipped on board and she followed. They took up the last available spaces on the benches. Gwynne uncoiled the mooring ropes and then jumped into the boat. He made his way to the stern and for a moment was lost in the darkness. Then an engine sputtered and roared to life. The boat turned sharply and moved towards the open sea. Pan watched the wake developing. She was tempted to trail her hand into the water, but resisted. Gwynne hadn't forbidden it, but she felt he would disapprove. So she kept her back straight, gripped the bench with two hands and looked back towards where The School must lie. She thought she could see the wall, but then the night swallowed everything. Within five minutes they were alone with the sound of an engine, the susurration of the sea and an upturned bowl of stars.

Nate bent his head towards Pan.

'Fishing trip?' he whispered. 'I wonder if there's a cooler on board with fresh bait and some cokes.'

'We're here to say goodbye to Cara,' Pan replied.

Nate was silent for about thirty seconds. 'For real?' he said finally.

'We were told she'd be buried at sea. We were also told that we'd be kept informed about arrangements. Why else would our group be here?'

'Cara's body is on board with us?'

Pan pointed to the broad expanse of tarpaulin.

'She's under there.'

Her voice must have carried because although no one spoke all eyes were fixed on the centre of the boat. It was Nate who eventually broke the tension.

'I'm glad,' he said. 'I couldn't bear the thought of her ... going, without us being there to see her off. I'm surprised, though. I didn't think The School would be so concerned about our feelings.'

'They're not,' said Pan flatly. 'There's another reason for us being here.'

'Yes?' said Wei-Lin.

'I don't know,' said Pan. 'I guess we'll find out.'

'You know something?' The voice was Jen's. 'I'm tired of your crap, Pandora. All this air of mystery. "I know things, but I don't know how I know things." It's all about you, isn't it? All the time. Can't you go five minutes without demanding that you're the centre of attention? Reckon you could do that for us, Pandora?'

'Cut it out.' Nate's voice was uncharacteristically sharp. 'The last thing we need right now is conflict between us. Cara deserves better.'

'Cara deserved better than to freeze to death up on some goddamn mountain,' said Jen. 'You knew where to find her, Pandora. Care to explain that?'

'I can't,' said Pan.

'Nate's right,' said Wei-Lin. 'Let's show some dignity, guys.'

The engine suddenly throttled back from a whine to an idle. The boat's momentum continued to take them forward, but it slowed considerably. The bow wave settled. From the back of the boat, Gwynne's voice rose.

'Good advice,' he said. 'Suggest you take it.'

He stood and the boat rocked slightly before settling. Gwynne moved towards the centre of the boat and put his hands behind his back. The group watched and no one said a word. Gwynne sniffed and glanced down at the tarpaulin at his feet.

'Give me a hand,' he said.

Sam and Karl got to their feet and took hold of the canvas edge at the boat's prow. They rolled it back, passed the tarpaulin to Wei-Lin and Sanjit, who in turn rolled it towards Pan, Nate and Jen. Then they stood and looked down at what had been revealed.

The sky was dusted with stars and the moon was a thin sliver suspended at the edge of a cloud. The light was sufficient to make out the pale and shrouded form, wrapped like a cocoon and washed with silver. Pan felt a sob rise in her throat, but choked it back. The body shape beneath the white sheet was secured with rope at the feet and the chest. It all seemed so desperately final.

'Need help,' said Gwynne.

'Don't touch her,' said Nate, his voice low yet authoritative. 'Just . . . don't touch her.' He bent down to the outline of Cara's shoulders, slipped his hands between the shroud and the deck. The rest of the group arranged themselves around the body and when they lifted, the weight appeared negligible. Gwynne stood to one side.

'Careful,' he said. 'Don't go to the side. Shift of weight will tip the boat. We could all go over. Be gentle.'

No one said anything, but they obeyed the instruction. Even so, the boat rocked alarmingly. Jen, who held Cara's feet, carefully dropped to her knees, and the others followed her example. For a moment they were a silent tableau.

'Anyone want to say anything?' asked Gwynne.

There was silence and Pan was glad. None of the group had known Cara very well. Anyway, whatever anyone said now would be irrelevant to Cara's life and her death. It was best to deal in thoughts. Pan made a silent promise. *I will find out how you died, Cara. I will find out and if anyone else had a hand in it, I will bring them to justice. You have my word.*

Cara's body was eased into the water, Jen taking most of the weight as the others slid the shrouded form towards her. The white shape dipped beneath the surface of the sea and the darkness swallowed her. *You have my word*, thought Pan. One by one, the group got to their feet and took up their original positions on the benches. Still there was silence, though Sam wiped her eyes with the back of one hand, and Karl put an arm around her shoulders. Gwynne stood in the place where Cara's body had rested.

'Sorry,' he said. 'For what it's worth.' There was no reply. He sniffed and wiped at his nose. 'Okay, listen up,' he continued. 'This was not the sole purpose. There's a mission.' Pan could feel Jen's eyes on her, but she didn't look away from Gwynne. 'To a place where there may be survivors. *May*. The helicopter pilot reported movement. But it's heavily wooded. Helicopter can't land. Your task: explore, locate and rescue survivors. If any . . .'

'Wait,' said Nate. 'We are the least experienced group in The School. Don't get me wrong, I'm happy to look for survivors, but wouldn't it be more sensible to use a party that has greater . . . skills than us?'

'Correct,' said Gwynne. 'But small is good. Can't split up an existing group. They need to bond. Like you. Anyway, chances of finding anyone are slim. Think of mission as exercise in survival.'

'Why is a small group an advantage?' asked Wei-Lin.

'Survivors may not be friendly,' Gwynne replied. 'Maybe survivalists and therefore dangerous. Shoot first, ask questions later. Happened before. So small group means easier to hide.' He sniffed again. 'Probably safe, but we don't take chances.'

Gwynne allowed the silence that greeted his words to last for a few seconds. 'Dawn when we arrive,' he continued. 'I leave you and come back in seventy-two hours. Exactly. You must wait for the boat. I *won't* wait. Really important. You're not there, you'll be left. Clear?'

Nate laughed. 'Call this a good pastoral care program?' he said. 'If you're late, you're dead.'

Gwynne didn't even turn to face him. 'We'll come back with another group to find you. If you're still alive. But takes time. So lesson's simple. Don't be late.'

He moved to a long box, like a workman's toolbox, that had also been under the tarpaulin. 'In this box,' he continued, 'are basic survival tools. Compass, rope, axe, boning knife, full canteen of water and fishing equipment - line and hooks. Oh, and Wei-Lin - a longbow and arrows. So, weapons and a means of finding food. Identify a water source asap. Remember your training.'

'Is that all we get?' asked Jen.

'That's it,' replied Gwynne. 'I told you. A survival exercise. Locating survivors unlikely. Use your initiative. You'll be fine.'

He didn't wait for a response, but moved to the boat's stern and the engine's whine increased and the boat picked up speed.

The group was silent for a minute and then Nate laughed. 'It's better than cleaning out septic tanks,' he said. 'Which is what Pan and I faced back at The School. Whatya reckon, Pan?'

'I'm not sure,' she said. 'Either way, we're deep in the shit.'

Nate laughed again. 'Be positive, people,' he said. 'And get some shut-eye while the going's good.' He leaned back on the bench, crossed his ankles and shut his eyes. No one said anything.

Too much has happened, thought Pan. *And we haven't had time to process any of it*. But Nate was right. It was sensible to get rest while it was available, though Pan doubted she would be able to sleep. Maybe the others felt the same, but they nonetheless shifted into different positions. Wei-Lin curled herself up on a small portion of her bench. Karl, Sam, Sanjit and Jen lay down on the decking.

Pan stretched out her legs and rested her head on Nate's shoulder. His body was warm. It felt tender and secure. Within minutes the sea rocked her to sleep and for once she didn't dream.

Chapter 19

Pan jerked upright, her heart hammering. It felt as though she'd been asleep for only a matter of minutes, though her neck was sore from where she'd been resting against Nate. For a second, she didn't know what had woken her, but then she saw Gwynne kicking at the legs of those who remained sleeping. She stretched and tried to get the kinks out of her muscles.

It was close to dawn and the sky was tinged with orange. Nate put his hands on her shoulders and kneaded, gently.

'Best to get those muscles unknotted,' he said. 'I have a feeling we're all going to need to be loose.'

'Feels good,' said Pan.

'And my fee is very reasonable. Don't worry. It doesn't mean we're engaged or anything.'

Pan smiled. 'Are we there yet?'

'I guess,' said Nate. 'Look.' He pointed over her shoulder to her right. Pan turned. Maybe two hundred metres away, just discernible in the diffused light, a dark land mass loomed. It was impossible to make out details. The other members of the group were standing now, stretching legs and arching backs. They too glanced at the land.

'Listen up,' said Gwynne. 'Out of this boat in thirty seconds. Under your own steam or with a helping hand from me. Take survival items, get going. In seventy-two hours, at exactly six a.m., I return. I wait five minutes. If you're not here, I leave. Even if you're in the water, swimming. Understood? Right. Go.'

There was a scramble for the items in the box. Wei-Lin took the bow and the quiver of arrows and the others divided up the items at random. Pan got the rope. Jen was the first over the side. She swam towards the shore with strong and confident strokes. Pan sighed. She couldn't swim like that, particularly since she'd be weighed down with a rope. Pan was more of a breaststroke swimmer, slow but steady. She coiled the rope up and wore it like a sash on her left shoulder so that it drooped over her right hip. There was no point thinking too much. She had no doubt that Gwynne would see through on his promise to throw her overboard if she took too long. Already the others were striking for shore. Nate had dived from the side of the boat and scarcely made a ripple as he entered the water. His freestyle was strong and Pan was sure he would outstrip even Jen. She jumped into the water and gasped at the cold. The rope almost immediately doubled in weight and dragged her down. She kicked back to the surface and followed the others in her desperately slow breast stroke. *I'm the weak link*, she thought. *The others know it and they will resent me for it. Even Nate.*

It seemed to take forever, but she finally felt sand beneath her feet and waded up onto a beach. The others were waiting for her and Jen could scarcely conceal her impatience. But no one shouted and Pan understood that Gwynne's words had made an impact. *Survivalists. Shoot first and ask questions later.* They had no idea where they were or if there were enemies close by. It was important to keep absolutely quiet, but it was also important to get the hell off the beach and hide from potentially prying eyes. Even as she left the water the others were running for a dense thicket of trees, some forty metres from the shoreline. Pan hitched the rope more securely on her shoulder and followed.

The trees were in a patch of swamp land. The water level was just below Pan's knees. She was bitterly cold and already she could feel the sting of mosquitoes on her bare arms. This was going to be miserable but the first priority was to find shelter – somewhere relatively dry and private – where they could talk and make a plan. Nate immediately struck off inland, wading through the swamp. He carried the axe in his right hand and occasionally chopped at branches that hindered their progress. The others followed silently. Pan noticed Jen didn't bother to slap at the insects on her exposed skin. After ten minutes she didn't bother either. *Toughen up*, she told herself. *You will not be the weak link.*

It took only twenty minutes to find land that was relatively dry. The trees were densely bunched and the place seemed secure enough. Nate glanced around and his shoulders relaxed. He threw the axe down, took off his jacket and stripped out of his trousers. His body was tough and lean. There wasn't a spare ounce of fat on him. He put his clothes on the branch of the closest tree and spread them out. The others started doing the same. It was still bitterly cold, but their wet clothes were even colder. The tree canopy was too thick to allow a glimpse of the sky, so whatever sun was up there, if any, was of no use. Pan reluctantly stripped off to her underwear as well.

Finally, they squatted in a tight circle. Pan noticed that she was not the only one who was shivering uncontrollably.

'We need a fire,' she whispered.

'Not yet,' said Nate. He kept his voice low. 'Not until we know it's safe. Sam, you've got experience with orienteering so I want you to scout out the surrounding area. At least a kilometre in every direction.'

'And who put you in charge?' said Karl.

'No one,' admitted Nate. 'Maybe that's the first thing we should decide. I mean, I take it there is no one here who thinks we can do without a leader of some description?'

No one said anything.

'I'll take that as agreement,' Nate continued. 'So who wants the job?'

'Oh, come on, Nate,' said Jen. 'You're the one with a gift for leadership, apparently. This is just wasting time and I'm cold. The job's yours, so tell us what you want us to do.'

Nate looked around the group. They all nodded, with the exception of Sanjit who did not glance up. 'Okay,' said Nate. 'So, Sam, you're on reconnaissance. Be as quick as you can, but stealth is vital. What equipment will you need? The compass?'

'Karl.' She replied without hesitation.

Pan giggled, as did most of the group. Even Jen smiled.

'Karl is a piece of equipment now?' smiled Nate. 'Okay. I guess it makes sense to move in pairs, anyway. All those computer games you played, Karl? Now is the time to put your skills into practice. But remember this is the real world and you only get one life. Take the knife and the compass. Look out for each other and the first sign of trouble, get back here as quick as possible. Understood?'

They nodded. Jen slipped the knife from the waistband of her pants, flipped it and offered it, hilt-first, to Karl. He took it and handed over the water canteen. Sanjit passed the compass to Sam and she, in turn, handed him the fishing tackle.

'Go,' said Nate. 'The sooner we know it's safe, the sooner we can get a fire going.'

Sam nodded and slipped off into the undergrowth, Karl on her heels. Within twenty seconds they were lost to view. The remaining five huddled closer together.

'Love's young dream,' observed Nate. 'It's sweet. Right. Here are my thoughts. First priority is to establish if we are in immediate danger or if there are people around. We do nothing until Sam and Karl report back. If they give the all-clear, then we light a fire and dry our clothes. No smoke, though. Jen, do you know how to do that?'

She nodded. 'Gwynne covered fire-starting in our personal development sessions.'

'Okay,' continued Nate. 'Then we need to establish a base camp, close to water and preferably with shelter. Wei-Lin should check out the availability of game and, if possible, lay down supplies. After that, I guess it's a question of exploration, seeing if there are any survivors and whether they want to join us at The School.'

The group was silent for a moment, then a small voice spoke.

'We should ask Pan.'

It was Sanjit. He hadn't raised his head, and his hands were interlocked in his lap, writhing and twisting as if he were washing them. They all stared at him, astonished that he had spoken at all. They had become accustomed to him as a mute member of the group. Wei-Lin was the first to speak.

'Ask Pan what, Sanjit?'

He gave an almost imperceptible shrug. 'She knows things,' he said. 'She knew where Wei-Lin's watch was. She found Cara. I don't know . . . maybe she could use . . . whatever gift she has to see if there's anyone out there. Survivors.' He glanced up. 'It couldn't hurt.'

Jen snorted.

'It couldn't hurt,' Sanjit repeated.

'True enough,' said Nate. 'Wanna give it a go, Pan?'

'Jesus Christ,' said Jen through her teeth.

'I don't know,' Pan said. 'You know, if I'm to . . . get anything, then . . . But I'm not sure I will be able to. It's kinda weird . . .' She felt foolish even as she uttered the words. *You're not even making sense*, she thought. *You sound like a cheap mind-reading act, only confirming Jen's impression of you.* She swallowed. 'I need to empty my mind.'

'So empty it,' said Jen. 'Shouldn't be difficult.' She plucked a broad leaf from a shrub next to her, put it into her mouth then spat it out.

Ignore her, Pan thought. *Conflict is our enemy.* She closed her eyes and tried to clear her head of all thoughts. How had she done it when she'd found her way into the mind of the falcon? Or when she'd fought Jen that time? She couldn't remember exactly. She took deep intakes of air and let the breath escape slowly and regularly. Immediately she thought of how she must appear to Jen and then she had to banish images of the contempt playing on her face. She forced the thought away and tried to focus. The whine of a circling mosquito broke her concentration. Pan shook her head and opened her eyes. It was useless.

'Anything?' asked Wei-Lin.

'Sorry.'

'Maybe having an audience doesn't help,' suggested Nate. 'Why don't you find a place nearby where you can be alone? Not too far. We have to stick together.'

'It's no good,' said Pan.

'I believe in you, Pan,' said Nate. 'Give it one more go. As Sanjit said, it can't hurt.'

Pan shrugged, stood and walked away. She didn't have to go far. The trees were so dense it wasn't difficult to find a private spot yet still remain close to the team. She sat behind a tree and hugged herself. The cold seemed to be getting worse, if anything. She hoped that Sam and Karl would be back soon. The idea of a fire and warm clothes was very appealing. She closed her eyes and tried once again to put the thought to one side. Why was it so difficult to clear her mind? She concentrated on her breathing. One long, slow breath in. Hold it. Then gradually exhale. Keep the rhythm, focus on the breathing. In and out. In and out.

This time there was no dramatic sense of occupying or being occupied. No slam of spirit into flesh. Just a vague feeling of danger. Close and getting closer. Pan concentrated upon letting the images, the impressions, in. If she thought too much they would simply disappear. Keep the breathing regular. The grainy darkness behind her eyelids softened and resolved into dim shapes. People moving through the forest. She couldn't make out any details, just the shifting of shadows and the rustle of foliage. She caught a glimpse of the barrel of a gun. Ten people, maybe more. She heard distant whispers but couldn't distinguish words. She couldn't even be sure they were talking in English. The images were as fragile as soap bubbles. One small disturbance and they would burst. Pan tried to release her mind further. The images firmed. She saw her team running. Running away from something. Soldiers? Were they soldiers? That gun. Maybe. Running for their lives? She saw Jen glance over her shoulder as if afraid of what she might see behind her. Wei-Lin, an arrow nocked on her bow. Nate gripping the axe. And then the images folded and only a sense remained. Not even a sense. But for all that, Pan *knew*. She knew that one of her group would not leave this place. Only six would return to The School.

She had no idea who would be lost.

Pan opened her eyes. The cold hit her once again and she shivered, though whether that was from the temperature or the aftermath of her vision she could not tell. *There is something wrong about all of this*, she thought. *There is something wrong about everything.* She tried to pin it down, but it slipped away immediately, leaving only the overwhelming cold and a sense of terror.

Pan got slowly to her feet. Her legs were almost blue, dotted with goosebumps. What could she say to the rest of the team? She couldn't tell them that one of them would be left here. It could serve no useful purpose. But she *could* mention the feeling that they were not alone. It mightn't help much and would probably provoke Jen's scorn, but it was information she could share.

Pan arrived back at the group just as Karl burst through a gap in the forest. Almost immediately, Sam appeared at his heels. A sense of urgency was stamped on their faces.

'A village,' Karl hissed, dropping to his haunches in front of the team. 'Less than a kilometre away. You need to see it.'

'People?' asked Nate.

'Oh, yes,' said Karl. 'But they're all dead. At least, we think they're all dead.'

~~~

They moved slowly, in single file, through the forest. Karl led the way, Sam at his shoulder, and Pan brought up the rear. Sanjit was ahead of her. Even when walking, he kept his head bowed. What had he said was his speciality? Technology. That figured. Pan could see him in front of a computer. But battling nature? Sanjit against the wilderness? There'd only be one winner in that contest.

She hadn't had the opportunity to share her vision with the team and she was grateful. When all was said and done it wasn't much of a vision at all. Nate had immediately ordered everyone to get dressed. Their clothes seemed even colder than they had been before, though Pan wouldn't have thought that possible. She shivered uncontrollably as she pulled on her camouflage pants. Jen didn't seem to be affected. Shivering, Pan imagined, would have been an unacceptable sign of weakness for that girl.

The team moved steadily and silently. They made little noise as they walked, and Pan couldn't hear anything else moving in the forest. Maybe it was a consequence of the vaguely disquieting silence, but Pan felt an itch between her shoulder blades as if someone was watching. She tried to shake the feeling as evidence of an overactive imagination and concentrate on Sanjit's bowed head.

After less than ten minutes, Karl raised a hand in warning and the group slowed to a halt. He jerked his hand towards the foliage in front of his face and put a finger to his lips. Then he moved slowly forward and parted the leaves of a massive fern. The others crowded towards him. They were on the edge of a large clearing. The first thing that Pan noticed was the smell. It was sweet and sickly and caught at her throat. It took her a moment to place it. Death. The sickly sweet smell of corrupting flesh. The second thing she was aware of was a faint humming, a steady drone, like a power tool being operated far off in the distance. Flies. Dotted around the village were clouds of blackness, swarming and gathering over mounds on the earth. Bodies. Pan lifted the neck of her T-shirt and pulled it up over her mouth. Wei-Lin and Sam did the same. She glanced at Sanjit. His face had turned pale and he opened and closed his mouth. His Adam's apple jerked up and down as if he was fighting a gag reflex, though he hadn't covered his face. She put a hand on his shoulder but he didn't react.

Nate beckoned the group away. It was a relief when Karl let the fronds fall back and the clearing was hidden from view. Pan concentrated on her breathing. She recognised that she was close to hyperventilating, and focusing on the rhythm of each breath helped calm her.

'I want us to spread out around the circumference of the clearing,' said Nate. 'Karl, you go to the opposite side, at twelve o'clock to where we are now. Sam at three o'clock. Pan at nine o'clock. Jen, Sanjit and Wei-Lin at four, seven and eleven respectively. Move quietly. When you get in position, observe only. If you see anything at all, any signs of life, report back to me, here at six o'clock. We wait thirty minutes. If nothing is reported I will enter the clearing. Watch for me. When that happens we move into the clearing together. Understood?'

They all nodded.

'Go,' said Nate.

Pan crept off to her left with Sanjit and Wei-Lin. They said nothing, concentrating on making no noise. Sanjit stepped on a broken branch and the sharp snap made them freeze. Pan cocked her head and tried to listen above the hammering of her heart. The forest was silent, eerily so. Even the sound of buzzing flies was muted by the trees. It was almost a relief to know that Sanjit was even worse at this kind of thing than she was. She might be a weak link in the water, but he was even weaker on the land. It wasn't a noble thought and she tried to banish it. Thirty seconds passed and they moved off again. After a couple of minutes, Pan tapped Sanjit on the shoulder. She pointed to the ground and Sanjit nodded that he understood. He got down on hands and knees and then lowered himself to the forest floor. Carefully, he crawled on his belly towards the clearing. Pan and Wei-Lin moved on.

When Pan estimated that she must be close enough to nine o'clock she patted Wei-Lin on the back. Wei-Lin nodded and continued, while Pan followed Sanjit's example and lowered herself to her belly. She inched towards the clearing, using her elbows to get purchase on the rotten mulch that made up most of the undergrowth. She carefully parted the leaves and looked out at the village. There were five or six buildings made of plastic siding. They looked like the small cabins found on some camping sites. Wooden steps led up to the front doors, which were encased in flyscreen. The building closest to her had its door open, but she couldn't see anything of the interior, because the angle was wrong. She thought for a moment about moving ten metres to her right to get a better view but decided against it. The interior would almost certainly be in darkness anyway and she didn't want to risk further movement. Pan scanned the perimeter, but couldn't see any signs of the others, who must have taken up their positions by now. She returned her gaze to the village. There were seven bodies that she could detect, all covered in flies. They were scattered randomly about the clearing, though one was on the bottom step of one of the buildings, as if the person had been trying to seek sanctuary within or was trying to flee something inside. Pan shuddered.

Almost directly opposite her position she noticed a narrow track leading out of the village and into the forest. A motorbike leaned on its kickstand close to the track. It was a curious and jarring reminder of a normality that the rest of the scene belied. Pan could imagine someone walking out of one of the buildings, sitting astride it and kick-starting it, before riding off. She glanced at her watch. Twenty minutes to go. She tried to let her mind clear, see if there was anything her intuition could tell her about the village, but she drew a blank. She let her eyes rove over the clearing, paying particular attention to her peripheral vision. There was no movement anywhere. Her clothes clung to her skin in an icy embrace and it took an effort of will to stop her teeth chattering. As she watched she tried to understand what this village was for. Apart from the motorbike, there was no machinery that she could see. The buildings indicated this might be a residential facility but it was also clear this wasn't a tourist destination. No proper roads, for one thing. In which case it might be accommodation for workers. But what kind of workplace would be around here? Logging, perhaps. But the path out seemed very narrow and there was no evidence of logging machinery. Unless there were chainsaws in the huts. They'd get more information when they searched the buildings. Pan rested her head on her arms and tried to ignore the mosquitoes whining around her ears.

Nate entered the clearing after exactly half an hour. He moved slowly, his head scanning every direction. Almost immediately the others appeared at their respective positions around the clearing's circumference. Pan got to her feet and followed. They converged at the centre, close to the largest building. Pan had to make a small detour to avoid a corpse. As she approached, the cloud of flies lifted and then settled again. She kept her eyes averted.

'We search each building in turn,' said Nate. 'Sam, Karl and Wei-Lin stay outside and keep watch. Yell if you hear or see anything. The rest of us get in and get out as quickly as possible. Any questions?'

There were none. Nate hefted the axe in his hand. Wei-Lin had an arrow nocked, though she kept the bow angled towards the ground. Karl moved behind the building and Sam took up a position to the side. Nate nodded his head towards the steps of the nearest building.

'I go first. When inside we spread out. No speaking unless you find something of interest. Right, let's do it.'

He moved confidently up the steps and gripped the door handle, turned it and entered. Pan was on his heels. As soon as he was inside he broke to the left. Pan moved straight ahead. The light inside the building was not good and it took a few moments for Pan's eyes to adjust. It was an office space. A desk sat in front of a small window, a leather chair in position. There was a filing cabinet to one side and a few leaflets pinned to a corkboard. The leaflets weren't in English, and Pan didn't recognise the language. She backed out and found Nate coming from the room to her left. He raised his eyebrows and she shook her head. Nothing. Jen and Sanjit joined them.

'Nothing,' said Jen.

'Okay,' said Nate. 'On to the next.'

They found a man in the last building they checked. It had been designed as basic sleeping accommodation. Three beds, little more than cots, had been squeezed into the cramped space. He lay half in and half out of the third. Dark stains, dried blood, spotted the bedding and chequered the plain wooden flooring. At first the man appeared dead, his pallor deathly white, but then he took a shuddering intake of air. It was a dreadful sound, like gravel rattling on metal. Nate and the others instinctively drew away in revulsion. The man's hand twitched and his eyelids fluttered open. He seemed to be staring straight at Pan, the whites of his eyes, bloodshot, the pupils black pinpricks. Nate knelt by the bed and took his hand, but he gave no reaction other than the tearing rasp of his breathing. Pan closed her eyes and fought a rising sense of panic. This was so familiar. She knew what was about to happen. The man's body would convulse and his frame would become racked with coughing. It would tear him apart, the pressure of blood building in his lungs too great to withstand. She felt tears well behind her lids. The relief teacher. All her nightmares. All her worst nightmares in the flesh.

The cough, when it came, was more violent than she could have imagined. It doubled the man up. A fountain of blood spewed from his mouth, a thick geyser that soaked Nate's shirt. Nate dropped the man's hand and gazed down at the spreading crimson stain on his chest. All of them were frozen by horror. The man slumped again, his hand trailing on the floor, fingers dipped in blood. The silence this time was absolute.

The images snapped into Pan's mind, caused her head to swivel to the door. Men approaching. Leaves being parted, boots crushing undergrowth, the lazy swing of a weapon, a sash of bullets like strange ceremonial decoration. A cry from outside pierced the quiet and Pan didn't know which had come first, her premonition or the shout of warning.

'Company!' It was Sam's voice, tinged in urgency.

Nate jumped to his feet and rushed to the door. He left a trail of bloody footprints. Pan shuddered and followed. They burst onto the front steps. After the relative darkness of the cabin, the light was blinding. Sam, Wei-Lin and

Karl had formed a small group in front of the steps. Sam held the boning knife loosely in her right hand, Wei-Lin's bow was half-raised and they stared towards the far end of the clearing. Pan shielded her eyes and followed their line of sight.

A group of men stood just inside the clearing. There were about ten of them and they, too, seemed frozen in the act of movement, as if stunned by the sight of other people. Jen took a step back and spoke quietly, though her gaze did not deviate from the newcomers.

'What now, Nate?'

'I don't know,' he replied.

Pan understood his hesitation. Were these people friendly, survivors of the disease that had killed their friends and family? Or did they present a threat? While they watched, one of the group raised his hand in greeting. He shouted something and took a couple of steps forward.

'Run!' yelled Pan.

For a moment, no one moved.

'Why?' said Karl.

'Because they mean to kill us all,' said Pan. 'Trust me. Run!'

She jumped off the verandah and sprinted for the forest. She was dimly aware of further shouts from the men. Glancing back, she saw the rest of her team hard on her heels. Further back she saw the group of men starting to run themselves. One was raising a gun to his shoulder. She increased her pace. She didn't hear the bullet. All she was aware of was a rush of wind past her left ear, a violent pressure in the air. Then the dull crack followed immediately. It sounded vaguely absurd, like a child's toy gun. The second shot gouged a splinter in the tree a metre to her right. But then she was in the forest, crashing through bushes, ignoring the slap of branches against her face. She risked another glance. Nate and the others were right behind her. The forest closed around them.

They were safe. For the time being.

Chapter 20

Nate drew level with her.

'Calm your breathing, Pan,' he said. 'Focus on each breath. Anxiety and panic will build up acid in your muscles. Stay loose.'

Pan felt a flash of annoyance. Did nothing disturb his equanimity? Not even running for his life, with armed men hard on his heels? How could he stay so goddamn . . . composed? But she knew his advice was sound. The panic and adrenaline had made her breath ragged and already there was a serious stitch in her side. After a minute, the stitch subsided and her breathing became easier. Nate moved effortlessly past her. He turned his head and spoke to the rest of the team.

'Follow me. Wei-Lin, stay at the back of the group. Watch for pursuit. If you see anyone, kill them. Understood?' He didn't wait for a reply, but crashed off through the forest to his left. Pan didn't understand the reason for the change of direction. The forest was uniformly dense and one direction seemed as good as any other. But she followed.

The next time they stopped, Jen turned to Nate. When she spoke it was without any evidence of breathlessness.

'You have a plan, boss?' she said.

Nate smiled.

'Nothing so grand, I'm afraid, Jen. Just trying to keep us alive.'

'So why this direction?'

'If I've got my bearings right, then we should stumble across that path - the one out of the village - fairly soon.'

'And?'

'We follow it. Crashing through the forest, we might as well put up neon signs. Broken branches, slashed leaves, all the evidence of flight. Any idiot could track us. We might be able to outrun them for a while, but eventually they'll catch us. If we can get on the path, we should leave far fewer signs. We run along it for a while, then take off into the forest again. If nothing else, it will slow them down.'

'The gift of leadership, huh?'

'Scarcely. We are still in deep shit. Look, enough talking. Jen, keep an eye on the others, particularly Sanjit. Okay?'

Jen nodded and dropped back. Pan lowered her head and kept her gaze on the back of Nate's boots as he took off again. She tried to empty her mind and allow her body to follow the rhythm of his feet as they rose and fell. The initial rush of panic had subsided, to be replaced by a strong sense of deja vu. *Running, pursuit.* Trying to get away from someone or something that meant her harm. Suddenly the recurrent dream she had been experiencing back at The School sprang to mind. And something else. Something that Cara had written in her journal. *The dreams that don't make sense.* Pan couldn't shake the feeling that she was on the verge of a discovery, an enlightenment. But there was no time to pay it any attention.

A shout behind them caused Nate to stop. He barely paused before retracing his steps. Pan skidded to a halt and then doubled back too. There were no signs of the others and for a moment she was surprised; then again, the forest was so thick that even a gap of a few metres was sufficient to provide cover. She stepped up her pace.

It was Sanjit. He had stumbled. He lay in a crumpled heap, clutching his right ankle. Karl helped him to his feet, an arm around his chest. Jen and Sam stood a few metres away, frozen in indecision. Pan ran past Wei-Lin, who was staring over Karl's head and into the forest. The sound of pursuit was loud, the crash of bodies forcing themselves through foliage, guttural sounds of men issuing orders. Pan felt the tingle of imminent disaster. Time slowed.

When the man burst through the foliage he was only five metres from Sanjit and Karl. He stopped. For a bizarre moment, they all watched each other. The man was sweating. His face glistened and drops of sweat had formed on the end of his beard. He was wearing army fatigues, though they were stained and torn. Then the man reached over his right shoulder and pulled out a machete. Its blade was spotted with rust, but it looked deadly. He balanced himself on the balls of his feet and glanced around the group. Then he grinned and took a step forward.

The arrow took him in the neck. Its shaft penetrated halfway through before jamming. The arrowhead glistened red on one side of his neck and the fletchings on the other side shivered for a moment before stilling. The man stiffened as if surprised. An expression of astonishment passed over his face and he reached a hand tentatively towards his head. His mouth opened. No sound came out, but a thin stream of blood trickled from his lips. The machete slipped from his fingers and then his legs crumpled.

Nate sprinted forward and lifted Sanjit in one easy movement. He threw him over his left shoulder.

'Move, people,' he yelled. 'Now.'

Pan turned to follow him. She saw Wei-Lin standing stock still. Paralysed. Her bow was dangling from her left hand and her gaze was fixed on the body. The man's hands still twitched and one foot scrambled ineffectually at the ground. Pan grabbed Wei-Lin by the wrist and dragged her along. For a couple of moments it seemed as if she was still frozen, but then she shuddered and started running. Pan risked a glance at her face, which was twisted, eyes wide and brimming with panic. Her breath came in ragged gasps.

'Breathe, Wei-Lin,' she said. 'Stay loose.'

Pan dropped back a couple of steps so she couldn't tell if her words had had any effect. She worried that Wei-Lin would simply stop again, fixed by the enormity of her actions, and Pan knew she must look out for her. This put Pan last in the group and she felt her back as a broad target. A bullet would bring her down before she knew what was happening and her shoulder blades itched in anticipation.

They burst onto the path. The leaves suddenly disappeared and a beaten track, only a metre wide, lay before them. Nate stopped and glanced in both directions. Even with Sanjit's body over his shoulder he hadn't tired.

'This way,' he said and took off to his left. The others followed. Pan considered his choice of direction. The path to their right had a bend only twenty or so metres away, whereas the way he had chosen left them vulnerable for at least one hundred and fifty. It wasn't logical. Pan prayed the men had stopped to help their fallen comrade. Seconds might prove vital if they weren't to be spotted before they rounded the bend. *The rest of the team will be thinking the same*, she thought, *yet they obeyed without question. He* is *a leader.* She might have smiled at the thought but the sense that a bullet could, at any moment, punch the life out of her choked the impulse before it could quicken.

It felt like the longest one hundred and fifty metres of her life, but they made it. As Pan turned the bend she realised she had been holding her breath and she forced her lungs to empty. Wei-Lin was staggering slightly, weaving across the track, and Pan knew she would not be able to keep running much longer. Whatever plan Nate had, if any, she hoped they would be able to stop soon before their bodies shut down. She wasn't altogether sure their minds hadn't done so already.

The group rounded another slight bend in the path and Pan saw the clearing of the village only twenty or thirty metres ahead. Nate stopped ten metres short and pushed his way into the forest on his right, Jen, Karl and Sam following. Wei-Lin stumbled and almost fell. Pan caught her by the arm, led her after the others. They brushed aside broad fern leaves, ignoring branches that snagged on their clothing. Wei-Lin's breath rasped. It was the sound of panic, close to hyperventilation.

They came to a small area of undergrowth dotted with saplings and small ferns, clear enough to allow the group to sit. Nate eased Sanjit off his shoulder and rested him gently on the ground, his back against a tree. Then he sat and covered his face with his hands. Wei-Lin dropped to the gound and did the same. The others sat cross-legged. No one said anything.

Two minutes passed and then Nate shuddered and lifted his face. When he spoke his voice was barely a whisper and the group had to edge forward to hear him.

'This is as good a place as any,' he said. 'We'll make this our base until we're sure we've lost them.'

'The village is so close,' said Jen. 'Is this wise?'

'I figured they wouldn't count on us returning here,' Nate replied. 'Especially since it was counter-intuitive to turn left.' *That's why he exposed us for longer than necessary,* thought Pan.

'A gamble,' said Karl.

'Anywhere's a gamble,' Nate said. 'I think the odds are slightly better here.'

'So what now?' asked Sam. 'We sit here and hope they don't find us?'

'No,' said Nate. 'Two of us will leave in about half an hour, assuming we remain undiscovered. The way I see it, we are in need of water and food. It's possible to do without the latter, but we must all be dehydrated. A water supply is essential. Another reason why I brought us back here. The village must be close to water. It wouldn't make sense if it wasn't.' He scratched at his face. 'Also, bodies.

Disease. Not great for uncontaminated water. I'm hoping for a stream. Running water is our only chance. Even then, we'll have to make sure there are no bodies upstream to pollute the supply.'

'I'll go,' said Jen.

'No,' said Nate. 'I'm not taking volunteers. Sam and Wei-Lin will go. A sense of direction and hunting, remember? It's what we need right now.'

Wei-Lin shook her head. 'I can't.'

'You can,' said Nate. He cupped Wei-Lin's chin and raised her eyes to his. 'You saved our lives back there, Wei-Lin.'

'I killed a man.' Her voice shook and one large tear spilled down her cheek, splashed on Nate's hand.

'Yes, you did.' Nate didn't let his gaze shift from her eyes. 'You had no choice. You know that, don't you? No choice at all. And if the situation arises again, you will have to do the same.'

'I didn't think it would be so . . . hard,' she said. 'It was so . . . hard.' Pan put her arms around Wei-Lin's shoulders, but she didn't seem to notice. Her body trembled.

'If you'd found it easy,' said Nate, 'then I'd be seriously worried about you. But this isn't over, Wei-Lin. Not nearly. We came through back there. I'm sorry, but now we need you to come through again. Food, kiddo. A bird, a mammal. Hell, a frog would do. But we need to eat and you're the best person for the job. You must go out there.'

Wei-Lin nodded. Then she laughed, but it came out wrong.

'One arrow down. Only five left.'

Nate mussed her hair.

'Make them count, kiddo,' he said.

She nodded.

Karl, Sam, Wei-Lin and Jen lay down and closed their eyes, though it was doubtful anyone slept. Nate sat cross-legged, staring in the direction of the village. There was nothing to see, even though they couldn't have been more than ten or fifteen metres from the perimeter. But Pan knew he was listening. The silence of the forest was deep, and if anything moved out there, it was almost certain they'd hear it.

~ ~ ~

After half an hour, Wei-Lin and Sam got to their feet. Wei-Lin seemed more composed, but her body was still tight and strained. Pan thought it would take a very long time before she was back to her normal self. If ever. Sam took the water canteen and Karl handed over the compass.

'To help you find your way back to the village,' he explained. 'Be quick, okay?'

Sam nodded and put the compass in her pocket. Wei-Lin checked her arrows, smoothing the fletchings almost lovingly. Then she hitched the bow over her left shoulder and they were gone. The sound of their departure was almost deafening and Pan felt her blood tingle in anxiety. But then all was quiet. She glanced over at Sanjit. The boy's face was drawn in pain. He had torn strips from his shirt and bound his ankle tightly, but he was still pale.

'I'm fine,' he said in answer to Pan's unspoken question. If anything his voice was even quieter than normal. She smiled at him. Nate hitched himself towards her and brought his mouth close to her ear.

'Do you sense anything, Pan?' he whispered.

She shook her head. 'Where the hell is this place?' she said. 'And what are we really doing here? I mean, Gwynne's story about possible survivors doesn't make much sense. If that was the case, wouldn't the helicopter have checked it out more thoroughly? I thought the search for survivors took precedence over everything. It just doesn't add up - sending a bunch of inexperienced kids into a place like this.'

Nate frowned.

'I hear you,' he said. 'And saying he'll leave us behind even if we're almost at the rendezvous point? If you've only got ten thousand survivors, then putting some at risk - and not doing everything possible to rescue them if they're in danger - appears illogical. Hell, I don't know, Pan. All I can deal with is the immediate situation. I'll worry about the rest later. At the moment it's reasonable to assume that what we saw in the village was the aftermath of the virus and those guys chasing us are survivors. Maybe The School knew that. Maybe we were sent here to test our survival skills after all. You know, see firsthand what has happened to the world and have some experience dealing with the kinds of people who are left.'

'But you said it, Nate,' said Pan. 'That's an unacceptable gamble given there are so few of us. No, it's all wrong. I know it.'

'Why?'

'A couple of things. First of all, why did those people attack us? I mean, come on, Nate. Assume you are a survivor of a horrendous virus that has wiped everyone out. As far as you know, there is only a small band of survivors. Then, suddenly, you see a group of seven kids, alive. Why attack? You'd think the first reaction would be to hug people rather than try to kill them.'

Nate scratched his head.

'Yeah, but that's assuming they're normal and reasonable people. Maybe living through all that, seeing your friends and family die, would change you. Fundamentally. Perhaps they've regressed, become militant survivalists willing to attack anyone they perceive as a threat. People who would sooner shoot than talk under the best of circumstances. After all of this . . . I dunno, Pan. It's bound to screw with your mind.'

'All of their minds?' asked Pan.

Nate shrugged. 'Maybe. I read a book in high school. *Lord of the Flies.* These kids are marooned on a desert island and although they try to stay civilised it all turns to shit in no time. They kill each other; do the nastiest stuff for no reason other than the desire to hurt. And from what I remember, that was the point the book was making. We think we are civilised, but when the restraints of civilisation are removed, we find the animal in all of us isn't buried deep at all.'

'I don't believe it.'

'You don't?'

'No. There's no way you'd have read a book in high school.'

Nate laughed and then choked it off. 'Maybe I dreamed it. Or watched the movie,' he said. 'So, what else?'

'What?'

'You said a couple of things. What's the other?'

Pan ran a hand through her hair. It felt grainy and matted.

'Statistics,' she said. 'The maths don't add up.'

'The math? What do you mean?'

'The School told us that billions died from the virus and only ten thousand survived.' She put up her hands in a gesture of helplessness. 'Hey, I can't work out the percentages, but it's tiny, all right? The ratio of survivors to fatalities. But that village we saw. It had, what, seven or eight bodies?' She remembered the man in the bed and the spume of blood arching through the air. Pan shivered. 'And the people chasing us. Ten of them, right? If that ratio holds good that would be the survival rate in a city of many millions. Okay, we don't know what may lie a kilometre or two down that track, but I seriously doubt we'll stumble on New York City. How do you explain so many survivors?'

Nate chewed on that for a few moments, his brow furrowed in concentration. Then he shrugged again.

'Maybe most of them are still going to die. Maybe they joined up from a much larger area. Maybe this is all of the survivors from a radius of two thousand miles around. I don't know, Pan. And you don't either. We don't have enough information.'

Except she did know. There was something very wrong about this place, this situation, but all she had were feelings. Feelings and a few dubious statistical ideas probably based upon fundamental misconceptions.

There was a rustle close by and she stiffened. Before any of the group had a chance to react, Sam and Wei-Lin entered the clearing. Pan was impressed. She hadn't heard anything until they were right on top of them. The two girls sat down close to Nate.

'How did it go?' he asked.

'Water okay,' replied Sam. 'We found a stream maybe half a kilometre from here. Clear running water.'

'You checked upstream?'

'As far as we could and we didn't find any bodies. But, as you know, we can't be certain that there wasn't pollution further up. Not unless we traced the stream back to its source and that simply wasn't practical.'

Nate rubbed at one eye. 'I guess those survivors must have a decent water supply. Maybe that's why they stayed around here, so your source might well be good. Whatever, we can't be certain. Perhaps we should boil it.'

'I drank at the stream,' said Wei-Lin. 'Tasted good to me and I've had no reaction in the last half hour.'

Jen grabbed the water canteen from Sam's hand and unscrewed the cap. She sniffed the contents and then took a small sip, wiped her mouth with the back of her hand and passed the canteen on to Sanjit.

'No guarantees in this situation,' she said. 'It's all a risk and we have no means to light a fire and boil it. Not while those guys are out there and looking for us. Way too risky.'

Nate shrugged. 'Maybe you're right,' he said. 'But drink slowly, guys. Sip, don't gulp. Every time we have to refill this we are exposed, and I want to keep that to a minimum. What about food?'

Wei-Lin frowned. 'Not so good on that account,' she said. 'We didn't see any animals. Heard scuffling, but that was all. I looked out for birds as well. Saw a few, but they were out of my range. Sorry, but I reckon it's the nature of forests. Everything avoids you when they hear you coming. Maybe if we had some traps . . .'

Nate spread his hands. 'I know,' he said. 'We're not exactly well-equipped. But there must be something to eat in this goddamn place.'

'We found berries,' said Sam. She unknotted the jacket she was carrying over her shoulder. 'Some kind of blackberries. A few had been pecked at by birds, so we figured they must be good. I had a couple and they are slightly bitter, but okay.' She unrolled the jacket to reveal maybe a couple of kilos of berries in the centre. They looked like hard red knots of blood. 'Better than nothing,' she added.

They divided the berries between them, but Pan couldn't eat half before she felt slightly nauseous. She gave the rest to Sanjit who had regained some colour, though his face was still drawn in pain.

'How's the ankle?' she asked.

He gave a wry smile. 'Okay if I don't put weight on it.'

'And if you do?'

'Not okay.'

'Just rest it, all right?'

Sanjit put his head down again. Pan wondered how he had coped with The School's regime. There was much about him that reminded her of Cara - a loner, lost in his own thoughts, inadequate in the skills The School valued most: physical fitness and psychological strength. What kind of horrors had he been through and what depths of loneliness had he plumbed? Pan remembered how she had let Cara down, had not been a good enough friend. Or, indeed, any kind of friend at all. She resolved that this could not, would not, happen to Sanjit. She shivered. *One of us will not return to The School.*

'I'm a burden,' said Sanjit as if reading her mind. He didn't meet her eyes, but examined the ground beneath his splayed legs. 'I fell and put the rest of you in danger. And someone died as a result. Now I can't move. It would have been best if you'd left me there. Maybe it's best to leave me now.'

Pan framed the words, but stopped them in time. *You are not a burden and it would not have been best to leave you.* The words were patronising and they wouldn't fool him. What would keep them together was honesty, and anyway, he deserved that much.

'Yes, you are a burden now,' she said. 'But that ankle injury could have happened to anyone. It wasn't your fault. To leave you would have been wrong. To leave you now would be inhumane. We are a team and we do not leave anyone behind.'

He glanced up at her then and smiled. But it was a difficult smile to read.

'Just rest,' she said again. She squeezed his shoulder and returned to Nate's side.

'Sanjit can't move yet,' she said. 'He can't put weight on that ankle.'

Nate nodded. 'I figured. Look, I think it would be a good idea to stay here overnight anyway. We have no idea where those men are and there seems no compelling reason to move. It's not like there is a specific mission we have to achieve.' He sighed. 'Roaming around for the sake of it is dangerous. I'll talk to the others, see what ideas they have, but that's the way I'm thinking.'

'He might be better in the morning. I don't think he's broken anything. Rest is all he needs.'

Nate nodded and got to his feet in one fluid movement. He went to each of the group and whispered in their ears, listened to their responses. Finally he came back and sat down at Pan's side.

'It's agreed. No one is happy about it. Like me, they prefer action to inaction. But no one could suggest a better alternative. I've told them to sleep. We are all running on adrenaline and it's not just Sanjit who needs rest. I'm taking the first watch. Jen insists on taking the second.'

'I'll do the third,' replied Pan.

'Okay. In the meantime, get some sleep.'

Right, thought Pan. *I'm freezing, my clothes are damp, my stomach is empty and we are being hunted. Not the best conditions for sleep.*

She fashioned a makeshift pillow from the rotting leaves and twigs that littered the forest floor. The ground was hard and lumpy and something dug painfully into her side. Shifting position did nothing to relieve the discomfort. She curled up, sighed and closed her eyes. It was hopeless, she decided. But sleep plucked her almost instantly.

And she dreamed.

~~~

At first she dreamed of Cara. Cara was running around a track at The School, far behind Pan. Cara was crying out, but Pan couldn't hear the words. The wind picked up the sound and swept it away. Pan slowed to allow Cara to catch up, but every time she looked over her shoulder the distance between them was increasing. Eventually she stopped. But, although Cara continued to run, she continued to recede. She was waving, gesticulating wildly. Her urgency was palpable. Yet Pan could only watch as she steadily shrank. Eventually, Cara disappeared from view and all sounds, apart from the moaning of the wind, faded and died. When Pan turned back she saw Cara's diary at her feet. She picked it up. Cara's name was written on the cover in large, childish script. Pan opened it to the first page. HELP ME was written in crayon, but as she watched, the crayon's colouring changed, became deep red and liquid. The letters dripped down the page, the word melting into blood. Pan watched as her hands were stained.

The image changed and she found herself in the group as they ran through the forest. Pan jogged behind Nate and she could see Sanjit's face as he bounced on Nate's shoulder. His eyes were wide open and he was mouthing something at her. She edged closer to catch his words. 'Read my journal,' said Sanjit. 'Read my journal.' He said it in barely more than a whisper but his eyes implored her with an urgency that belied the softness of his speech. 'Read my journal.' Pan nodded and he smiled, but he did not stop his repetition of the words. Nate turned and it wasn't Nate at all. It was the man Wei-Lin had shot. His beard was badged with blood and Pan could see the arrow head jutting through his neck. The man smiled at her through blood-stained teeth.

Then the scene shifted again and Pan was back in her recurring dream. She was in the police car and a handcuffed man was being brought towards her.

'Don't bring him here,' she yelled. 'Please. Don't let him anywhere near me.'

The female police officer slid into the back seat next to her.

'It's okay,' she said. 'He's cuffed. See? And we'll put him in the front. He can't get to you. You're safe.'

But Pan didn't feel safe. The closer they got, the less safe she felt. The man was crouched over in pain. His eyes were red, inflamed and puffy. But the officer with the moustache was not being gentle. He gripped him tightly, pulled him around to the passenger side of the police car, placed his hand on the man's head and thrust him into the seat. Pan shuddered. The officer closed the door and walked around to the driver's side. He got in the car, belted himself in, turned to the prisoner next to him.

'You have the right to remain silent,' he said. 'But anything you do say may be taken down and used in a court of law. Do you understand?'

The man nodded. Pan was grateful she couldn't see his face. The car pulled away, lights still flashing. The driver turned his head and smiled at Pan in the back seat. A gold tooth glinted.

'I've always wanted to say that,' he said.

And the sense of wrongness flooded over Pan again. Perhaps she had simply been too traumatised to notice properly, her instincts, her gift buried beneath adrenaline and pain. But now it swamped her, screamed in her mind, twisted her gut. Police officers didn't use those words when they arrested someone. That was old-fashioned. Like something out of an 80s TV series.

'How did you know I sprayed his eyes?' she asked.

But she knew the answer already. Her sense of the wrongness of the situation heightened. Part of her had known from the moment she had seen the police car. The police were not here to save her. Pain flashed in her left thigh. It was intense. But all pains were intense now. She glanced down at the syringe in her leg. A numbness was *spreading through her body. It was a beautiful numbness. It filled her, took away pain. The sunlight changed, became buttery. Colours flashing past the window melted together. Even the words of the others in the car, when they came, were cool, wrapped in cotton.*

'Take these cuffs off.'

'Not yet. You don't deserve it.'

'The bitch sprayed me in the eyes.'

'Good. I hope it hurts.'

'It stings like hell.'

'You have any idea what a cock up this whole operation is? Have you? Ten agents. To get one schoolgirl. And you failed. A whole street in uproar. Dozens of witnesses. I have no idea how this mess is going to be cleaned up. But I have a fair idea of what our superiors are going to say. This is a disaster and you are responsible.'

'We got her.'

'I got her.'

'I need to wipe my eyes.'

'I suggest you shut the hell up. If you don't, I'll spray your goddamn eyes myself.'

The words fluttered around in Pan's head, floated and then broke up into small fragments and dissolved. Finally, all pain was gone and she welcomed the darkness.

~ ~ ~

When the hand shook her she bolted upright and gasped. Immediately a hand clasped over her mouth and she felt a surge of panic. Jen's face loomed within the darkness and she pressed her mouth close to Pan's ear.

'Quiet, Pandora,' whispered Jen. 'It's only me. It's time for your watch.'

Pan heard the thudding of her heart and the race of blood in her ears. She swallowed and nodded. Jen took her hand away and Pan worked hard to resist the urge to take deep and violent breaths. Slowly, the drumming of her panic subsided.

'What time is it?' Pan whispered.

'Eight o'clock. You have three hours on. Karl is next. Nate decided that we wouldn't ask Sanjit tonight. He needs the rest. Tell Karl when you wake him.'

Pan stretched and tried to get rid of the aches in her muscles. She stood and twisted her head from side to side, working out the kinks. It didn't help much. She paced the clearing, stepping over the sleeping forms of the team. After a few moments she returned to the tree and sat down again. The rough bark on her back was sufficiently uncomfortable to ensure there was little chance of drifting off. Pan sat and listened to the faint sounds of forest nightlife, creatures scurrying. But ultimately she couldn't resist her own internal mental scurrying.

Pan tried to remember the details of her dream. It had been so vivid but already it was fading. She tried to recall the images. Running through a forest. Cara and Sanjit. A journal. A policeman and a car, a needle. The fine points were elusive, but the feeling remained strong. There was something in those dreams. Some hint, some clue that would explain everything. She made up her mind that she would talk to Sanjit. A journal? Sanjit had never mentioned anything about a journal. He had scarcely spoken at all. But it was a feeling and Pan trusted it.

She hugged herself. Her clothes were finally dry, but it was still cold in that forest. At least there was no wind.

The forest offered that advantage, that protection. And it wasn't raining. *Be grateful for that*, she thought. *Hoard the small mercies.*

When Pan first heard the sound, it was difficult to pin it down. There was something familiar about it, but it seemed out of context. Not a man-made sound. And not coming from the direction of the village. She strained her ears. It wasn't the men returning. It didn't smell of danger at all. And then she realised. It was a faint drumming, a quiet and insistent beat. She understood at the same time the rain began to filter through the forest. A large drop hit her on the head and rolled down the back of her shirt. She pulled her collar up and hugged herself tighter. The foliage was dense enough to afford some protection, but only if the rain remained light.

Oh God, she thought. *Hoard the small mercies and something steals them.*

No one stirred despite the rain. Pan made herself as small as possible and stared into the darkness.

Chapter 21

The rain had stopped by morning, but everyone was clammy and uncomfortable. The mosquitoes were out in force, too. Pan's exposed flesh was mottled with bites and itching like crazy. She looked around the rest of the group and all she saw was misery. What sleep they'd had did not seem to have refreshed them much. Eyes were bloodshot and faces drawn in fatigue and hunger. Pan's stomach rumbled. When was the last time she had eaten a proper meal? Back at The School. It was almost funny. The food at The School was insipid and often inadequate but now it seemed like the height of gastronomic luxury, a five-star meal in a three-hat restaurant. She groaned and tried to put thoughts of food out of mind.

Nate beckoned them all together. Sanjit attempted to get to his feet, but as soon as he put weight on his injured ankle, his face twisted in pain. Nate pulled out a branch from the undergrowth by his feet. When Pan looked closer she realised it wasn't a branch, but a crude crutch. At the top was a triangular contraption, bound together with rope and packed with some kind of material to form a cushion for the armpit. Halfway down the shaft was another piece of wood, also tied on, that was clearly designed for a hand hold. Nate looked apologetic as he passed it over.

'The best I could do, I'm afraid, Sanjit. It's a bit rustic, but it should take your weight.'

Sanjit took the stick and propped it under his right armpit. He kept his right leg slightly off the ground and attempted a few steps. He made ungainly progress, but at least he could move.

'Works well, Nate,' he said. 'Thanks.'

'When did you do that?' asked Sam.

'During my watch,' Nate replied. He shrugged. 'While I was working I was also doing some thinking.'

'Multi-tasking?' said Karl. 'Is there no end to this man's talent?'

'Yeah, right,' said Nate. 'Wisecrack all you like, if that keeps up the troops' morale.'

'Let's hear the plan,' said Jen. She looked in no mood for banter. Her face was grim and she scratched at her right forearm, which was a livid red. 'I'm tired, I'm hungry, I'm wet and cold. I could do with a plan of action.'

'Ah,' said Nate. 'You may be disappointed then because action doesn't play a great part in what I was thinking. But let's talk it over. Here's the way I see it. We've established that there *are* survivors here, and they are hostile. I reckon we've done what we can and need to report back. That means waiting around for slightly less than forty-eight hours before we meet Gwynne at the agreed rendezvous point and go home.'

Home, thought Pan. *A strange word to describe The School*. It didn't feel like home to her. It felt like a prison.

She tried to focus on what Nate was saying. 'The hostiles are better armed and better equipped than we are. Our best option is to avoid confrontation. We also need water and food. Shelter would be welcome as well. Under other circumstances I'd suggest we stay in the village, despite the dead bodies. There's shelter and a water supply not far off. But the fact that the hostiles returned here is not a good sign and I don't think it's worth the risk.'

'Could you get to the plan, please Nate?' said Jen. 'We know the situation we are in.'

'I propose we make our way back to the beach, explore the surrounding area. It is possible we might find a cave. There are cliffs near where we made shore. A cave in a cliff would be ideal. We could light a fire, get warm and dry. There are two further advantages. We could try to catch fish, since there doesn't seem to be much in the way of game in this forest. And we would be on hand when Gwynne returns. We need to meet him at precisely six a.m. The worst possible scenario would be to miss that appointment.'

Silence greeted his words. Sam broke it after about thirty seconds.

'And the disadvantages?'

'Ah,' said Nate. 'Yes. One or two. Vulnerability is the main one. The beach is exposed, and clearly the longer we're on it, the greater the chances of discovery. And say we are lucky enough to find a cave. There would only be one way out. We could be trapped in there if the hostiles came looking. Plus, we are a long way from water unless we find another stream.'

The group mulled things over. It was Wei-Lin who spoke first.

'I like the idea. This is now all about survival. I reckon we stand more chance on the beach. It's got to be better than sitting in this forest.'

One by one, the team nodded their agreement.

'Okay,' said Nate. 'We go first to the stream that Wei-Lin and Sam found. We stock up as much as possible on water. Everyone drinks enough to be comfortable and then we ration the water in the canteen. After that we go back to the beach. Sanjit? Will you be able to find the way?'

Sam handed over the compass and Sanjit shook it a couple of times and glanced at the display. He nodded. *Nate's giving him something to do*, thought Pan. *Bolstering his self-esteem.*

'Right,' Nate continued. 'We move slowly, partly because Sanjit is unable to walk quickly, but mainly because I want no mistakes. We are not in a hurry and we must never forget that there are killers out there. Wei-Lin, I want you to take up the position you had yesterday. Last of the group. Watch our backs.'

There was little further discussion. The team finished what was left of the berries, which had gone soft and mushy overnight. Pan ate her share this time. Her stomach felt cavernous and she fought the sensation of nausea, swallowing the bitter goo with grim determination.

Sam led the way out of the clearing, followed by Nate and Jen. Pan walked beside Sanjit. Karl and Wei-Lin brought up the rear. Progress was slow. Occasionally, Nate would slow the leaders down so that the gap between the team members did not become too great. Pan was tempted to talk to Sanjit. The impression left by her dream played on her mind and she wanted to ask him about a journal.

It felt important. But they were moving with extreme caution, detouring to avoid areas that would have caused too much rustling. Everyone kept quiet and she didn't want to risk even whispering.

After twenty minutes Pan heard a new sound. Water. Running water. Sam proceeded carefully. She put one foot precisely in front of the other, parting the branches with exaggerated care. The sound of the stream might also mask other sounds, Pan realised. They did not want to burst out of the forest and into the arms of men in camouflage gear and deadly weapons. If she were intent on ambushing someone, it's what she would do. Stake out the place she knew they had to come to, eventually. The water source. Sam parted a final branch and the stream was before them. She stuck her head out gingerly and surveyed the area. Then she waved a hand and stepped out of the forest.

The stream was small but fast flowing. The group did not waste any more time than necessary. Pan knew they almost certainly felt the same way she did. Vulnerable. After so long under cover, the open space, even though it was small, felt threatening, as if at any moment danger would spring from the forest and claim them. They knelt at the stream's edge and sucked greedily at the water. It was cold and deliciously fresh. After she had drunk her fill, Pan ducked her head under the current. It was so cold that she felt a pain in her temples, but she kept her head under. When she came up for air, she saw Jen filling the water canteen. Nate beckoned and they slid back into the forest. Pan glanced up once at the sky. It seemed so long since she had last seen it. It was dark, cloud-filled and threatening. She shivered.

Under cover again, Sanjit took the compass from his pocket and examined it. After a few moments he pointed into the depths of the forest. Nate nodded and moved forward. Pan noted that he still held the axe. His grip was relaxed but determined.

They walked for an hour, stopping occasionally to check their direction. Once or twice, Sanjit made small adjustments. There was still no sign of pursuit. Pan forced herself to focus, to keep listening for any sounds that might indicate danger. But there was nothing. Towards the end of the hour, Wei-Lin shot a bird. The thrum of the bowstring caused Pan to stiffen and her heart to race. There was a brief and terrifyingly loud rustling of leaves and branches as the bird fell. Wei-Lin stepped past Pan and into the undergrowth, and when she returned she was holding the bird aloft triumphantly. The arrow had hit it clean in the chest. Nate came and inspected the bird.

'Good job,' he said. 'I'm tempted to eat it raw, but we should wait until we can build a fire.'

It wasn't a large bird. Some kind of wood pigeon, and it wouldn't go far between seven, but the group's spirits rose perceptibly. Wei-Lin removed the arrow, cleaned it on her shirt and inspected it for damage. Satisfied, she returned it to her quiver. Then she took a small piece of cord from her pocket, tied it around the bird's legs and hitched it to her belt. The group moved on for another ten minutes before Nate called a halt.

'We should be close, shouldn't we?' he asked Sanjit.

'Should be,' the boy replied. 'But all a compass does is tell us direction. Not distance. According to my calculations, we travelled due North from the beach to our first resting point, then it was south-east to the village. From the village we went north-east to the stream. We are now travelling south-west. Basic geometry. We must be close to the beach, but I can't guarantee we'll hit it at exactly the right place.'

It was the longest speech that Sanjit had made. Pan wondered whether that was a sign of new-found confidence or whether he was simply more comfortable when talking about things he understood.

Nate nodded. 'The forest seems to have thinned out over the last mile or so,' he said. 'And I think I can detect a hint of saltwater in the air.'

He didn't sound convinced and Pan couldn't smell anything.

'Right,' Nate continued. 'You guys stay here and I'll scout ahead. If we're close, I want to check the beach is clear before we all go trooping out. Keep the noise down. I'll be gone a maximum of half an hour. If I don't return, then don't come looking for me. Stay hidden and wait for Gwynne.'

He slipped off. The group members glanced at each other and sat. Karl and Sam huddled together. Wei-Lin crouched on her haunches and examined her bow, checking the string and then inspecting the arrows. Jen stood, arms folded, her face like thunder. Sanjit hopped a couple of steps and then sat at the base of a tree. He placed the crutch at his side. Pan gave it a quick glance. Some of the padding was coming off, but otherwise it was holding up well. Nate had done a good job. Pan eased herself down next to Sanjit.

'How's the ankle?' she asked.

'Better,' he replied. 'I'm not ready to do without the crutch yet, but it's definitely improving.'

'Good.' There was a silence.

'Sanjit?' said Pan. 'Do you mind if I ask you a question? Do you by any chance keep a journal?'

'A journal?'

'Yeah. A diary about what happened?'

Sanjit looked puzzled. 'No,' he said. 'Why do you ask?'

Why do *I ask?* thought Pan. She couldn't think of a suitable response.

'I'm curious about what people remember, I guess,' she said after a lengthy pause.

'I'm not,' he replied.

'Why not?'

'I don't know. Partly because the memories are too painful. And partly because it doesn't do any good to dwell on the past. This, the here and now, is what we have to deal with and it takes up all my energy coping with that.'

Pan nodded. 'I understand,' she said. 'But I think it would help me if you would share something of what you remember.' And Pan felt that was true, though she had no idea why. Sanjit frowned once more and plucked at the fraying edge of his bandage. He unravelled a thread and twisted it around his finger.

'I won't talk about my close family,' he said eventually. 'Or how they . . . died.'

'That's fine,' said Pan. 'What about anything you remember afterwards. How long was it before you were rescued, brought to The School?'

'A few weeks.'

'How did you survive?'

'I lived in Darwin. Everyone called it a city, but it wasn't much more than a country town. One hundred thousand people and I was the only survivor. I know that because I spent two weeks checking. Surviving wasn't a problem. There was plenty of food and shelter in a place designed for so many people, but with a population of one. I ate better than I had ever done before. Or since. My physical health was fine ...'

'But your mind?' Pan prompted.

Sanjit twisted the thread tighter. Pan noticed that the tip of his finger was white as his circulation became choked. She reached over and gently took the thread off him. Sanjit gazed incuriously at his finger as it filled with blood.

'A hundred thousand dead people. One living boy.' His voice was small and close to breaking. 'That's a lot of ghosts to deal with. A lot of fear. A lot of loneliness.' He shuddered. 'I don't want to talk about this anymore.'

'Did you see anyone alive?'

'A few. But they died. And that made it worse. Like I was given hope and then it was snatched away. Like everything else.'

'Any memory in particular?' Pan knew this conversation was coming to an end, and although she hated pushing she couldn't help herself. Sanjit stayed quiet so long Pan thought he wasn't going to respond. Maybe she had gone too far and he had locked some interior door against her. But then he spoke, though he didn't raise his head.

'I found my cousin. She was alive. She was sitting next to her mother, my aunt, playing with a doll. My aunt must have been dead for many days. Her face . . .' Sanjit swallowed. 'But my cousin was talking to her doll. Gently. She kept smoothing back its hair. She rocked it. Her dress was covered in blood and she was coughing. And every time she coughed the stain down her dress became worse.'

'What colour was her dress?'

'It was red. It was nearly all red. But at some point it had been white.' Sanjit raised his head and met Pan's eyes. 'I'm done,' he said matter-of-factly. 'I'm not talking anymore.'

Pan opened her mouth, though she had no idea what she was going to say. As it turned out, she didn't get the chance. Nate slipped into the clearing and squatted down on his haunches. The group drew closer.

'Good work, Sanjit,' said Nate. 'The beach is very close. Deserted, as far as I can tell. And the best news. There is a cave. Not huge but reasonably inconspicuous. It's big enough to keep the rain off us and we could build a fire in there. When it's dark. We can't risk anyone seeing the smoke. Let's move, people.'

It was a relief to leave the forest. When Pan saw the ocean stretching away to the horizon, it was easier to breathe and her spirits rose. The beach was totally deserted and there were no footprints to indicate any recent human visitation. The tide must have swept away any signs of their landing. The sky was grey, blanketed with high rain clouds and a few seagulls circled aimlessly. Rain was coming. Again. Nate led them along the edge of the beach, close to the tree line for cover. The cliffs weren't very high – no more than three metres.

The cave was small, but Nate was right. They could all fit in it and the entrance was relatively well hidden. The group huddled inside and looked around. The sand was clear and there was enough room for them all to sleep, though they would be cramped. Nonetheless, it would be much better than the uncomfortable forest floor.

'There's no driftwood in here,' said Nate, 'so I figure the tide won't come up this high. It's covered and it's fairly safe from prying eyes. Okay. Anyone got any suggestions about what we do now?'

'We need to be prepared for someone sneaking up on us,' said Jen. 'I propose we have someone on watch at all times, day and night. Three-hour shifts. Lying on top of the cliff would be the best position. We can see for a distance, but it would be difficult to spot us. Plus, it would be easy to raise the alarm.'

'Good,' said Nate. 'Anything else?'

'I'll collect wood for a fire,' said Karl. 'I want to get dry and warm as soon as possible.'

'If someone's on watch,' said Wei-Lin, 'I'll try my hand at fishing. We've only got that wood pigeon and it won't be enough. While you are fetching wood, Karl, keep an eye out for anything edible. Tubers of any kind. Maybe wild onions or mushrooms. Anything to bulk out a pigeon stew.'

Karl nodded and Nate grinned.

'We sound like a team, guys,' he said. 'I'll retrace our steps and smooth out the sand, hide our tracks. Karl, you do the same after you get the firewood. Sanjit, I want you to pluck and clean the bird. Do you know how to do that?'

Sanjit shook his head. Jen stood above him, hands on hips.

'Jesus, Sanjit, what's to know?' she asked, her voice strained. It was as if she was deliberately injecting incredulity into her tone. 'Get rid of the feathers and the guts. It ain't rocket science.'

Sanjit flushed. 'I've never done it, but I'll try.'

'Good,' said Nate. He flashed Jen a look as if to tell her to back off. She stalked off to the cave's entrance and stared out at the ocean, arms folded across her chest. 'I'll take first watch,' she said without turning around. 'I'll whistle if I spot anything.' And then she was gone. For a brief while the team could hear her scrambling up the cliff face, but then silence descended once more.

'What's her problem?' said Sam.

'It's too passive for her,' said Nate. 'She's not comfortable doing nothing.' He turned to Pan. 'Are you okay, kiddo?' he said. 'You're very quiet.'

'I'm fine,' said Pan, though she wasn't. Things were starting to come together in her mind, the jigsaw pieces slotting into position. The picture was still hazy and full of holes and many of the pieces didn't fit seamlessly. What she needed was quiet to work things out, but she also knew the day would not bring time for contemplation. The long hours in the night were another matter. 'What do you want me to do? I could help Wei-Lin with the fishing.'

'Give Sanjit a hand,' Nate replied. 'I don't want us to be out of this cave in pairs. We'll be too easy to spot.'

The next couple of hours were productive. Karl returned with an armful of wood and went off immediately to get another. Sanjit and Pan did their best to pluck and clean the wood pigeon. Sanjit screwed up his face at the mess of entrails, but he kept at the task. Pan took the guts out to the side of the cave and buried them in sand as deeply as she could. The carcass of the bird looked mangled, but it was the best they could do and Sanjit placed it on a ledge when they were finished. Almost immediately flies appeared, so Pan snuck out and returned with some broad leaves to wrap the bird in.

When Wei-Lin returned she was glowing with pride. She held up her hand-line and three fish dangled, their scales catching the light and flashing fitfully.

'No idea what they are,' she said, 'and I don't care. Dinner is suddenly more adventurous.'

Sanjit and Pan offered to clean the fish, but Wei-Lin waved them away. She scraped the boning knife's blade clean with sand and then expertly gutted the fish. Pan glanced at the time and tapped Nate on the shoulder.

'I'm taking second watch,' she said and he nodded.

Erosion had pitted the cliff face so there were plenty of hand and footholds and she climbed the few metres in a matter of seconds. Jen was lying on her stomach, her head protruding over the edge. She barely acknowledged Pan as she scrambled up and lay down beside her.

'Seen anything?' asked Pan.

'Nothing,' replied Jen. 'All quiet. Too quiet.'

'I'll take over.'

'Okay.' But she didn't move. The girls lay together, unspeaking for a few minutes. Then Jen turned her face. Her mouth was only centimetres from Pan's.

'I keep thinking about that fight,' she said. 'You know? Where you kicked my arse. If I didn't know any better, I'd think you were better trained than me. That you were some kind of martial arts expert. You now, from before. Those moves were like nothing I've ever seen. How did you do it?'

Pan turned her head to the beach. She scanned the shoreline and kept the forest in the periphery of her vision. Nothing moved.

'The truth?' she said.

Jen snorted. 'No, lie to me. Of course the truth.'

'I don't know. It's difficult to explain. I cleared my mind, I looked into your eyes. I sort of ... I let my body react, as though it was operating independently of me. And I instinctively knew what you were going to do and how to counter it. I know it sounds dumb. But I don't know any other way of explaining it.'

'You're right. It sounds dumb.'

'Thanks.'

'How did you know Cara was up that mountain if you had nothing to do with her disappearance?'

Pan stiffened and fought a surge of anger. She forced her muscles to relax. This was a subject that everyone avoided. Only Jen had the courage to ask straight out.

'I didn't kill her,' she said quietly. 'If that's what you think.'

'But you knew where her body was.'

'Yes.'

'Your intuition again, right?'

'Yes. Look, Jen. I know you don't believe me, but to be honest, I don't care anymore whether you do or you don't.'

'All right. Let's assume for a moment that you do have this sixth sense. What does it tell you about this place? I mean, you went off into one of your trances back in the forest. Did you *sense* anything?'

'One of us will remain here.' She regretted it as soon as the words came out.

When Jen spoke, there was nothing in her voice that indicated shock or surprise. 'Do you know who?'

'No. I'm guessing it's not me, but that's all there is. A feeling. A sense that only six of us will leave this island.'

And suddenly, it came to her. Why the feeling had appeared so strange when she'd first experienced it. This was new territory. In the past, her intuitions had been based on events that had already occurred – the finding of Wei-Lin's watch, her location of Cara's body. Never before had she seen into the future. Yet her knowledge of the men on the island, the sense they meant them harm and, above all, the premonition that one of the party would remain behind … Pan shivered. *What is happening to me?* she thought. *I am changing.* The thought was at once terrifying and strangely empowering. Pan shook her head. This was something she'd have to examine later. Jen had said something, but she'd missed it.

'Sorry?' she said.

'I said what makes you think this is an island?'

'I don't know.' Until Pan had said the word she had no idea she'd even been thinking it. More food for thought. But it felt right. This *was* an island.

'You don't know much, do you? Maybe you assume it's an island simply because we came by boat?'

Pan scrambled to her feet. Her head was too full of possibilities to focus properly on Jen's scorn.

'Look, you asked. I answered. This is my watch, so why don't you just leave?'

But Jen didn't leave. Not immediately. She plucked a thin piece of grass from the cliff top and stuck it in her mouth, chewed slowly.

Pan suddenly felt very exposed, confused and not a little foolish. She lay down again.

'The smart money would be on Sanjit,' said Jen.

'I guess.'

Jen spat the grass from her mouth and got to her feet.

'Keep your eyes out,' she said. 'And, Pandora? I hope you're wrong, but if it comes true ... well, I might have to rethink my opinion of you.' She shifted her body and dropped over the cliff face. A moment later her face reappeared. 'Unless you kill that person, of course. There's always that to think about.'

Pan settled down on the cliff top and glanced at her watch. Two hours and forty-five minutes. Plenty of thinking time, with no distractions. She felt on the verge of a breakthrough. It was a strong feeling and she was beginning to believe that strong feelings were her greatest asset.

~ ~ ~

Night fell quickly and Nate gave the order to light the fire. Jen took a small flint from her pocket and used the knife to strike sparks onto a nest of wood shavings. As soon as a spark caught, she brought her face to the wood and blew gently. The nest glowed and tiny licks of flame spread. Jen put more shavings on top and a thin trickle of smoke emerged. Within ten minutes a fire blazed at the side of the cave. The smoke was a problem. It gathered in the roof and spread downwards so that everyone's eyes stung and watered. It was slightly better towards the back of the cave, but still unpleasant. Sam took the broad leaf that Nate had used to sweep away their tracks on the beach and used it as a makeshift fan. It helped a little. The smoke drifted out of the cave's entrance. If it had been light, it would have betrayed their position immediately. But darkness was on their side and the fire, they hoped, was far enough back in the cave that no glow would be apparent to anyone from a distance.

Wei-Lin took on the role of cook. Karl had found some roots that might be edible, but her plan of making a wood pigeon stew had to be abandoned because they had nothing to cook it in. So she stuffed the potato-like vegetables into the bird's cavity and skewered the carcass shut with a thin branch. Nate had fashioned a couple of wooden forks over the fire and Wei-Lin placed the skewer onto the forks. Within moments, fat dripped from the bird and made sizzling noises in the fire. Sanjit volunteered to rotate the bird on its spit while Wei-Lin prepared the fish. The group, with the exception of Sam who was on watch, huddled around the fire. Gradually, Pan was starting to feel warm and dry.

It wasn't the greatest meal Pan had ever eaten but it was a feast under the circumstances. Parts of the bird were slightly overcooked, but by the time they'd finished there was nothing left except bones. Jen even broke the carcass apart to suck out what juice remained. Pan had taken Sam's share up to the cliff top. The fire died down and the smoke problem eased. The cave still wasn't exactly warm, but it was a vast improvement on spending the night out of doors. Pan felt even better when a steady rain fell, though she experienced a twinge of sympathy for Sam. They spread themselves out as best they could and settled in to sleep. Nate slept close to Pan. She could hear the faint murmur of his breath. Once or twice, she felt his breath on her cheek.

~ ~ ~

Pan woke at five o'clock. She carefully rose and stepped over the sleeping forms around her. There was barely room to place her feet. The entrance to the cave was nearly as dark as the interior. She climbed the few metres to the top of the cliff and found Karl slumped on the ground. For a moment her heart raced until she saw his chest rising and falling in a steady rhythm. *Falling asleep on duty*, she thought. *He put us all at risk.*

It took a moment to control her anger. *Cut him some slack*, she thought. They had all had an exhausting day and Karl must have risen at three in the morning. There were mitigating factors. She considered shaking him awake, but thought better of it. Let him sleep. She was up now and they didn't need two on watch. She'd wake him when the others stirred and his dereliction of duty could remain their secret.

Pan climbed down to the beach and watched the sky. No one would see her if she stayed close to the cliff. A few stars shone hard and bright through the gaps of cloud cover. It was peaceful. The gentle whisper of the ocean. The clean and fresh air. At The School there was always an underlying smell of something unpleasant - sweat, mainly. She walked towards the sea. Darkness was still a good cover, though she could see the first streaks of dawn against the horizon. In half an hour the sun would rise. She sat on the sand at the water's edge, waves lapping against her toes. She thought things through again, all the ideas that had come to her on her watch and in those times when she had woken in the night and couldn't get back to sleep. Most of her conclusions lacked any corroborating evidence. Huge questions remained unanswered. But she felt certain her line of thought was, in the main, correct. But she also knew she couldn't say anything to the others. Not yet. The main problem was who to trust. If she was right about The School, it was difficult to trust anyone. Even yourself. Perhaps especially yourself.

Dawn gave the air a grainy luminescence. As soon as the entrance to the cave became visible, Pan climbed back up the cliff and woke Karl. He jerked upright as soon as her hand touched his arm. Realising what he'd done, he blushed.

'I was just resting my eyes,' he whispered.

'I know,' Pan replied. 'I've been on watch.'

Karl rubbed at his eyes. 'Sorry.'

'You're lucky. It's all quiet. Why don't you go down to the cave? And if anyone's up yet, tell them I'm in the market for a full English breakfast.'

Karl smiled. 'I'll pass it on,' he said.

Pan watched the ocean. There was something relaxing about the way the waves rolled in and retreated, like the sea itself was breathing. She found it almost hypnotic. Pan tried to keep her mind alert to any movement in her peripheral vision, but her gaze kept returning to the ocean. She was certain that if anything moved along the beach she would spot it. Of course, if anything approached from behind, from out of the forest, they were all in trouble. When the sun was up, Wei-Lin came out of the cave with her hand line and made her way to the water line. She waved up at Pan and Pan waved back. Wei-Lin waded into the ocean up to her waist and threw out her line. Pan wondered what she was using for bait. Maybe she'd kept some of the fish guts from the previous meal. Pan forced herself not to watch, afraid she'd jinx Wei-Lin's luck. Anyway, she needed to keep a lookout. And watch the ocean and let the thoughts weave through her head.

The rest of her watch passed quickly. Wei-Lin returned with two small fish on her line. She shrugged apologetically as she approached the cave entrance. Pan gave her a thumbs-up. Within another half hour the smell of cooking fish drifted to her nostrils. They must have used the ashes of the fire to roast them, she thought. Sam brought her share up to her. It was pitifully small, but Pan's stomach rumbled in anticipation.

'I was told to tell you the full English is off the menu,' Sam said.

'Poached eggs with bacon?'

'Off.'

'Corn fritters?'

'Off.'

'How about a tiny sliver of almost cooked and wholly unidentifiable fish?'

'A wise choice, madam.'

When she'd finished breakfast, Pan felt hungrier than before. They needed meat. Maybe Wei-Lin could give the forest another chance. There had to be something in there. A pig, maybe. She wished she hadn't mentioned bacon to Sam. The thought was torture.

It was Wei-Lin who eventually scrambled up the cliff to relieve her. 'They've been discussing a plan for today,' she told Pan. 'See what you think.'

When Pan climbed down, Jen was sharpening the knife against the cliff face. She was doing so with fierce concentration, rubbing first one edge and then the other. Her face was set and Pan thought she detected anger in her every movement. The rest of the team looked tired and dispirited.

'We've decided that we need to top up the water supply and see if we can find something to eat out there,' Nate said to Pan. He jerked his head in the general direction of the forest.

'Sounds sensible,' Pan replied. 'I was just thinking we could do with something other than fish on the menu. Who's going?'

'Wei-Lin and Jen,' said Nate. 'The rest of us are staying put.'

Pan raised her eyebrows. Jen stopped honing the blade and slipped the knife into her waistband.

'If I don't do something,' she said, 'I am going to go completely crazy. Sitting around is doing my head in. Jesus, at least at The School I could do something. Run or practise weapons-training. Even the philosophy classes were better than being stuck here, following the second hand on my watch.'

'She wants action,' said Karl.

'No, really?' said Pan.

'As long as you don't go looking for it, Jen, okay?' said Nate. 'You hear me? You go to the river, you mark your way by making cuts in the trees as we agreed. If you find food, great. Go for it. But you do not take risks, is that understood? This is about getting there and getting back without detection.'

'What? You think I'll go looking for those guys?' said Jen.

'It's crossed my mind. Yes. But you have a responsibility to all of us, okay? Stealth and speed, Jen. Stealth and speed. Avoid conflict.'

'Yeah, yeah,' said Jen. 'I hear you.' She walked to the back of the cave and picked up Wei-Lin's bow and quiver. 'Is someone going to take over her watch?' she said, 'because I want to get going as soon as possible.'

'I'll do it,' said Nate. He sighed. 'Take care of each other. And for Chrissake, find us something to eat. Hell, insects will do.'

Jen smiled. 'I'll get us something better than insects,' she said.

'Do you want the compass?' asked Sanjit. He reached into his pocket and pulled it out. 'We don't need it.'

Jen glanced down at him. 'Nah,' she said. 'Keep it. You might need it to find your way out of the cave.'

'Jen . . .' said Nate.

'Yeah, I know. Be nice. He's hurt his leg. Poor boy. Can't even do his watch duty.' She shook her head and left. Nate sighed again and followed. Pan heard them scrambling up the cliff face. She sat down next to Sanjit.

'She didn't mean it,' she said. 'She just gets . . . frustrated.'

'I know,' said Sanjit. 'Just as I know she did mean it.'

Pan laughed. 'Yeah, I guess she did. But trust me, the rest of us don't think that way.'

'Maybe you should,' said Sanjit, and Pan couldn't think of a suitable reply.

She turned to Sam and Karl, who were sitting at the cave's entrance and staring out towards the sea. They held hands. Pan suddenly felt something of the anger that Jen had expressed. This was pointless. It was frustrating. And the longer it went on, the worse it was going to get. Irritation, followed by argument? The sense of being a team was starting to fall apart. Boredom was a dangerous thing, an insidious drain on their strength. They all felt it, but only Jen had the honesty to express it so forcefully. Pan almost envied her. She sighed, squeezed Sanjit's shoulder and left the cave. She climbed the cliff face. She hoped Nate wouldn't object to two sentries, and there was nothing for her to do down there anyway. She lay down at his side.

'What was that about the cuts in the trees?' she asked.

'Sam wanted us to keep the compass with the larger group, in case we had to relocate. We worked out the likeliest path back to the river, given what we remembered from yesterday. Wei-Lin suggested there might be game beyond the river - further away from the village.' He scratched his head. 'So, once they get to the river, they are heading into the unknown, and the cuts on the trees are to help them find their way back.'

'Jen is so angry.'

'Yeah,' said Nate. 'She is. It worries me. She'll get us all into trouble unless she learns to curb that temper.'

'Are you going to talk to her?'

Nate smiled. 'Not me,' he said. 'I value my life too much.'

After that, they didn't say much. Pan rested her head on her forearms and gazed at the sea. She had memories of doing exactly this, but they were scrambled and vague. A family occasion, maybe. Sitting on a beach with her mother and her brother, a completely blue sky and people splashing in the foam. Surfing. Ice creams. Rubbing lotion into her mother's back. The memories were slippery and she felt her eyelids drooping closed. A weariness overcame her. Sea, a big sky and nothing to do. Somewhere at the back of her mind, she knew it had always made her tired.

Nate's voice jolted her from a doziness that was accelerating towards deep sleep.

'We've got company, Pan,' he said. 'Get the others. Now!'

Chapter 22

She wasn't sure whether she heard it first or saw it. A motorbike, its engine a distant whine, far off to her left, just a speck on the beach, following the shoreline. For a moment she was paralysed. Not by fear, though that came quickly enough. But rather by the unexpectedness of company. The ocean had done that. Made the world seem empty. The motorbike was coming towards them, its back wheel weaving and drifting slightly in the sand.

'Now!' repeated Nate. His voice wasn't loud, but there was no mistaking the urgency in it.

Pan edged over the cliff face and shimmied down. She dropped the last metre or so and landed with a grunt. Sam and Karl were as she had left them, sitting close together, staring at the sea.

'They're coming,' said Pan. 'Get up the cliff face now.'

She didn't wait for an answer but ran into the cave. Sanjit had curled up in the corner and was sleeping, deeply, as far as Pan could tell. She shook him by the arm. He woke with a startled expression and tried, instinctively, to get to his feet.

'Hurry,' said Pan. 'A motorbike. Coming this way.'

She helped him to his feet. He grabbed the makeshift crutch and hobbled to the front of the cave. *His ankle hasn't improved*, Pan thought. *He is still the weak link.* This was going to be difficult. Outside, she took the crutch off him and threw it up onto the cliff face - there was no time to worry about who she might hit. Then she grabbed him under the arm and helped him find purchase on the cliff face. He made better progress than might be expected given his injury. Adrenaline, probably. He favoured his better foot, but still made it to the top in good time. Pan followed.

The team lay side by side next to Nate. All of them were watching the progress of the motorbike. It was much closer now.

'Damn it!' muttered Nate. 'I knew I should have disabled that thing. It would have been so easy. Slash both tyres. Goddamn.'

'Too late to worry about that now,' said Sam. 'What do we do?'

Nate was silent for a moment. It was clear he was deciding upon the best course of action. Pan was glad she wasn't a leader. Too much responsibility. One mistake and everyone suffers. Maybe everyone dies. Nate screwed up his eyes in concentration.

'Is that what I think it is?' he asked.

Everyone looked in the direction of the motorbike. Behind it, painfully slow in comparison, a group of men stalked the shoreline. Seven or eight, it was difficult to tell at that distance. The motorbike was probably about three hundred metres ahead of the group and was closing rapidly on the cave.

'Too late to get rid of the evidence of our occupation,' muttered Nate. It was as if he was talking to himself, speaking aloud only to clarify his thought processes. 'Footprints coming from the sea. Wei-Lin's fishing expedition. And we forgot to get rid of the traces. They are bound to spot it. No. Only one option.' He turned to the rest of the group. 'The forest. Sanjit, how's the leg?'

'Okay. Not too bad. Improving.'

'No, I mean, can you run?'

Sanjit thought for a moment, balancing the impulse towards honesty with the desire to give good news. He plumped for honesty.

'I don't think so.'

Nate's eyes cleared. When he spoke it was authoritative.

'Right. We crawl to the forest. No one is to get up until we have cover. If we can see them, they can see us. Once into the forest, we try to find the marks that Jen and Wei-Lin have made. It is important that we find them. We do not split up, we keep close. I will help Sanjit. Karl, you stay at the rear and you take the axe. Protect our backs. Okay, guys. Let's move.'

It was probably only about twenty or thirty metres to the forest's edge, but the crawl seemed to take forever. The worst part for Pan was taking her eyes off the pursuing group. The louder the drone of the motorbike's engine, the more vulnerable she felt. As soon as they made it to the forest, they got to their feet and headed into the interior, Pan and Sam taking the lead. The impulse to run as fast as they could was almost overpowering, but they were aware of Nate's and Sanjit's slow progress behind them.

Sanjit's face was screwed in pain, but he was limping along courageously. Nate was at his side offering quiet encouragement. Karl was at the back of the group. He kept casting his eyes behind and he gripped the axe firmly in his right hand. Their pace was reasonable, but it would be inadequate if they were being actively pursued. And they all knew it. Ten or fifteen minutes, Pan estimated. The motorbike would reach the cave in less than three or four. She wondered if the rider would wait for the rest of the group to catch up. An inspection of the cave would reveal that whoever had been there had left recently. After that realisation, it would be easy to guess which way they had gone. There was only one path that they could have taken to escape – the path they were on now. Fifteen minutes, if they were lucky, and they could expect the sounds of pursuit. The thought almost made Pan run faster and she had to deliberately slow her pace. The group could not split up. They had to look out for each other. But they needed a plan and they needed it quickly. *Or a miracle*, she thought. She slowed a little and waited for Nate and Sanjit to catch up.

'I know,' said Nate. 'I know. We have to do something.'

'Leave me,' said Sanjit. 'We can't get away. What's the point of all of us getting caught because of one weak link?'

'Because we are a team,' said Nate. 'And that means we do not leave anyone behind.' He pointed to a gash on a tree a few metres ahead. 'This way.'

Wei-Lin and Jen. They are on this path, Pan thought. *We are leading our pursuers straight to them.* She glanced at Nate's face as they pushed further on into the forest. The thought must also have occurred to him.

'I know what you're thinking, Pan,' he said. 'Don't worry. It's under control.'

Pan had no idea how it was under control. Whichever way she looked at it, the notion of control just didn't figure. But she followed him. It was twenty minutes before they heard the sound of pursuit. Faint at first, the distant rustling of branches, but getting louder and closer. Nate slowed and brought the group together into a huddle.

'Listen up,' he whispered. 'I don't want a discussion. I don't want a debate. This is what is going to happen. You will all go in that direction.' He gestured to his left. 'Find somewhere to hide. Dig down into the undergrowth, cover yourself with leaves. Or climb a tree. Be quick. Stay there until it's safe. Then stay longer. I'm talking a minimum of an hour. Listen up for Wei-Lin and Jen. If you don't hear them after an hour, follow the gashes in the trees until you do.'

'But—'

'No time, Karl. When you meet up with Jen and Wei-Lin, head for the beach, quietly. But don't leave the forest. They will probably have left someone to keep guard. Wait until five-thirty in the morning and then swim out to the meeting point, wait for Gwynne. His arrival will attract attention and I don't want you guys on the beach when that happens. Is that understood?'

'What about you?' said Sam.

'I'm the decoy. I'll run through the forest, away from the path that Wei-Lin and Jen have left. With luck they'll follow me.'

Pan knew what he wasn't saying. Without luck, their pursuers would split up and search until they found them all. He was banking on them being undisciplined. He was betting all their lives on it.

'What happened to "the team stays together"?' said Karl.

'I'll meet you at the rendezvous point at six in the morning.' Nate continued as if Karl hadn't spoken. 'They won't be able to track me all day and all night. I *will* lose them. But I will not join you until the last possible moment. Now go. Quickly. Hide. And don't make a sound.'

His tone didn't brook any argument. And the plan made sense. They knew that. Perhaps if Sanjit had been fully fit they could have outrun them as a group, but under these circumstances, it was not an option. Nate's plan was their only chance. The group made to leave and Nate grabbed Pan's arm as she turned away.

'You are in charge, Pan, until you find Jen. Then she is. Tell her.'

Pan nodded. Nate suddenly leaned forward and kissed her on the lips. It was over almost before she was aware what was happening. Her mouth tingled and a shiver ran down her spine. Nate stepped back and grinned.

'I'm in no danger,' he said. 'It's what I do, Pan. Run. No one can run like me. No one can run as fast or as long. You know that.'

'You should take a weapon.'

'No. I won't need one and it would slow me down. Trust me, I'll run them ragged. I'll lead them all over the island. Now go and hide.'

And then he was gone. He struck off to his right and pounded through the undergrowth. The noise he made was an assault on her ears, but Pan guessed that was the point. She turned and followed the other members of the group. Sanjit was still limping. In fact, his ankle appeared to have got worse from putting it under so much strain. It was clear that he was slowing with each step and it could only be a matter of minutes before he was forced to stop entirely. Pan urged him on, got him to lean on her shoulder and relieve some of the weight. She could hear the men, much closer and loud with danger.

They found an area where the leaf fall was deep, a brown and yellow drift of rotting vegetation. Pan stood guard as they buried themselves under the litter. She smoothed leaves over the humps in the undergrowth until they blended completely into the forest floor. When she was satisfied, she dug down and covered herself as best she could. It was possible they might have left tracks to their hiding place, but Pan hoped the very noisy Nate was leading them in the opposite direction. Someone would have to step on them before they were discovered.

The forest floor smelled of dampness and rot. Pan felt insects crawling over her neck and face and she had to resist the temptation to sneeze. She closed her eyes and held her breath. The noise of thumping feet was much louder now and she prayed that Wei-Lin and Jen would hear them approaching. She heard voices, speaking in that same guttural language she'd heard back at the village. They sounded out of breath already, which was an encouraging sign. Nate was right. There was no way they could catch him. They might have guns and supplies, but they didn't have his legs. The noise drowned out any that Nate might be making, but Pan knew he would be creating plenty to draw them away. The footsteps gradually faded.

After what felt like fifteen minutes, she could hear only the sound of her own breathing and the thumping of her heart. Pan waited another ten before she rose from the drift of leaves.

Even though she knew the others were buried, it was still difficult to spot them. She moved from one mound to the other and whispered the all-clear. Nate had specified an hour but her survival instinct overwhelmed her intention to follow his orders. They needed to keep guard, to watch for the return of Wei-Lin and Jen. She was in charge now. Until Jen came back. The group didn't speak. They brushed the remains of leaves and earth from their faces and sat quietly. A tree, wounded by a white gash, was within eyesight, and they watched and listened.

~~~

The girls appeared without warning, and once again Pan was impressed with the silence of their movements. When Karl stood up to greet them, Jen instinctively adopted a fighting pose. The knife flashed in her hand and she crouched, knees spread and balanced on her toes. Even when she recognised the group she did not entirely relax. Pan explained what had happened and Jen accepted the leadership role without comment. She agreed that they must hide in the forest until Gwynne turned up. Pan glanced at her watch. It was just past ten in the morning. They had twenty hours to remain undiscovered.

Wei-Lin held up the two birds she had killed, but they all knew there was no way they could cook what she had caught. She dropped them in the undergrowth and buried the carcasses beneath leaves. The group watched and their stomachs tightened.

Jen led them very carefully back towards the beach and the cliff. They made camp just inside the cover of the forest, protected by the heavy shadows, but still able to see through the leaves towards the beach. Nothing moved. Pan could see the top of the cliff where they had kept watch, but it was deserted. If Nate was right, there would be a guard within a few metres, probably hiding in the cave itself in case they returned. All they could do was sit and watch and wait. Somewhere Nate was leading the group of men away from them, but no sounds of that chase could be heard. The silence meant safety. For now. The hours crept by and the sun disappeared behind thick cloud.

And then it rained.

None of them slept at all that night. Occasionally, Pan would stretch her muscles very carefully when cramp threatened. She sipped water, but it didn't do much to keep her hunger at bay. Only when her bladder was bursting did she steal off through the undergrowth to relieve herself. The temptation to move to a more comfortable hiding place was almost unbearable. The cave was dry and relatively warm, but she had had to endure the cold rain that had soaked through to her skin. She couldn't even sneeze, though once or twice she had to fight hard against the impulse.

Sometime before dawn, Pan saw tendrils of smoke creep above the cliff face and dissolve in the air. She nudged Jen and pointed. Everyone in the group peered towards the cave. Nobody said anything. They hugged themselves and huddled closer for warmth.

At five in the morning, Jen beckoned Pan away from the group. They took ten minutes to move just a few metres. Jen put her mouth up to Pan's ear.

'The situation will have to be dealt with. Sooner or later. And sooner is better. I'll do it now.'

'If there's more than one guard, you'll need help,' Pan whispered.

For a moment it seemed like Jen would argue, but then she nodded.

'I'll check it out first. But if it's just one, I'll deal with him immediately.'

Pan squeezed Jen's arm. There *was* no alternative and Jen was the logical choice. With luck, the sounds of the sea and the patter of falling rain would mask her approach. She watched as Jen moved quietly towards the cave. She took fifteen minutes to crawl the distance to the top of the cliff, and once there she eased herself over the edge. Pan held her breath and waited, her ears straining for any sound. But she heard nothing.

Suddenly a dark shape was moving towards them and the whole group froze. When Jen spoke, it was in an urgent whisper.

'One guard,' she said. 'Now it's clear. We should move.'

She wiped the blade of the knife against her leg before tucking it back into her waistband. Pan looked away from the dark stain on her pants.

The group rose as one and moved out of the forest towards the cliff. On the horizon, the very first tinges of pink were smeared on the border of sea and sky. One by one they dropped over the cliff edge and climbed down. The cave's mouth yawned before them but no one looked inside. Jen led them down to the sea's edge. She bent her head to her watch.

'Right,' she said. 'Dawn will be here in twenty minutes and we don't want to be on the beach when that happens.

We swim out now and tread water. Wait for Gwynne. Anyone have any problems with that?'

Pan did. She wasn't sure if she could tread water for so long and the cold would be intense. Sanjit was another concern. He wasn't strong to start with and his leg was getting worse and worse. She'd noticed during the night that his ankle was badly swollen. But at least once he was in the water, he wouldn't have to put weight on it, and perhaps the cold would help with the swelling. If they could survive hypothermia then this was the safest course of action. So she said nothing. Karl went first. He held the axe in his hand until he was waist deep in the water and then he dropped it. There was nothing to be gained by keeping their weapons and it would only make swimming more difficult. Pan followed and dropped the rope in about the same spot. She was glad to get rid of it. It had been of virtually no use and she wouldn't miss its weight. As she kicked off into deeper water the cold gripped her like a vice. It took her breath away and all the muscles in her body stiffened. *Relax*, she thought. *Stay loose.* She didn't glance back, but she knew the others were following. She concentrated on the dark form of Karl as he swam out. Her breaststroke was still painfully slow, and he was outstripping her with every stroke. Soon Jen overtook her, and then Wei-Lin and Sam. Sanjit would be the only member of the group slower than her. She worried about him, but there was nothing she could do. Pan doubted she could keep someone else afloat. She doubted if she would be able to keep herself afloat. So she swam and tried to empty her mind of everything other than the thought of one stroke following another.

The sea was calm and the swell minimal. When Pan caught up to the rest of the group the undersides of the clouds were tinged with gold. Day was dawning. She turned in the water and was relieved to see Sanjit ten metres behind her. His face was screwed up in pain. He laboured up to them and trod water. Pan was aware of the depth of the ocean beneath her and a dim fear surfaced in her mind. The thought of movement in the darkness underneath. Her legs dangling and scissoring beneath the waves. She fought down panic.

No one said anything. They bobbed in the gentle swell, some looking out to sea for Gwynne's arrival, others looking towards shore. Where was Nate? They were only a few minutes short of the rendezvous time and he should have been there by now. Unless something had happened. *Only six will leave this place*, Pan thought. *Only six.* The sky lightened moment by moment.

'He's here,' said Jen. They had been silent so long that the sound of her voice was a shock. Pan looked along the beach line. Nothing. She turned in the water and heard the sound of the boat's engine. Even though the water was calm, the swell meant she could see little beyond a hundred metres. Gwynne's arrival - she assumed it was Gwynne - would be invisible for some time yet. The sound rose in intensity and Jen started waving her arms above her head. Pan turned her gaze and fixed it on the beach. The shore remained stubbornly empty.

When the boat arrived it did so dramatically, looming above them. The engine throttled down and the boat turned in the water and idled. Gwynne peered over the side, held out a hand without speaking. Jen swam to Sanjit and looped her arms around him. He was exhausted, his head lolling, eyes almost closed. Gwynne leaned further and took his arm, hefted him onto the side of the boat and then inside. Sanjit flopped like a landed fish. The others followed, needing various degrees of help. Jen stayed in the water until everyone else was in the boat. Then she put both arms onto the side and hauled herself out of the water. There was a pile of thermal blankets in the bottom of the boat, the metallic sheen glinting in the pale sun. One by one they took a blanket and wrapped themselves up. Sam and Karl lay Sanjit down and covered him. His eyes were fully closed by now and his breathing was laboured.

'Where's Nate?' said Gwynne.

'He's still out there,' said Jen. 'We wait.'

Gwynne examined his watch. 'Nine minutes,' he said. 'If he's not here by then, we go.'

No one replied. They all watched the shoreline and shivered. The seconds ticked by and became minutes. Gwynne looked at his watch again and opened his mouth to speak. Then he closed it. Out of the forest a figure appeared. It was running towards the beach. Running fast. Pan recognised the easy lope, the angle of the body as it moved across the land.

Nate.

Jen stood up in the boat, but she didn't say anything. A group of figures burst out of the forest about thirty metres behind the lone runner. They were moving fast, but Nate was putting distance between himself and his pursuers. One of the chasers stopped. A distinctive pop sounded. A gun. But Nate didn't stop running. He was racing along the water's edge towards them. Another shot rang out. Another miss. Now they could see him clearly from the boat. Nate had spotted them as well and was judging when would be the best time to strike the water. He was a strong swimmer. They wouldn't catch him once he was in the ocean, but they would get closer while they were still running along the shore. He was trying to maximise his chances before he became a slower-moving target in the sea. Jen muttered under her breath. The group watched and felt powerless.

Nate thrashed through the shallows and plunged into the sea. Immediately he was swimming towards them, his arms scything through the water in powerful strokes. The men kept running. When they reached the point where Nate had entered the water they stopped and one man stepped forward. He raised the gun to his shoulder and took careful aim. The seconds stretched. The only movement was the rhythmic dip of Nate's head as he took a breath and the thrust of one arm after another through the waves.

He was about a third of the way to the boat when the shot rang out. For a moment, the group thought he had missed again. Nate's arm rose, bent at the elbow, ready to strike the water one more time. But then his body stiffened and the arm fell. His body shuddered in the water and stilled.

'No!' yelled Jen. She turned to Gwynne. 'Take the boat in. Now. There's still time.'

Gwynne wiped his nose with the back of his hand. He gazed out across the water. The men were already wading out towards Nate's body.

'Too dangerous. The deadline has passed,' he said. 'We leave.'

'No,' repeated Jen. 'We won't leave him behind. We will not.' But Gwynne took no notice. He moved to the stern and the engine roared. He swung the boat around in a tight arc and headed away from the beach. Jen moved to jump into the water, but Karl and Sam grabbed her arms. Even so, she writhed furiously to break their hold. By the time she freed herself, Nate's body was almost lost to view. She appeared to collapse in upon herself. She slumped, resigned, at Gwynne's side and watched as the land fell away.

No one spoke.

Chapter 23

Pan sat up the front of the boat as far away from the group as she could and watched the sea as it flashed with dazzling shards of sunlight. She was dimly aware of the sounds behind her, the drone of the boat's engine and faint, intermittent sobbing. It might have been Sam.

Pan's focus turned inwards.

Something had happened when that shot rang out and Nate's body slumped in the water. The rest of the pieces had slotted together. All those fragments had circled in her mind, assumed new shapes and come together. There were gaps. Some of the pieces were still missing, but the general pattern had formed in an instant, like an epiphany.

It took her breath away.

Pan wondered how much Cara had already worked out. There was so much more to her than anyone could have thought, and Pan was convinced that her own gift of intuition was even more developed in Cara. She had simply hidden it better and her shyness meant that no one pressed her to disclose more than she was prepared to reveal. She'd locked herself up in her own mind. Even her journal did not provide a key to her inner thoughts. Had The School suspected? Had The School killed her on the basis of those suspicions? That was one missing piece, but it was a mystery Pan was determined to solve.

A quotation sprang to her mind. *When you have eliminated the impossible, whatever remains, however improbable, must be the truth.* She thought it was Sherlock Holmes who'd said that, but it didn't really matter.

Her dreams and her memories. They were the key. Why did she doubt her own memories? Why did she trust her dreams more than her memories? It took a monumental effort of will to break her mind's certainty that what she remembered must be true and that what she dreamed must be fantasy. Three memories, shared by three people independently. Sanjit remembered a child in a white dress, playing with a doll. So did Pan. So, according to her journal, did Cara. What were the odds of three people remembering the same thing? Not impossible, but staggeringly improbable. Cara had said during that conversation outside the shower block that she didn't trust her memories. She'd said that some of her dreams made more sense. The dream she recorded in her journal of being chased? The same dream that haunted Pan most nights, the men in suits running after her, the policeman with the gold tooth, the injection in the back seat of the police car. What if that was true and the memories of the relief teacher in Melbourne, the streets littered with bodies, the policeman who killed himself in front of her eyes . . . what if *they* were the dreams?

Other things, small things. How could Dr Morgan

get a shuffling machine when vital supplies were almost non-existent? Where did Gwynne's protective equipment for stick-fighting come from? The guarded wall, the mysterious village and the story they'd been fed about why it was impossible for students to visit it. *Evil lives beyond the wall*, Dr Macredie had said. How did they know immediately that the wall had been breached when she and Nate had been caught? Cara again. *The watches are wrong.* The watches issued to each student. What if they were tracking devices, intended to monitor everyone's movement? Would that explain why Cara had left hers behind the night she disappeared? Nate had said they were on an island. How did he know? What if he knew their destination before they set out? Nate had flirted with her. What if that was his job, his own individual mission? What if he hadn't died back there, but his death was faked because his mission was over?

Pan stared at the water and turned all the ideas over in her head. The conclusion was absurd, but that didn't make it wrong. The students were not survivors. They had been abducted, the memories of abduction suppressed, replaced with false memories of a virus that had wiped out billions. A virus that didn't exist. And, if that was so, the world was going on out there as it always had. Her mother and Danny were alive. The students believed what they remembered and the wall kept them all as prisoners.

Their memories were an elaborate fabrication. Pan *knew* it.

Everything was built on a monumental lie.

And The School was the biggest lie of all.

Barry Jonsberg's young adult novels, *The Whole Business with Kiffo and the Pitbull* and *It's Not All About YOU, Calma!* were shortlisted for the CBCA Book of the Year, Older Readers, awards. *It's Not All About YOU, Calma!* also won the Adelaide Festival Award for Children's Literature, *Dreamrider* was shortlisted in the NSW Premier's Awards for the Ethel Turner Prize and *Cassie* (Girlfriend Fiction) was shortlisted for the Children's Peace Literature Award. *Being Here* won the 2011 QLD Premier's Young Adult Book Award and was shortlisted for the 2012 Prime Minister's Award. *My Life as an Alphabet* won the 2013 Gold Inky, the 2013 Children's Peace Literature Award, Older Readers and the 2014 Victorian Premier's Literary Awards.

Barry lives in Darwin with his wife, children and two dogs. His books have been published in the USA, the UK, France, Poland, Germany, Hungary, Brazil, Turkey and China.